D0450058

594

Celeste's Harlem Renaissance

CELESTE'S HARLEM RENAISSANCE

A NOVEL

by Eleanora E. Tate

Beverly Hills, California 90210

Little, Brown and Company

Hachette Book Group USA
1271 Avenue of the Americas, New York, NY 10020
Visit our Web site at www.lb-kids.com

First Edition: April 2007

Library of Congress Cataloging-in-Publication Data

Tate, Eleanora E.
Celeste's Harlem Renaissance : a novel / by Eleanora E. Tate. — 1st ed.
    p. cm.
Summary: In 1921, thirteen-year-old Celeste leaves North Carolina to stay
with her glamorous Aunt Valentina in Harlem, New York, where she discovers
the vibrant Harlem Renaissance in full swing, even though her aunt's life is not
exactly what she was led to believe.
ISBN-13: 978-0-316-52394-3
ISBN-10: 0-316-52394-1
[1. Coming of age — Fiction. 2. Aunts — Fiction. 3. Harlem (New
York, N.Y.) — History — 20th century — Fiction. 4. Harlem Renaissance —
Fiction. 5. African Americans — Fiction.]   I. Title.
PZ7.T21117Ce 2007
[Fic] — dc22

                                                         2006017622

10 9 8 7 6 5 4 3 2 1

Q-FF

Printed in the United States of America

Chapter One

"Scoot your big bucket over, Cece, and let me have more room," Evalina yelled. I'd settled myself in the Bivenses' wagon first! But I moved closer to Angel Mae. Evalina was the kind of girl who *had* to have her way. She'da sat on me otherwise. Lissa, the Bivenses' mean albino mule, swung her head around in her straw hat and glared at us.

"Please don't get this mule riled up," Mrs. Bivens said, and puffed on her pipe. "About the only time she wants to move is when she sees me pack my herb bags in the wagon. Then she won't take more'n ten steps until we stick sprigs of sage in her hat. She likes the smell of sage. I'm down to my last leaves."

My neighbor Mrs. Smithfield, in the front seat by Mrs. Bivens, glanced around at us, too. She was a short, pleasant-faced woman with gray eyes, and so fair-skinned that she was often mistaken for being white. "Everybody ready? Leon couldn't come. All right. They're ready." She straightened her woolen cap on her head and pulled her heavy coat closer around her. When Mrs. Bivens clucked and snapped the reins, Lissa brayed, then slowly clopped off.

"Cece, put that bonnet on!" Aunt Society's clacker bell tongue followed us. "You don't need to get any darker from this sun, even if it *is* chilly!"

I snatched off my red and white cap and slapped the scratchy gray woolen bonnet onto my head while Evalina snickered. Mrs. Bivens grunted. Leave it to Aunt Society to embarrass me in front of everybody. I hated that old bonnet. I'd take it off and put my cap back on after I got out of her sight. Aunt Society would go up to heaven — or down to the Devil's Pit of Never-Ending Fire — criticizing my dark skin color. She allowed that she was tangerine-colored, and was she ever proud of that! To me she just looked wrinkled-up orange.

But this was a special Sunday, and I wasn't going to let either my aunt or the sun ruin it. I was a winner! Me, Evalina, Angel Mae, and Leon had written winning essays about our state capitol in the annual contest sponsored by our Butterflies Club at school. Mrs. Smithfield, who was a cook for the governor, was taking us winners on a tour of our state capitol here in Raleigh right now. This was a great honor, our teacher Mrs. Bracy kept telling us, because not many Colored children got to see the inside of the capitol up close, like we would. Lands sake, I'd never won anything before. Momma was smiling down at me from heaven, and Poppa was proud of me. Aunt Society hadn't said a word.

When we drove up Hargett Street past the Colored section of City Cemetery, I looked over toward where Momma and my baby brother, Emmanuel, lay, like I always did. Grandma and Grandpa Lassiter, Momma's parents, were in there, too. Momma stayed sickly after Emmanuel's birth, but I didn't hold it against him. He passed a week later. That was four years ago, when I was nine years old. I promised Momma in her last days before she passed on two years ago that I would take good care of Poppa, and I will, no matter what. He and Aunt Society were the only family I had left. Well, I had Aunt Valentina Lassiter, Momma's younger sister, but she lived in New York City.

We passed Hamlin's Drug, the Masonic Hall, the Royal Theater, and the Stackhouse Hotel, where Poppa worked. I waved, in case he was looking out a window. Hope he wasn't coughing. He'd had a bad bout this morning when he woke up.

"Now, children, look to your manners," Mrs. Smithfield was saying. "Anybody with gum or candy in her mouth swallow it now. And don't touch anything. We want those guards to see you three are the best-behaved Colored girls in Raleigh."

We said, "Yes, ma'am." My stomach was squeezed into knots, like it got whenever I went around strange people and places. Aunt Society said that was due to either the devil or tapeworms in my belly, but I knew better on both cases.

"Will we see the new governor and his daughter Angelina?" Evalina asked, sniffing. She always kept a cold all winter and never had a handkerchief, so her eyes watered and her nose was a mess. I hoped she wouldn't be snotting inside the capitol building. At least she wore her nicest coat — the brown velour one with the matching cap. Which was nicer than mine. I just had my plain ole blue corduroy coat and cap with the missing pompons.

"We don't go round to the governor's private quarters anymore," Mrs. Smithfield said, "not after some White schoolchildren caught a governor still in bed." After Mrs. Bivens let us off at the capitol building, we entered through a back door past the guards. We stopped in a circular hallway called the rotunda. Building the capitol began in the 1790s, Mrs. Smithfield said. It caught fire in 1831. It was completed in 1840. "And, Evalina, before you ask, no, I wasn't around when it was built."

Evalina closed her mouth, smiling. Mrs. Smithfield handed her a handkerchief. Colored people like my Grandpa Lassiter helped to build the capitol, she said. I smiled proudly. We followed her up the stairs. "I'm glad I don't have to scrub this place," I whispered to Angel Mae. "After I scrub our kitchen and bedroom floors, my knees look like tree bark."

On the second floor we peered into the House of Representatives chambers. "After the Civil War many Colored men got elected to the House and passed laws right in this room," Mrs. Smithfield told us. "One of Cece's great-uncles also served in the House and —"

"Only men?" Angel Mae frowned. "If I'd been around, I'd have voted for a lady."

"Well, women only got to vote in 1920, remember. This is 1921, but things are still slow for us Colored," Mrs. Smithfield explained.

I started to speak, but Evalina spoke over me again, then Mrs. Smithfield got to jabbering some more. When things got quiet, I said, "When I get grown maybe I'll run for the legislature."

"Ole mousey *you*?" Evalina arched up her eyebrows. "If you tried to give a speech, nobody'd hear you."

I shut up again. *Well, I am going to be a doctor,* I added, to myself. Evalina and her big mouth, always talking over me! I had also wanted to say that Momma used to tell me about my great-uncle what's-his-name in the House. Never mind now.

Mrs. Smithfield said that a ghost man in old-timey clothes haunted the capitol. "But I've never seen any ghosts," she said while I peered around looking for anything shadowy. "Ghosts don't eat, so they got no business in *my* kitchen," she said. Upstairs was a room that used to hold samples of every rock, mineral, and plant in North Carolina, she told us. "But when General Sherman came through, people said his men stole all that stuff. I'm sorry about the rocks, but I'm sure glad he came, 'cause he helped to free our people from slavery."

"Yay for General Sherman!" Evalina yelled, then clapped her hand over her mouth. Nobody else but the guards were around, but Evalina's big mouth must have bothered Mrs. Smithfield a little, because she hurried us through the rest of the tour. The next thing I knew we were climbing back into Mrs. Bivens's wagon. I didn't mind. I'd seen enough. She dropped me off at the Stackhouse so I could walk home with Poppa. I sat down on a bench to wait. This way I wouldn't have to help Aunt Society fix dinner. I was her captive in the kitchen. She poked, pinched, and plucked at me just like she did a dead chicken.

I waved at Mr. Hortimus Stackhouse, the hotel owner, and he waved back. He stood talking with some men in his blue serge suit and straw hat near the hotel entrance. Mr. Stackhouse built this grand four-story hotel for us Colored. It had a drugstore, where I worked with Poppa on Wednesday afternoons and on Saturdays, a barber chair, and a shoe-shine stand. He was the richest Colored man in town. Well, he and Mr. Lightner, who was building another big place, too. He already had Lightner's Office Building.

I heard someone playing "Over There," one of Poppa's favorite war tunes, on the hotel piano. He and Momma gave recitals there on Sunday afternoons, Poppa on violin, Momma on piano.

I played violin, too. I'd named mine Dede, after Edmund Dede, a violinist from New Orleans. Dede and I knew all the songs my folks had played, but we'd never played with them in public. We did at home, though, until Momma got too sick to sit at the piano.

After she passed, Poppa gave away our piano and packed away his violin. Whenever Dede and I played, I thought about Momma. I wished Poppa would play with me sometimes. Maybe I'd ask him again tonight. Maybe he'd learn how to play my poem "Forsythia," which I wrote in honor of our yellow bush in the front yard, and set to music.

I hummed "Forsythia." After we'd won the school essay contest, Angel Mae, Evalina, and I had entered "Forsythia" and some other things in the *Brownies' Book* magazine children's writing contest in New York, but we hadn't heard anything yet.

I loosened my coat in the warm sunshine and listened to the piano player. Once upon a time I'd even wanted to be a concert violinist. But have all those eyes staring at me? It'd be hard enough for me to stand up in church and say my lines in the Easter program coming up March 27. Although Poppa and I were members of St. Paul African Methodist Episcopal, we almost always attended Aunt Society's Baptist church now — when he and Aunt Society were up to going.

Poppa left the hotel coughing and pulling his black sweater coat close around him like he was cold. But I saw sweat on his thin face. "Hi, Poppa. You all right?"

"Just a little gas, girlio, just a little gas," he said, smiling at me, which made the long dimples that I loved crease his cheeks.

"That's what you always say, from being mustard gassed in the war." I loved to smell his army uniform when he wore it to the Great Negro State Fair here every year with the other Colored soldiers. But I never smelled what I figured was mustard gas. "I wish you'd go on and see Dr. Pope, so we'd know for sure."

"Doctors just like to stick folks with needles and cut, cut, cut. They can't cure what I got." He pulled a small bottle of Cheney's Expectorant from his jacket pocket and drank from it. He'd been drinking that stuff for years, but it didn't seem to help. "Now quit jabbering about me, and tell what you saw at the capitol."

So I did, especially the part about the ghost. "Poppa, do you vote?"

"Try to," he said. "When they let me."

"But Momma couldn't, because she was a Colored woman, huh." He nodded.

I believed in keeping promises. I promised myself that when I got old enough, I'd vote, no matter what. They ought to have things figured out for us Colored women by then.

Momma, who had been a root worker and a midwife, said people with bad coughs like Poppa's had consumption, also called tuberculosis. TB. Momma could show everybody else how to fix and drink which kind of tea and how to swab on which kind of salve to ease aching joints and spider bites. Why couldn't she have been able to find a tea or salve to help herself after she had Emmanuel?

As we walked on Hargett toward home, we saw the Smithfields sitting on their front porch. Mr. Smithfield, a railroad porter who traveled from Atlanta to New York, waved at us. He was a plump, handsome, dark-skinned man with a thick mustache, always joking. You know how folks have good neighbors and bad neighbors? Though Evalina was my friend, her family let their ducks and chickens and dogs poop everywhere. Other bad neighbors dumped their cookstove ashes in our backyard by our grape arbor. The Smithfields, though, were our *good* neighbors, praise the Lord.

"Time for you to bake the governor some more pecan pies and Lady Baltimore cake," Poppa told Mrs. Smithfield, and coughed. "So you can bring us what he doesn't eat."

"I'll do that come Wednesday," she said. "Taylor, you really ought to do something about that cough."

"A piece of pecan pie'll take care of it." He laughed.

"Say, Taylor, when's Valentina coming back down to visit?" Mr. Smithfield asked. "That girl must truly love New York. She still living in that mansion and singing and dancing and driving that Pierce-Arrow? Now, that's a fine car!"

"As far as I know, she's still doing all that," Poppa replied. "Be nice to see her, but she loves the big city and the fast life. You know how badly she wants to break into the big time and be on Broadway. She's doing those little cafés and plays and joints and rent parties and working for that ole fat opera singer."

"I'd love to see her, too," I said. "Remember one time when she was here how she showed us those Harlem dances, and let me try on her fake mink fur? She even put a little of her rouge and face powder and perfume on me." Momma said I looked pretty, but when Aunt Society came over to our house from hers around the corner, she said I looked like a clown. That set off a big fight between her and Aunt Valentina.

"Cece, you wanna live in New York and wear rouge?" Mr. Smithfield laughed.

"Oh, I'd love the rouge, but I'd never leave Poppa!"

"We sure Lord do miss your momma," Mrs. Smithfield said kindly. "Elizabeth was like a sister to me, too."

Poppa cleared his throat. "We better get on, girlio. You know how Society hates to wait on us for her supper."

"Lord have mercy on your taste buds," Mr. Smithfield said.

Before we reached our house, I told Poppa what Aunt Society had said about my color and the sun. "Seems like she can't have a good day unless she can say something mean to me." I kicked a rock.

"Too bad when she was raising me and my brothers back in Morehead City that she didn't get some practice raising girls, too. Pray for her to have more patience and understanding with you, and you with her."

"All she likes to do with me is raise Cain," I fussed. Glancing toward our kitchen window, I lowered my voice. "I'm praying that the Lord'll find a way for me to not have to be bothered with her clacking tongue!"

"Here, quit that talk. You pray for something like that and you might have it come back on you, and not in a good way. But I know what you mean. She makes me want to pull out every hair of my mustache with her yapping and fussing."

"She'da had a conniption, too, if she'd heard us bragging on Aunt Valentina," I added.

After Momma got down sick, Aunt Society started coming over every day to our house from hers to help clean up and cook. She threw out the cosmetics Aunt Valentina had left us. She said they would corrupt us like they had Aunt Valentina. According to that ole bat, Aunt Valentina was a loose woman whose powder, perfume, and hoochie-coochie dancing would send her to the Devil's Pit of Never-Ending Fire. I figured if somebody as nice as Aunt Valentina had to go down there, Aunt Society would be waiting to meet her.

As soon as we got into the kitchen, Aunt Society started banging the pots and pans and snapping at me. "Didn't I tell you to wear your bonnet to keep you out of that sun? You don't listen to a thing I say." She brushed at a spot of grease on her apron dress.

"Let her be, Society. The sun's going down," Poppa said. "Cece, turn on the lights. It's dark in here." He winked at me. I smiled back at him, grateful.

After I washed my hands, I poured hot water from the teakettle on the stove into the teapot, and dropped sassafras bark, a stick of cinnamon, and a teaspoon of honey into it for Poppa's tea. Momma had taught me that sassafras tea strengthened and purified the blood in the spring. Poppa drank it all year long. Then I helped Aunt Society carry supper to the table. Didn't take us long to eat, because Poppa usually just picked at his food. I knocked mine down quick so I wouldn't have to waste my taste buds on her rubbery chicken, watery greens, hard corn bread, and mushy turnips. My aunt gobbled hers down, too, but that was because she claimed she liked what she fixed. Nobody talked much at the table. Not since Momma passed. My aunt said she couldn't stand all that jibber jabber around her food.

Sunday was when Aunt Society let us sit in the parlor. It was the prettiest room in the house, reserved for guests, special occasions, and Sundays, with shelves of our books, the Thomas Day sideboard where we displayed Momma's fanciest dishes, and our best rocking chairs and couch. Momma's piano had been in there, too.

Poppa lay down on the couch with his tea. "Turn on the Westrand, Cece," he said. That was Poppa's radio. He called it "the Westrand" like he owned the whole company. I carefully fiddled with the knobs, trying to bring in the *Sunday Evening Serenade* program from Pittsburgh, Pennsylvania, while the radio popped, screeched, and spat static. "Maybe one day we'll hear Aunt Valentina singing on a New York station," I murmured to Poppa.

Aunt Society rolled in in her wheelchair, with her lap full of muslin cloth to make into sheets. She was the only person I knew who loved to sit in a wheelchair, even though she didn't need to. When she went to her own or a sewing customer's house, she set everything in her wheelchair and pushed it where she needed to go.

She poked me on the shoulder. "Straighten that thing out," she said, pointing to the Westrand.

"I'm trying." I rubbed my arm. Her bony fingers felt as sharp as her sewing needles. By the time I had the Westrand right, the show was already on. I wrapped myself in Momma's ivory-colored cashmere shawl and curled up in her rocking chair. "Isn't that one of James Reese Europe's songs, Poppa?"

"Cece, be quiet so we can hear," Aunt Society ordered. "That Mr. Europe was our most famous Colored composer and conductor," she added. She poked her sewing needle in and out of the cloth in time to the music. "He performed in New York and Boston before the war, and in France during it. Your Poppa saw Mr. Europe and his band."

You ole jabbering thing, you forgot you just told me to be quiet! I cupped my hand to my ear to hear better. She got the message and hushed up. The solemn notes of "Clair de Lune," one of my favorite songs, swept into the room. I stretched out in the rocker to better embrace the sound.

"Celeste, sit up like a lady," she barked. I sat up, trying not to frown. Scott Joplin's "Maple Leaf Rag" bounced over the airwaves next. I tapped my foot and snapped my fingers until she told me to stop. "Taylor, your child's soul will go straight to the Devil's Pit if she keeps listening to that new ragtime stuff. Turn it off till another song comes on."

"Nothing's wrong with ragtime. I guess she takes after me, 'cause I like it," Poppa replied. While Aunt Society grunted and humphed, I went back to tapping and snapping until the song ended.

After the last notes in the program faded, Aunt Society told me to turn off the Westrand and the electric lights. Momma kept our frosted carnival glass chandelier lights blazing and the radio on all Sunday evening. People used to drop in to talk and laugh. "Sunday used to be fun," I said.

"Sunday's supposed to be set aside for the Lord, and ain't nothing fun about that," Aunt Society replied as she lit the oil lamps. Greasy oil stink flared up around me. My clothes always reeked of it. The oil funked up my bed worse than the lard she slicked down on what was left of my thin hair.

I wiggled onto the couch beside Poppa. On this pretty spring night I wasn't ready to go to bed with a cloud of oily smoke dangling over my head yet. "Poppa, tell me that balloon story again."

Aunt Society looked up from her sewing. "Not that old stale tale again, Taylor. You need to rest."

"I been resting since I got home," Poppa told her. He turned to me. "In 1883 a little girl and her folks were staying at the Morehead Hotel by the bay. This child wasn't more than two or three years old. Her daddy bought her a bunch of red balloons from a vendor fella and gave 'em to her. He tied the strings around her waist. Right off those balloons lifted her clear up in the air! They carried her over trees, church steeples, the lighthouse, over the bay. She screamed and screamed. Her daddy ran in circles, jumping up to grab after her. Her momma fainted." He paused, shaking his head.

"Some fishermen hopped into boats and paddled after her, but their boats couldn't keep up with that wind blowing those balloons so hard. There was only one thing left to do. Know what it was?" He raised his eyebrows at me, then continued. "Shoot the balloons one by one, and bring her down before she got blown out to sea."

I wrapped my arms around Poppa's right arm and laid my cheek against his shoulder, feeling his bones against my face. What if Poppa changed the story, and the men shot *her* instead of the balloons? I imagined myself clutching balloons above the waves while poisonous Portuguese man-of-war jellyfish circled hungrily beneath me.

"Each balloon they shot brought the girl closer to the water. Suddenly she disappeared. The men paddled around and called out her name. But it was like the tide had swept her out to sea, and the sea had sucked her down.

"Feeling sad, they headed back to shore. That's when they saw her sittin' on the sand, wet and scared but all right. The people back at the Morehead Hotel saw the men returning with the little girl and cheered so hard her momma came out of her faint. When they put her child in her arms, Momma fainted again, and so did her daddy."

"No such thing happened, Cece." Aunt Society shook her head, as always. "Filling your girl's head full of such nonsense."

"You weren't any older than that girl, so how would you know? Society, you can sure kill a happy mood. Girlio, why you like that story so?"

"'Cause I love balloons."

"I do, too." He laughed until he started to cough.

After we told each other good night, I ladled out hot water from the pot on the stove into a basin and carried it into my room to wash up. It was warmer there than in our tiny lavatory. Afterward, I took out Dede and, thinking about the balloon girl and Poppa, softly played my song poem, "Forsythia." How awful it would be if something happened so that Poppa and I couldn't get to each other! I thought about that and played louder and slower until Aunt Society yelled, "Put down that thing and go to bed, Celeste!"

"Yes, ma'am." In bed I decided that the next time I wrote in my journal, I'd draw a picture of Momma in heaven dressed in white, with wings and a halo. Poppa and I'd hold yellow and red balloons, floating in the sky after her. And at the bottom of the page I'd draw Aunt Society in her wheelchair, sewing, and crying, "Come back, Celeste, come back!"

Chapter
Two

Wednesday after school found me working with Poppa at the Stackhouse Hotel drugstore. I'd make fifty cents today and on Saturdays, sweeping and scrubbing the floor, washing containers, and dusting and straightening everything. Right now, though, I was skimming through our Colored newspapers — the Raleigh *Independent*, the *Baltimore Afro-American*, the *New York Age*, and the *Chicago Defender*. I always searched through the *New York Age* to check for articles about the *Brownies' Book* magazine contest that we Butterflies Club writers had entered. We still hadn't received any word of the results.

Besides newspapers and medicine, people bought white sugar, Mrs. Smithfield's Lady Baltimore cakes and cinnamon loaves, fragrant Parisian soaps wrapped in dainty lavender paper, men's socks and ladies' silk stockings, hair baubles and ribbons, needles and thread, teeth cleaning powder, decorative pencils and writing tablets, mints, red and black licorice, peppermint sticks, and sodas. Part of my money came right back to the pharmacy because I loved to buy licorice, pencils, and paper. Being employed in the pharmacy was more fun than work.

When I finished skimming the papers, I stepped over to the corner to get the broom. Mr. Hodges, the pharmacist, was talking to Poppa. "No, Taylor, you go see Dr. Pope right away. Your cough's getting worse. That's not mustard gas. That's galloping consumption. I can't have you spreading disease among my customers."

"But you don't understand," Poppa said. I had to strain to hear him. "I can't afford to take off any more time."

"Better go while you can, before you get flat on your back sick and can't. You can't keep fooling me. Or Stack, either."

"Well, he hasn't said anything to me," Poppa said. I knew that "Stack" was Mr. Stackhouse.

"Consumption lays quiet in you for years, until you get sick from something else," Mr. Hodges went on. "Or run-down. You're a pile of bones, man! If Dr. Pope says you have it, we can get you into Coopers Colored Sanitarium outside of Oxford. We'll try to make do here till you get back. You should have Cece and Society looked at, too."

Poppa leave me? For how long? What would happen to him? What would happen to me? Was tuberculosis galloping around in me, too? Heart fluttering, I grabbed up the broom and began sweeping just any which way. My broom handle knocked a glass beaker to the floor, where it shattered.

"Pay attention to what you're doing," Poppa said, looking up from where he was filling small white envelopes with powder.

"Yes, sir. Sorry." As I cleaned up the glass, I felt like I was brushing up pieces of my heart. How could I pay attention to anything with Poppa sick and maybe leaving me — like Momma did? I pulled the medical encyclopedia from the bookcase. Galloping consumption germs passed through cough droplets spread through the air, I read. It could affect not just the lungs but almost any other organ in the body. Sick people's breath, handkerchiefs, hands, and homes were crawling with germs. Working at the drugstore, Poppa shook sick folks' hands, talked with sick folks, and made deliveries to sick folks' homes. And he sure hadn't been eating right since Momma left us, not with Aunt Society cooking. After sliding the book back, I began dusting, but it was hard to keep my mind on what I was doing.

As we walked home, I kept glancing at Poppa. "I'm sorry I broke that beaker. You can keep the money I made today. Will that be enough?"

"Don't worry about that. You heard us talking and that got you upset. Don't pay Hodges any mind. He's a worrywart."

"But he said you'd have to leave. Can't you be treated at home? I'll take care of you. What'll happen to me if you have to go? I won't have my family anymore!"

"My sweet little girlio, just like your momma. I know how important family is to you. It is to me, too. You and me, we're a team, huh." When he coughed and wiped his mouth, red spots stained his handkerchief. I'd never seen him cough blood before. Suddenly the day felt colder. He leaned against me and we staggered home. I made him sit down on the porch so he could rest, and rushed into the kitchen. Aunt Society glanced up, frowning, from her sewing machine. "Girl, don't I keep telling you not —"

"Poppa's sicker! Mr. Hodges thinks he's got galloping consumption and needs to leave!"

She jumped to her feet, her fingers pressed to her mouth. "Oh, precious Jesus, I knew he had it. Where is — Taylor! Oh, you're gonna die!"

Poppa had entered the kitchen behind me. "What'd you tell her, Cece?" he snapped.

"Enough for me to know you need help now." She dropped the sheets on the table and went past me to Poppa, and made him sit down at the table. "Cece, from now on wash his clothes separate from ours, and no more kissing him, you hear?"

"Listen here, Society, I haven't even been diagnosed yet. I haven't left, and I'm gonna keep on kissing my child." His thin face had gotten so tight with anger that his dimples disappeared. I could see his cheekbones sharper.

"And what about this girl?" she went on. "I can't raise her by myself. She's so headstrong and sneaky I won't be able to do a thing with her if you're not here."

Me? Headstrong and sneaky? How could she say that when she controlled every move I made? I poured hot water into Poppa's cup and tried to keep my mouth shut. I wished I had kept quiet about Poppa's attack, too.

"I got to lay down." Poppa rose from the table. "No, Society, leave me alone. I can get there myself." He moved slowly to the couch in the parlor.

Aunt Society looked at me with a squinty half smile, half frown. "If he has to be in a sanitarium, I'll move back to my own home," she said. "We'll close up this house till Taylor gets back. And you, we can hire you out to stay with two ladies I know near Roxboro. You can cook and clean for them. One's portly and only has one leg, so she won't move around much. It'll be quite nice and bring us money."

My hand shook and made Poppa's teacup clatter. "No, ma'am, I don't want to do that," I whispered. "I want to stay here with you and Poppa." Well, not necessarily her. She could move back into her house around the corner.

She crossed her skinny arms. "Taylor won't be here, Cece! You can't stay in here alone. They could teach you to make beds correctly, empty the chamber pot, wash and iron clothes quicker, since it's just them two. Do a little hoeing, pick a little tobacco, feed the chickens, slop a hog or two, and such, for the one when she's too sick. The other sister's a missionary who comes and goes, so she could keep you on the straight and narrow. Don't you see? Accept the fact that you're not smart enough to be a doctor or even a nurse, Celeste. I'm just trying to help you get a trade. So you'll be useful to Taylor when he returns."

"You just don't want to be around me," I said quietly. "You never liked me anyway, because I'm a girl, and you can't raise girls, like Poppa said."

Aunt Society's mouth fell open, then she snapped, "Nonsense! That's what I mean about your sassy mouth. Now you" — she waved her bony fingers toward the parlor — "you go take his tea to him and hush up."

Slop hogs? I bit my lip to steady my hands, and took Poppa's tea to him. I set the cup on the lamp stand and eased down on the couch where he lay, his eyes closed. "She wants to send me away to wait on some ole one-legged tobacco farmwife and a missionary who's apt to ship me off to Russia! Poppa? Poppa?"

Poppa snored. Ole bat wants me to be like that girl Topsy in that book *Uncle Tom's Cabin* we read in school: slave away day and night, no home, no family. How could I save myself? Shivering, I stayed by Poppa until my aunt called me in to peel potatoes for supper.

The next day at school I couldn't talk to anybody about my terrible situation, not even Angel Mae. Being my best friend, she knew when something was wrong, but she didn't pester me about it. Angel Mae was what folks called "stout," because she was heavyset. When she hugged me, it was like I was being folded into a pillow.

She studied me with her big gray eyes. "Have you got any word yet from the *Brownies' Book* folks about our stuff?" she asked. I told her no.

After school I stopped by the Stackhouse to check on Poppa, but Mr. Hodges said he'd gone to see Dr. Pope — one of our best Colored doctors, and one of Poppa's good friends. I had a million questions to ask him, but I kept them in my head. I wished I could have gone with him. I didn't know what kind of tests he had to take, but I knew Poppa hated needles. I could have held his hand, maybe, to help him relax.

The second I dragged inside our house, Aunt Society rose from her sewing machine and cornered me. "That Miz Hugelburger and her sister out past Roxboro been needing a live-in girl for the longest," she began. "You should —"

"Please don't do this!" I dropped my schoolbag and twisted my skirt in my hands. "I promise I'll do whatever you say. I don't know what I'm doing wrong, but I won't do it anymore!"

"How you know what you're gonna do and not do? You can't think straight from one hour to the next." She returned to her sewing machine and talked over its whirring thump. "You're thirteen years old and yet to get your womanhood. You're all stopped up. Girls like you got torment going on inside stopped up like that. And then when you do get your womanhood, you'll go hog wild over every boy you see and bring shame on the family."

My face burned with embarrassment. I blew out my breath.

Old thing's gone completely batty. Where did she get such outrageous ideas? "Oh no, ma'am, I've never whistled or snapped my fingers or ever done anything flirtatious toward a boy! And boys hardly ever come around me anyway, 'cause I smell like lard and lamp oil."

"Hardly ever? So some do, eh?" She nodded her head vigorously, like she'd heard me confess some secret.

Stopped up! Ole crazy bat! I stamped across the kitchen to begin washing dishes while she kept on spouting off. I didn't want to get my womanhood, anyway, and have to wash out messy rags and feel bloated and cramped for days on end. Angel Mae got hers when she was eleven and had terrible cramps. My friend Swan, who lived back of us, got hers when she was nine.

"Cece, you need to be someplace where you can't get into mischief, or be with someone quicker than me to keep an eye on you. What would *you* do? Go live with your fancy Aunt Valentina in New York?" Aunt Society sneered out her name like she was flinging slime from her mouth.

I hadn't thought about Aunt Valentina. "Maybe she could come stay with me here," I said. Was hope on the horizon? "I could be home here, and you could come around but live in your own home. That way I'd still be with my family."

"That woman's no good for doing anything but causing trouble. Now set the table."

As I reached into the cupboard for the plates, an idea began to form. Aunt Valentina might be my only hope. But could I get word to her in time?

Chapter Three

Though I tried to stay awake in bed so I could talk to Poppa after Aunt Society turned in, I fell asleep. When I woke up the next morning, he had already left the house. Out the kitchen window I saw Aunt Society in the backyard hanging up clothes and fussing at the duck poop she had just stepped in. I quickly packed a sardine sandwich and apple into my schoolbag. I wasn't a breakfast eater, so after washing up and throwing on my clothes, I hurried out the front door.

"Bye, Aunt Society," I said low so I knew she wouldn't hear me. She'd label me as being headstrong for leaving like this, but I had to write a letter to Aunt Valentina, and I didn't dare do it at home. I ran to the Stackhouse Hotel and settled myself on a bench. Pulling my coat tighter against the March chill, I balanced my tablet carefully on my knees and began to write.

"Dear Aunt Valentina, I hope this letter reaches you in good health and in a pleasant disposition." Mrs. Bracy had taught us to be more courteous in our letters, but I was in a hurry. "Can you please come down? Poppa has TB and might have to go away." I told her about Aunt Society wanting to send me out to the country to slave under the one-legged tobacco farmer/missionary Hugelburger sisters. "I would be so very indebted to you if you would kindly reply in a rapid manner. I end this letter with much affection for you, my dearest aunt. Yours truly, your devoted niece Celeste." I folded the sheet, slid it into an envelope, addressed it, and went inside to Mr. Toodlums, the desk clerk.

Mr. Toodlums chewed on the ends of his handlebar mustache while he wrote in his ledgers. He was so busy chewing that I had to clear my throat twice to get his attention. "Poppa wants you to please put a stamp on this and mail it out," I said. I crossed my fingers behind my back and prayed the Lord wouldn't strike me down for telling a falsehood.

Mr. Toodlums nodded at the mail basket on the counter. I thanked him, dropped the letter into the basket, and ran on to school. Angel Mae, our school's back-door monitor, waved me in with only two minutes to reach my room and my seat before the tardy bell rang. I could barely keep my mind on what Mrs. Bracy was saying about our new governor.

At lunch with Evalina, Swan, and Angel Mae, I was so quiet and wiggly that even Evalina noticed. "You got chigger bugs on you already?" I shook my head. "Well, what's wrong with you not even said a word? We Butterflies supposed to know how to use words."

"Pipe down, Evalina! How could she use any words with you chattering all the time?" Swan told Evalina. A short, wiry girl, Swan wasn't afraid to talk back to Evalina.

"Poppa's sicker." What else did I dare say? I nibbled on my sandwich, but I wasn't much hungry.

The rest of the day crept along like half-frozen snails. When school finally ended, I burst out the door with Angel Mae, Evalina, and Swan. As we walked together, with them talking about clothes and homework and boys, I said nothing. What would happen if I had to go live with those Hugelburger women? I'd never get to see my friends, or Poppa, either! Tears popped out of my eyes, and of course everybody saw them. "Your pa's gonna be all right," Angel Mae clucked, rubbing my shoulder. I let them think I was crying about my father. Well, I was, but I was crying about them, too.

When we neared the Stackhouse, I saw Poppa standing outside with Mr. Stackhouse. He smiled a little when he saw me, but he didn't look very happy. Ignoring Aunt Society's commandment that running was unfeminine, I hiked up my dress and coat and hurried to him. "You all right, Poppa?"

"Speak to Mr. Stackhouse, too," he said. "Remember your manners."

"Good afternoon, Mr. Stackhouse." Angel Mae, Swan, and Evalina caught up to us and greeted Poppa and Mr. Stackhouse, too. "Poppa, what did the —"

"We'll talk about me later." He pulled my letter from his jacket pocket. My heart slid down to my knees. "And talk about this, too. You get on home. I'll be there directly."

"Yes, sir. Bye, Mr. Stackhouse." I left but I was in no hurry to go home. If Aunt Society knew about the letter, she'd pick and poke and pester me to pieces the minute I set my big toe onto the porch.

"Well, I'm gonna ask you again, what's the matter with you?" Evalina demanded as soon as we'd got onto the next block. "Fess up to something now, girl!"

"You in trouble over that letter?" Swan raised her eyebrows at me. "Did you write it?"

"You order from the Sears Roebuck catalogue again without sending money?" Angel Mae asked calmly.

"No, it's — it's calamitous!" I told them the whole horrible story, especially the part about the Hugelburger sisters. We came to the corner by the cemetery where we usually went our separate ways. "But Aunt Valentina can't get the letter 'cause Poppa didn't send it."

"You can stay with us," Swan offered kindly. Swan lived with her momma; her feebleminded great-grandmomma; her Uncle Jeff, who liked moonshine; his mangy hound dog, Alvin, who always had slobber dripping from his mouth; and Swan's own three cats who hated everybody, especially me. I thanked her, but I'd be better off with the hogs and chickens out in the country.

We said good-bye and I hauled myself on home. I entered through the kitchen door with my insides balled up. Where was she? I peered into the front room, and then I heard her talking with someone in the parlor about a blouse. So that's where she was. I tiptoed into my room and stayed there until I heard Poppa's footsteps on the porch. Then, I hurried into the kitchen to fix his tea just as Aunt Society's customer was leaving. I heard them exchange pleasantries, and then Poppa came into the kitchen, followed by Aunt Society, with the blouse still in her hands.

"What did the —" Aunt Society and I began at the same time. Poppa sat down at the kitchen table. "I want you both to keep my house absolutely quiet till after supper, and that's what I mean," he said in such a sharp voice that Aunt Society silently retreated to her room. I went to my room and tried to concentrate on my homework.

At supper Poppa scooted his navy beans and turnip greens around on his plate but hardly ate a thing. I stuffed scorched beans into my mouth, about to burst from the taste and the tension.

"Well." Poppa finally spoke. "They say I got consumption and they want me to go to Coopers for a spell."

The beans stuck in my throat. I couldn't have said anything anyway.

"I knew it wasn't war gas," Aunt Society declared. "Get your medical and military papers together, Taylor. And ask Mr. Stackhouse to drive you to Coopers. Cece, you boil his plates and silverware tonight. And, Taylor —"

"Didn't I tell you to be quiet?" Poppa said.

"I was just going to say that I'll move back to my own home while you're gone," Aunt Society said.

"What about me?" I whispered, hoping against hope.

"I told you already," Aunt Society said, fidgeting about in her wheelchair.

"Work for the Hugelburgers —"

"Just be quiet like Taylor told you," she said over me. "We'll talk about it later."

"Society, you're thinking and talking crazy again," Poppa said. "You're not going to get hired out nowhere, Cece. I telegrammed your message to Aunt Valentina and got an answer back."

Aunt Society dropped her fork. "You contacted that woman about our situation without asking me?"

"Oh, thank you, Poppa! When's she coming?" I sat up in my chair and swallowed the beans.

Poppa laid his thin hand on mine. "She wants you to live with her in New York till I'm better. She can't just pick up and leave."

I never thought Aunt Valentina would suggest that I go to New York. "But I want to stay here, closer to you and my friends."

Aunt Society folded her arms, nodding and frowning. "You get what you wish for, see? Always bragging on that woman with her sinful ways."

"Society, Valentina has a name." Poppa sighed. "Honey, look at it this way. New York's a wonderful city, with libraries, music, musicians, museums, beautiful clothes, great food, everything. That's why you wrote to her, wasn't it? To be with her?" He stood up unsteadily. "Now, before I forget, be sure tomorrow to let Mr. Hodges look you over."

Aunt Society poked me in my arm. "You think you'll lie around eating chocolate bonbons and having maid service up there with her, but you won't. She'll make you work in a factory twenty hours a day and take every penny you earn. She'll have you sleeping on the floor and wearing the same dress for weeks. So start packing, Sister Sassy. Send your soul right on to Jesus because the rest of you is going to New York."

"At least she likes me," I whispered. "Even if I am a girl."

"What?" Her voice got high. "See, Taylor!"

Right then Poppa had a coughing spell so severe we shut up to help him lie down on the couch. I ran to get his Cheney's medicine. Aunt Society rushed to get a blanket to cover him. Aunt Society and I didn't say another word to each other after that. We just sat in our chairs on each side of Poppa, and watched him.

Later, I rolled from one side of my bed to the other until I knocked Momma's folded-up quilt to the floor. True, I had always wanted to go to New York someday — but not right then!

Maybe I could just run away to Durham, Method, or Knightdale, those little towns outside Raleigh. I didn't know where else to go. And then what? Get lost and raggedy, eating out of pig troughs, drinking milk straight from the cow, sleeping in tobacco barns, and picking flies and fleas out of my lardy hair. Sounded like how things would be for me at the Hugelburgers.

At the drugstore Saturday I opened my mouth wide so Mr. Hodges could peer down my throat. Then he asked if I had pain in my lungs or stomach and did I cough very much. I shook my head. "All right, you can close your mouth. You look fine. No need for you to be examined by a doctor. I just gave you an eyeball checkup."

"Praise God," said Poppa, who'd been watching. He returned to filling bottles behind the counter.

"Is Poppa going to be all right?" I whispered to Mr. Hodges.

"I think so, if he can get fresh fruits and vegetables, rest, nursing care, and quiet," he muttered, making notes on a sheet of paper.

"I could go work at Coopers and be with Poppa. I'd learn more than slaving away on a tobacco farm with the Hugelburgers."

"Well, that's sweet, Cece, but you're too young to work in a sanitarium, or for the Hugelburgers, either. New York's much better."

That night, after we'd all retired, I slipped out of my bed and went to Poppa's. We talked about school and work and my aunts. "Does anybody know when I have to leave? Will I have to be on a train by myself? Will I have to leave before Easter?"

"Mr. Smithfield's working on finding free tickets for you so he can be with you all the way during his run. I figure you'll leave as soon as he gets the tickets." Poppa coughed softly. "Start laying out things now to take. Use my valise, the brown one. Sorry to say, you'll probably go before Easter. But you're too old for Easter baskets, anyway."

"I like more than only that. I like how we ate breakfast at church after sunrise services, and everybody wore their best clothes, our Sunday school program, and how Momma always looked —" I stopped. The last two Easters hadn't been the same without her. "Poppa, would Momma have wanted me to go to Aunt Valentina's?"

"I wondered if you'd ask. Under the circumstances, yes, she'd approve." He squeezed my arm. "Give me a smile, girlio, before you go back to bed. Your smile and your pretty hazel eyes are just like hers. Knowing you're in good hands and remembering your smile will help me get better quicker than anything else."

In the dim lamplight of my room I set out my most precious clothes and possessions to take: my yellow dress with the lace around the neck and wrists; the red velvet dress with the white buttons down the front; my Sunday silk stockings; the family picture of Poppa, Momma, and me; my Bible; and of course my schoolbag, violin, hairbrush, and comb.

Aunt Valentina had always been nice to me. Surely she wouldn't change now. Would she?

I kept trying to get up my courage and tell Angel Mae, Swan, and Evalina my sad news, but I couldn't. When we got to school that Monday, I told Mrs. Bracy that I'd be leaving, and she announced it to the rest of my class. At her words, Angel Mae shook her head, Swan gasped, and Evalina frowned up something terrible. I heard Leon say, "Goin' to the Big Apple! Cece's gonna be a flapper!" But nobody laughed. At first I felt special being singled out like that, then I got sad. These were my friends that I'd have to leave behind! For how long?

While she had the other kids working on arithmetic, Mrs. Bracy took me aside. "I'm going to miss you. You're such a good student."

"I'm gonna miss you, too," I whispered, trying not to cry.

She reached into her desk and pulled out a pretty writing tablet. Each page was trimmed with a thin border of delicate yellow and red flowers and fairies. Two sharpened pencils set in a small pocket attached to the tablet. "Write to us once in a while. New York is a fast, noisy city, Cece. Learn to speak up for yourself and don't be timid."

She hugged me, and I hugged her back. When we separated, I saw that her face was wet. I thanked her again and stuck the tablet into my schoolbag for safekeeping.

I found my friends in a corner of the school yard, talking about me. "You can go to the *Brownies' Book* office right away and find out about our poems and stuff," Swan said. "If they send you a letter here, your aunt might throw it away, or lose it. You shouldn't have any problem finding the office, 'cause I bet it's in a building the size of the Statue of Liberty."

I nodded, but how would I find their office in big ole New York? I'd read about New York's subway, but I didn't know how a subway worked. Did New York have a trolley service like ours here? Our trolley only ran on certain streets, and we

Coloreds sat in the back. Would I be able to find a seat anywhere, or would I have to stand until an empty one in our section was available?

"Speaking of us Butterflies, it won't be the same without you," Angel Mae said, "since you and your momma really started it."

"But Mrs. Bracy's been keeping it going at school okay. She had a hand in getting it started in the first place," I reminded her. "Her and Momma. Maybe she'll have special meetings for you after school's out."

"But it hasn't been the same without just us girls reading the *Brownies' Book* magazine together, and having our little tea parties, and going to the movies, stuff like that. At school we just meet and talk about writing and have to put up with Leon and those other boys."

"I don't mind that," Evalina broke in. "Leon's cute."

"Cece, promise you'll write just one letter to all three of us," said Swan, "so we won't miss out on anything. You know Evalina'll hog her letter and not share it. And write and tell us what it's like to live in a mansion and go to the zoos."

"All right, but you each write back to me, please, 'cause I'm gonna be lonely."

"What if you had to take one of those airplane things, instead of a train?" asked Angel Mae.

"I'd have heart palpitations on an airplane," I said, and shivered.

"You'll have heart palpitations on the train," Evalina broke in, "being as you've never been on one before."

"Hush up, Evie!" Angel Mae swung her arms around me. "I'm gonna miss you so much, Miss Mouse!" she cried. Swan and

Evalina hugged me, too. When we pulled apart, we wiped our faces on our coat sleeves.

"Aunt Society said manholes in New York don't have covers," I said, and sniffled, "so children fall into them, never to be seen again."

"If that was true, Mrs. Bracy or some other teacher would have told us when we studied New York in geography," Evalina retorted. That made us laugh.

"You'll be back by fall, 'cause you said your father'll be better by then, so maybe it won't be too bad." Swan tried to reassure me. "In the meantime, you'll be in the Colored people's capital. You can do anything there — write, play Dede, read every book in the world, and live high on the hog with your aunt. She's a famous actress and singer, ain't she?"

"Well, that's what Poppa and Mr. Smithfield said just a few days ago, and I know she wears fine clothes when she's here," I said, like I was reminding myself. "At least she did all that when she was here for Christmas the other year. I really don't know how famous she is."

"If you live in Harlem and sing and dance and live in a mansion, you ought to be famous," Angel Mae said. "Let's say our old Butterflies pledge, the one we did when it was only us girls meeting here at your place."

"All right, Butterflies, let's spread our wings," I ordered. We gathered in a circle, hands touching one another's shoulders. "We pledge to be beautiful and pure in spirit, thought, word, and deed," we said together. We lifted and lowered our arms like we were fluttering our wings. "Moment by moment, hour by hour, day by day, week by week, month by month, year by year, decade by decade, score by score. This is our solemn promise one and all."

I tried to think about how I should be excited, going to the Big Apple. I didn't feel excited. Just scared.

When I reached home, I saw Momma's sweetgrass basket sitting on the sideboard in the parlor. Aunt Society was in her wheelchair, her head bent over a bundle of white muslin, sewing furiously. She wore her red-and-white-checkered apron dress. Poppa stood with his valise in his hands, biting his lip.

I grew cold inside. "What's going on?"

"Mr. Smithfield found tickets," Poppa said. He tried to smile at me. "You have to leave this afternoon. It's time."

He pointed to the basket. "Mrs. Smithfield fixed your food. Check your valise to make sure your aunt's packed what you want. We'll try and send more later."

Leaving now? I hadn't even said good-bye to everybody! Numb, I opened the valise. I found our family picture and my Bible. Most of the clothes I'd set out were missing. That ole bat had packed heavy, long woolen stockings and underwear, and heavy sweaters. Was New York chilly all year? I wore my only pair of shoes. When I glanced around at Aunt Society, she dropped her eyes and wouldn't look back. She wanted me to look as dull as she looked when she stood by Aunt Valentina.

In the kitchen I wrapped echinacea leaves, sassafras bark, goldenseal root powder, and other herbs in scraps of brown paper. I didn't know what kind of medicine Aunt Valentina might have, so I figured I should be prepared. I hardly ever got sick, but I sure didn't want to in New York. I carried the herbs back to the parlor and tucked them in my schoolbag.

New York! This couldn't be real! My heart pounded with excitement and fear.

Just then I heard Mr. Bivens's bell outside. "Come along, Celeste." Aunt Society finally spoke. "Don't make Mr. Bivens wait."

Wringing my hands, I rushed into my room. I pulled my journal from under my mattress — where it had been safe from the ole bat's nose — picked up my one precious *Brownies' Book* magazine, and hid my journal in it. I strapped my only belt around my violin case so I could carry it more easily. My China-head doll? My parasol? The embroidered picture of the fishermen? All too big for the valise. Momma's shawl? No, Poppa might need it. Handkerchiefs! My dresses!

"Celeste!"

"Good-bye, room," I whispered. I carried my things into the front room and packed everything into the valise except for my violin. My heart twisted when I looked at Poppa. He rested his hand on my shoulder, then picked up the valise.

"Say good-bye to your aunt," he said. I dragged myself over to her and kissed her stiffly on her wrinkled cheek.

"God be with you till we meet again," she said. Her nose was unusually red. "You behave, stay out of the hot sun, and don't take on any of — her — sinful ways."

"Yes, ma'am," I said. When she dabbed at her eyes, my tears spilled out. I'd even miss her, I realized. She followed us out to the wagon, and handed Mr. Bivens my lunch basket. Poppa and I climbed into the wagon. When Mr. Bivens clucked, ole Lissa slowly drove us away. I looked around and waved at my aunt. She waved once, then returned to the porch.

I had a million things to say to Poppa, but I couldn't put anything into words. We silently leaned against each other until I saw the train station come into sight. "You'll be all right with Aunt Valentina," Poppa said. Then he burst out, "I wish she could have come down here, but she couldn't. I don't like you being so far off, but it can't be helped."

I lowered my head. Tears fell onto my clenched hands. He dropped an envelope on top of them. "Here. Stamps, some penny postcards. Write to me, your girlfriends, and your aunt. Be careful, girlio."

"Oh, Poppa, I'm scared. Don't make me go!" I fell over onto his shoulder. He rubbed and patted my back, but the wagon kept moving.

"It's just a test, girlio. All life's a test and you got to pass it, just like how you wrote in your poem 'Forsythia,' remember?"

"That was something I remembered from a St. Paul sermon," I whispered. I didn't believe those words.

The wagon slowed and stopped. Colored people strolled around on the train station platform, shouting over the train and motorcar noises. Poppa helped me down to the ground. I saw Mr. Smithfield in his black jacket, black pants, and black cap. He waved at us to come over. I heaved my feet along like I wore horseshoes instead of my Buster Browns. Mr. Bivens handed my valise to Mr. Smithfield and my lunch basket to me. I held tight to my schoolbag and violin.

Poppa whispered, "I love you, girlio. Gimme a kiss and a big smile. You'll be back soon and I'll be fine. Everything'll be all right."

I set down my stuff, and I wrapped my arms around his neck and squeezed until he coughed. My face was too crumpled up to give him a good smile. My tummy was twisted up so bad it probably looked like a pretzel. The next thing I knew, my things and I were stumbling up the train steps behind Mr. Smithfield. "You play my niece on this trip," he said. "Follow close, now."

Our Colored section of the train was crammed with grown folks, children, boxes, coal dust, and steamy air that reeked like rotten vegetables. Mr. Smithfield showed me to a seat by a woman and across from a frowning, skinny-as-a-beanpole, bald-headed boy pushing at three small children. The boy shoved at them as if he was trying to keep them stacked like the books on our bookshelves. "Don't talk to nobody but these nice folks here," Mr. Smithfield said. "I'll watch your valise."

The woman yawned and smiled at me. "That your kinfolks?" She pointed out the open window to Poppa and Mr. Bivens waving on the platform. As the train wheels screeched into motion, I waved back until I couldn't see my father or even the train station anymore. Mr. Smithfield shouted out greetings up and down the aisle while babies cried and people talked, laughed, and hollered. We rolled faster away from stores, streets, and people I had known all my life. Soon we were speeding past tobacco barns, people bent over in newly plowed fields, then woods.

Poppa was gone, and so was everything else that I loved.

Chapter Four

That bald-headed skinny boy nudged me with his shoe. "Stop that sniffling and moaning," he snapped. "You wake up these younguns and I'll make you rock 'em back to sleep. Anybody got a right to cry is me. You don't see me crying."

"Don't be barking at me," I wanted to say, but I didn't. I just stopped crying as best I could. He was right. Nobody else around me was boo-hooing like this. I noticed that he had the thickest eyelashes I'd ever seen on a boy. And a crease-like dimple in his right cheek, like Poppa had. I loved dimples, I guess because Poppa had them.

"If they wake up Momma, she'll pop a knot on my head, see," he explained, but not as snappy, nodding at the sleeping lady beside me. "Momma's knots hurt."

"I guess you got your hands full both ways," I told him.

"You're darn tootin' I do." He sounded almost proud. "Where you headed by yourself?"

I hesitated. I didn't even know this boy's name. Aunt Society had drilled me about "Don't talk to strangers on the trolleys, trains, and out on the street." I decided to remember my manners and not be a stranger. "My name's Celeste Lassiter Massey," I said politely. "And who are you?"

"Big Willie Madison. So, where you headed?"

"New York City, to visit my Aunt Valentina. She's —"

"Girl, you're talking so low I can't hear you," he said. "Speak up! But don't yell." He pointed to the sleeping children.

I repeated myself. What I wanted to ask was, "Why are you called Big Willie, being so skinny?"

"Aunt Valentina's a big Broadway star and a famous singer and dancer." Maybe I was stretching her reputation a bit, but it sounded right to me!

"This train's probably burning coal my daddy dug. He's a coal miner, see, the best around, and a union man. Him and his crew go way inside a mountain. He's also been so far down in the ground he says he almost hears folks talk Chinese." Big Willie grinned. "They call him Coal Dust Willie, 'cause everything he eats and breathes and wears is full of coal dust. We're going to Richmond, Virginia, then West Virginia to meet up with him for the summer, then we'll hike on back down here to Eagle Rock come fall."

"You mean he makes coal, like what they burn in stoves?" I liked his smile, too, showing that crooked front tooth. I liked that he was dressed neat, in a stylish brown knickerbocker knee-pants suit and stockings. A matching golf cap lay on a bag by him.

"You can't *make* coal." Big Willie snorted. "You dig it out the mountain or the ground first. My daddy's in the mines from can't see in the morning to can't see at night. He coughs a lot, and can spit it farther than anybody else."

He pointed to a black grape-sized bump on his dark brown chin. "See this big chunk a coal on my face? Daddy says that shows I was marked to be a miner, so I'm gonna work in the mines with him. What I really want to do is be a baseball player. I can fling a chunk of coal and hit a can off a fence twenty feet away, and I'm only fourteen. I can spit good, too. But I don't cough."

I was trying to take in everything he said. I knew a lot about oil and kerosene, but not much about the coal-mining process. I did know that any kind of dust wasn't good for the body, though. After all, I was going to be a doctor, and often read Mr. Hodges's medical encyclopedia and other books. Big Willie's father probably spit and coughed so much because of the coal dust in his lungs. "Baseball player sounds more like it, since you got those long arms," I told him. "I bet you're a good one."

He nodded slightly. "Better believe it! I'm gonna get on a team, too, after I'm through with the coal mines." He stopped talking to push his brothers and sister around again. Poppa played second base with the Raleigh Colored Rangers on Saturday afternoons, until Momma got sick. I bet Big Willie would hate being in a dark, dirty coal mine when he'd rather be out in the sunny, fresh air throwing balls. I kept my mouth shut about that part.

I was glad to talk with somebody my age — and a boy — for once. I liked bald-headed boys. Momma said you could see the shape of a man's brain better when he was bald-headed. If his head was round at the top and then narrowed toward the neck, that meant he had a big brain and was smart. Like Big Willie's head was. Him being so skinny — though at least he was tall — made me want to fix him a big meal and fatten him up.

Celeste, you're a mess, I told myself, and laughed inside. Wouldn't Aunt Society have a fit if she saw us and could read my thoughts! I smiled at him again and he smiled back. I closed my tear-swollen eyes, trying to imagine him pitching on Poppa's team. Maybe the train ride to New York wouldn't be so bad if everybody was as friendly as Big Willie was.

Next thing I knew I was waking up to the train jerking to a crawl, then halting, and Mr. Smithfield yelling, "Richmond! Richmond, Virginia! Everybody for Richmond, get off here." I struggled up straight from where I had been leaning against Mrs. Madison's shoulder.

"I didn't sleep, watching these kids. But you were cuttin' Zs louder than the train whistle," Big Willie said, and slapped his knee, cackling.

"Was not. Listen, when I get to New York I'm gonna write to my friends back home about you going to work in a coal mine."

"How're you gonna write about that when you never been in one?"

Well, he had a point there. I pulled Poppa's stamps envelope from my schoolbag, wrote Aunt Valentina's address on a penny postcard, and handed it to him. "How about you write to me when you get to the coal mines, and tell me what it's like? I'll pass the postcard on to my friends. I mean, if you want to."

"I reckon I can do that." He slapped his knee again, and woke up the kids.

Mr. Smithfield swayed over right then and touched Mrs. Madison on the arm, which probably saved Big Willie from getting that knot on his head. "You look happy, Celeste, so you must be getting along all right. We're here long enough to let folks on and off to refresh themselves. You need to do anything?"

I shook my head. I was hungry but I didn't want to eat yet. I was afraid I'd run out of food before I got to New York. I moved out of the way so Mrs. Madison could leave. She and Big Willie rounded up the triplets, bags, and boxes, and headed up the aisle. Big Willie clapped his cap onto his head. "Promise to write me back if I write to you," he hollered.

"I will!" Suddenly I remembered. "Come to the Great Negro State Fair in Raleigh in October if you're back in Eagle Rock. It has pitching contests. I'll be there!" Or at least I prayed I would. I hoped he heard me. They rounded a corner for the steps and then they were gone.

I waited in the now empty, dimly lit train car. Mr. Smithfield said it would be a while before the train would move. What if somebody got on and grabbed me? I pulled my schoolbag and Dede closer for comfort. What if a bat flew onto the train and got into my hair? Aunt Society said bats liked to pull out bad girls' hair. She sure pulled mine out, though I didn't consider myself bad. Ole bat! She washed and combed and yanked on my hair like she was out plowing a field.

But right then I could have even put up with her. And what if Aunt Valentina was as mean as Aunt Society said she was? What if she made me work all the time and fed me turnips and burnt bread? I turned my head to the window and burrowed my head in my coat. Poppa and my friends said I'd see and do exciting things, having such a wonderful, good-looking Aunt Valentina. I remembered how she'd looked the last time I saw her: shapely gams, which was what Mr. Smithfield called her legs; ginger-toned smooth skin; pretty white straight teeth; long black hair; and almond-shaped brown eyes, which made her look a little bit like she had Asian or Mexican in her. Though she didn't.

I guess I'd said so much about her to my friends over the years and talked about all New York City's great sights that they'd assumed I would be rip-roaring ready to go. But I wasn't. I just wanted to go home! *Well, pray for the best, Celeste,* I told myself. I tried to imagine myself standing on the Statue of Liberty torch and shaking hands with the bears and elephants at the Bronx Zoo. But all that stuff scared me, so instead I just daydreamed about the time when we Butterflies had gone to the movies one Christmas.

I must have dozed off, because off in the distance, then closer, I began to hear *Clickety, clackety, clack. Clickety, clackety, clack.* Beside me a tiny man wearing a top hat and beard danced. He sang in a high-pitched whine. Was I dreaming about Abe Lincoln? When his right arm jerked, his hat sprang up. He was tipping his hat to me!

Now I knew I was dreaming. Or was I having hysterics? Folks said girls and women had hysterics when they talked or acted strange or fell out foaming at the mouth. Aunt Society never foamed at the mouth, but she sure talked and acted strange a lot. I squeezed my eyes shut and this time kept them shut until Mr. Smithfield shook me. "You need to relieve yourself," he whispered. "You have another long ride ahead. Leave your stuff. It'll be safe."

I staggered after him into the cold early-morning light, but took Dede and my schoolbag with me. I could survive without my lunch but not without them. He pointed to an outhouse several yards away. My stomach was squirming and rolling again nervously. I hoped going to the outhouse would calm it down, but it didn't.

When I returned, several new people had come into our car.

One was a thin man in shirt and pants standing — I noted with a start — near my seat. When I sat down, he sat down beside me, smiling. Mr. Smithfield shook his hand. "Cece, this is Sandy Smalls, the puppet man. Mr. Smalls, my niece, Celeste."

I smiled back and nodded, but didn't speak. When Mr. Smalls opened a suitcase, I saw the tiny man — a wooden puppet! — inside. He wore a painted red-and-blue-striped suit and a white shirt. Mr. Smalls screwed a long, narrow stick into the puppet's back. Singing softly, Mr. Smalls made the puppet dance by flicking the stick and gently thumping on a wooden paddle that it stood on. The puppet's jointed arms and legs swung rapidly in time to the thumping and flicking. I had seen puppets like this at our state fair but never any so close.

"This is Mr. USA," he said as the train began to move. "Would you like to help him dance?" I thought I was too old for puppets, but not this time! I told him yes, softly, and took the stick. Mr. Smalls began humming again, patting his foot and rhythmically thumping the other end of the paddle situated on his knee. I flicked the stick a couple of times. "Oh, my goodness gracious!" I whispered when the puppet jumped. I stared, waiting. Then I realized that I had to move the stick to make the little man dance. This was fun!

Mr. USA and I danced until full daylight arrived, when around us folks and babies stirred, stretched, yawned, and talked. Mr. Smalls stored Mr. USA back in the suitcase.

"I'm going to write to my friends back home about you and your puppets after I reach New York."

"You gonna like where you're going?" he asked softly.

"I — well, it's because of Poppa," I said. I told him about Aunt

Society, too, and my poetry and the *Brownies' Book* magazine, Big Willie, and — oh, my little lips just flapped! I guess Mr. Smalls's kindly eyes made me spill the beans.

"When you're up in that big town thinking about home, talk to this little lady," he said. He opened his suitcase and lifted out a small wooden girl puppet with a yellow and red dress and black shoes painted on her square feet. He screwed a stick into her back and handed her and a paddle to me.

She was beautiful. "I shall keep her all my life," I breathed. Remembering to speak louder, I thanked him over and over. "What's her name?"

"Whatever you want to call her," he said. "I been making puppets since I was a boy. I'd carve them from pine splinters in the pine tar camps where me and my folks lived. We worked in camps outside Loris, Bucksport, and Conway, South Carolina. I sold 'em to make a little money. Now I just make 'em to give away. I get my real money from making tables, chairs, stuff like that. No more pine tar camps for me!"

"Did you know a man named Thomas Day? He made furniture, too. We have one of his sideboards in our parlor."

"I never knew him, but I know his work. Now, he's what you call a *real* furniture maker. He's a famous man."

I tucked the puppet in with Dede where she'd be safe. "I'll call her Miss Pinetar," I said.

My stomach growled. Mrs. Smithfield had fixed two thick slices of country ham, buttered yam cubes wrapped in collard green leaves, two boiled eggs, two corn bread squares, two slices of pecan pie, an orange — and six beautiful candy Easter eggs! She hadn't forgotten me. I ate one piece of ham, a few yam cubes, one piece of corn bread, just half of one slice of pie, and the blue Easter egg. I gave a red Easter egg and the other half of pie to Mr. Smalls, along with a penny postcard with Aunt Valentina's address. He promised to write. I could share his card with the Butterflies, too — if he wrote.

After that full meal, I fell asleep. When I woke up, Mr. Smalls was gone. Now a young woman with a hundred bags was crunched against me. How did she do that and me not hear her? But what I noticed most was that she had long, straight, thick black hair and smelled like vanilla.

She smiled at me and touched her hair. "Like it?" she asked in a friendly way. I nodded, wishing mine looked like that. "Mine was short like yours, until I began using Madam C. J. Walker products. Then it grew faster than the grass in my momma's backyard."

"Who's Madam C. J. Walker?" I asked, still staring.

"Madam was a businesswoman. She showed Colored women how to take better care of our hair. I'm Almadene Hardy, by the way. I'm a Madam C. J. Walker agent. I sell Walker products and train other women to be agents, too."

I told her my name. She showed me pictures of Mrs. Walker: one with her hair as short as mine, and one with her hair down her back; she showed me a picture of Mrs. Walker's business in Indianapolis, Indiana. "And here she is in her Model T Ford. She also had a mansion in Harlem. This Colored lady was a million-aire! She passed on in 1919, and we miss her so, but we keep her company alive. She personally trained me in the Walker hair care method."

"My momma died in January 1919," I whispered. "I wish I could get my hair to grow again. Momma said my hair was soft and needed special treatment. She kept it long and sweet-smelling. But she — Then my aunt started washing my hair with lye soap, caking it down with lard, and yanking the comb through my hair. The comb ended up with more of my hair than my head."

Mrs. Hardy shook her head sympathetically. Then she handed me two small jars. "This shampoo and salve will help. And this sheet teaches you how to care for your hair and scalp."

"Oh, thank you! Maybe you'll write and send me more information." I wrote my name and Aunt Valentina's address on a penny postcard and handed it to her.

She looked at the card. "One Hundred Thirty-sixth Street? That's the same street as the Walker salon," Mrs. Hardy said. "Maybe your aunt'll take you in for treatments now and then."

My face lit up. "It's a blessing to have met you," I told her, "which is what Momma said when she met nice people."

"Same to you," Mrs. Hardy replied.

After a while Mr. Smithfield appeared. "Washington, Washington, D.C., coming round the curve. Everybody gets off to make their next connection." He lowered his voice. "Miss Celeste, you too. I'll show you to the next train. You sit down on a bench inside close by."

My heart beat fast and my tummy repeated its pretzel twists. More strangers! I collected my schoolbag, my violin, and my lunch basket. Mr. Smithfield said he'd get my valise. Mrs. Hardy and I followed the other Colored folks down the steps, off the train, and into a bigger wave of people pushing, walking, and hurrying into the station. I felt like that tiny boat in the balloon story, being swept out to sea.

"I'll wait a bit here with you till the porter comes," Mrs. Hardy said, and I appreciated that. We sat on the bench, watching for Mr. Smithfield. But after several minutes, when he didn't show, she stood up. "I've got to go, Celeste. Don't talk to anybody, and keep close watch over your things. Maybe I'll come see you when I get to New York."

"Thank you for staying with me, ma'am. I hope to see you again," I whispered. "I really liked talking to you." As she turned to leave, I tried to think of something to keep her with me longer. "How often should I wash my hair?"

"At least twice a month. Read the sheets. Good-bye, honey!" She and her bags vanished into the crowd.

Sitting on the bench with my violin and my schoolbag clutched to my chest, my lunch basket hanging heavy on my arm, and my coat smothered around me, I felt like a slab of beef squashed between two thick bread and tomato slices. Seemed like all the people racing to and from the trains stared at me. Like that man in overalls by Gate A. Seemed like he'd been watching me ever since Mrs. Hardy left.

After forever, Mr. Smithfield arrived with my valise. "See that clock on the wall there? Your train is due in ten minutes. I'll be right back. Then you can go refresh yourself and get ready for the next go-round. All right?"

"Can't I come with you?"

Mr. Smithfield shook his head. "I got work to do." He smiled broadly, then removed a large gray metal whistle from his coat pocket. "Anybody try to bother you, blow! People'll come help."

I pulled the Walker hair jars from my coat pockets, tucked them into my valise, and dropped the whistle into my coat pocket, sighing. If somebody got after me, I'd be too afraid to blow that thing. Trains rolled in and out of the station with great thuds, roars, and grindings that kept me jumping. Men wheeling food carts yelled out what they had for sale. Everything but the clock's minute hand moved quickly. Suddenly I was thirsty. I glanced around for a Colored water fountain. When I turned back around, that man in the overalls stood right beside me! I jumped and gasped.

"Lemme carry your bag," he said, showing his yellow teeth. Brown stubble covered his pale face. He smelled like sour cabbage. He grabbed for my valise, but I clawed at it. He snatched at Dede's case and broke the strap. Dede crashed to the floor. He seized my schoolbag, but I kicked him in the shin. Swearing, he jerked my valise out of my hands and pulled my lunch basket off my arm, knocking me off the bench onto the floor, and left.

"Help, somebody! Mr. Smithfield!" I shouted, finally finding my voice. I scrambled around on the floor with scratched, stinging knees and an aching shoulder, grabbing my schoolbag and violin case, confused and terrified. My only picture of Momma, me, and Poppa together; my Bible; my clothes; the Walker salves; my food — gone! I finally thought to blow the whistle.

An elderly lady limped over to me. "Girlie, you all right?" she asked.

"That man — he stole everything!" I screamed. I saw Mr. Smithfield rushing to me. "My Bible, my —"

"What happened? What's wrong?" he asked.

"I saw that low-down scum steal her things," the woman cried. "Who left this chile out here by herself? Where's her people? Porter, call the police!"

Mr. Smithfield banged his hands together angrily, then shook his head. "Cece, are you hurt? I'll take a look at your knees in a minute. That scoundrel's gone for good. Right now I got to get you onto the next train before it pulls out. I —"

"But my things! He —"

"Come on now, Cece. I know it's bad, honey, but you got to come on."

Tears surged down my face. When I wrote my poem about life being a test, I didn't mean terrible things were supposed to happen to me. I was flunking this test! I stumbled after Mr. Smithfield. I couldn't wait to leave Washington, D.C.

Chapter Five

Mr. Smithfield steered me toward the car that would carry me on to New York. "Bad things can't be stopped sometimes," he said. "That ole devil waits around every bush to steal our joy. Just be glad you didn't get hurt worse than you did. Look, I'll round you up something more to eat right quick."

"But can't you keep looking? Maybe that robber threw away Poppa's bag when he didn't find money in it."

"I'll scout around but I don't expect to find it. If he threw it down, probably somebody else picked it up. Now you sit tight and I'll be right back."

"What if another robber comes and pesters me? Can't you please stay with me?"

"I can't go look and stay at the same time," he said. "Use that whistle."

I sat down until he left the car, then I stood back up with the whistle in my mouth, trembling. The cold wind whipped around my legs like it thought it was still outside. What if that awful devil was hiding in here, waiting to steal the little bit I had left? Or a hobo slipped on and grabbed my schoolbag and Dede? *Dear Lord and Dear Momma, watch over me. Pray for angels and watch out for devils. Robbers, stay away!*

In a few minutes a woman got on, then a few more people. Several smiled at me. I sat down, but kept the whistle clenched between my teeth until I felt too silly, and took it out. Mr. Smithfield brought me a chunk of cheese, a fork, a can of sardines, half an apple, and water in a tin cup. He said he checked some trash buckets but didn't see any of my things. "Stay warm. It'll keep getting colder. You're goin' north, baby! You might even see snow."

Snow? I had only seen snow in Raleigh a few times. When I had walked in it, my feet had nearly frozen, even though I'd stuffed rags into my shoes. As I munched on the sardines, and shivered, I thought about my other pairs of heavy stockings and my old gray woolen bonnet in the valise. I wished I had put on the stockings and the bonnet, but it was too late now. What would Aunt Valentina think when she saw me with only the clothes I was wearing, bad breath, and messy hair? Wouldn't a fancy entertainer like her be scandalized to be seen with raggedy, smelly me?

I didn't have a brush or comb, talcum powder, or even salt to rinse my mouth. I hadn't packed any herbs in my schoolbag for sour breath. My scratched knees burned under my torn stockings, and my shoulder hurt. Poppa would say I was a case! My eyes teared up, thinking of him. He'd be so upset when he heard. At least I still had my schoolbag and Dede. If that stinky scoundrel had stolen my writing things and Dede, I think I'd have had to give up the ghost and die right there in the train.

Well, I knew one thing. I wasn't going to leave my seat again until I reached New York. I didn't care what Mr. Smithfield said.

Nobody'd steal anything else from me, either. I'd stab them with the fork first.

Like little mousey me could stab someone! That made me laugh.

The train finally rumbled off for Baltimore. We stopped at several stations but I didn't move. I finally warmed up enough to doze off a little. I don't remember where the train stopped next, but I woke up with a change of mind about leaving my seat. I signaled Mr. Smithfield and he motioned to a woman sitting a few seats ahead of me to take me to the outhouse.

When I got back, I asked Mr. Smithfield how big Harlem was. "Big, honey, big. So big Harlem could swallow up Raleigh and still be starving," he told me. "But you got to step lively so hooligans won't steal from you like that man did. Most are fine people. So enjoy the music, walk fast, and eat lots of down-home Harlem food."

I nodded at his words and warnings. Sounded like I'd be looking for the *Brownies' Book* office a long time. I thought of Aunt Society's predictions about factory sweatshops and hog slop, too. Besides open manholes, now I'd have to watch for thieves. The old bat had warned me about staying away from strangers, even in Raleigh. I'd been trying to do that all along, but what if these crazy people up here wouldn't stay away from *me*? *Pray for the best, Miss Celeste,* I told myself. The closer we chugged toward New York, the harder I prayed.

We stopped somewhere when the train broke down, and stayed there several hours. Finally we headed out again. We stopped *again* and stayed put for several more hours. My neck was about to break trying to hold up my head. Next thing I knew,

Mr. Smithfield was shaking my shoulder to wake me up. New York! Harlem station! On wobbly legs I followed Mr. Smithfield down the train steps. The cold wind slapped me in the face. "I don't see your aunt," he said, rubbing his hands together. "You see her? Maybe she got caught up in traffic." He stopped a pretty lady in a fur coat and pointed to me. She shook her head. He stopped some other women, too, but none of them were Aunt Valentina. He told me to sit down on a nearby bench, and against my better judgment, I did. Cold again, I watched for ugly men in overalls who smelled like cabbage.

Where was she? Had she changed her mind? What if she didn't show up at all? I felt like sinking into the platform floor, but that was too much like falling into a manhole, so I sat up straight.

Mr. Smithfield returned this time with a bent-over woman in an expensive-looking red wool coat with a white lambs' hair collar, and a matching large red hat. The woman gazed at me, then enveloped me into her coat in a tight hug. She smelled like her familiar lemonade and cherries. Yes, here was Aunt Valentina! But why was she so crooked? "My beautiful Celeste!"

"You're here! I —"

"Oh, good, you brought your violin," she went on in her soft, sweet voice that was always so comforting. "We'll make good music together." When she turned me loose and stared into my face, I gasped. For an instant I thought I saw my mother. "Where's your other bags?"

Before I could explain how a robber stole my things when Mr. Smithfield left me on a bench, Mr. Smithfield told his version about how he had had to take care of his passengers and couldn't

★ 53 ★

stay with me, when the thief attacked. "Oh, I'm so sorry," Aunt Valentina said as she hooked her arm through Mr. Smithfield's, and took me by the hand. "But we'll take care of everything. I'm glad you didn't get hurt."

"He hurt my shoulder, and when —"

"I imagine you'll have to get back to work now, Alton," Aunt Valentina broke in. "Or are you free for a while?"

Mr. Smithfield peered down at my aunt with a toothy smile on his face. "Well, I do have some free time before I head on," he said.

She handed him a small piece of paper. "Please contact me next time you're in town," she said. By now we had reached the station entrance. "As much as I'd love to invite you to my, uh, home, Cece and I have some pressing engagements to attend to."

Mr. Smithfield opened and closed his mouth, then lowered his head. "I see." He cleared his throat, straightened his cap, then patted me on the shoulder. "Take good care of yourself, Miss Cece, and I hope to see you back home soon." He tipped his cap to us and walked away fast.

"Bye, Mr. Smithfield." I kept calling to him until Aunt Valentina tugged on my arm.

"Still an ole flirt," she murmured, shaking her head. "Well, Cece, now we're off on a grand adventure. Shall we?"

"Yes, ma'am," I said. Now it was just me. And her. And New York. Not only my tummy, but now all of me was in knots. "Aunt Valentina, what color is your new motorcar? Will I have my own room in your mansion?"

She didn't answer, but instead hurried me up the cold street through the crowds so fast I could barely get my words out.

Folks were still out — at night! Back home everybody would probably be asleep by now. I smelled rotten fish and sour vegetables from the trash cans lining the sidewalks and the snow-clumped alleys.

We walked and we walked and we walked. My sore shoulders and knees, and my bare ears, fingers, and cheeks began to ache in the freezing air. And my dogs were barking!

I got up my courage. "Aunt Valentina, are we almost to your mansion? I'm tired."

"No, we have to make a stop first. Come on now, we're late."

"Late for what?"

She stopped under a streetlamp. She wasn't smiling now. She wore that blank look grown folks like Mrs. Bracy and Mr. Hodges use when they're trying not to show how mad or irritated they are. "Celeste, your train was so late I left my job twice to get you. I'm bent over now because I strained something in my back so bad last night it feels like a fire burning my spine. You have to come help me work."

"I'm going to the theater to help you dance? Or sing?" Thrilled and alarmed, I tried to imagine myself onstage kicking up my legs with a feather boa around my shoulders. No, indeedy! Not Miss Mouse! "Oh, I couldn't do that, Aunt Valentina. But maybe we could ride in your car to ease your back? Mr. Smithfield said it was a Pierce-Arrow."

"I don't have a car anymore. No more questions!" she snapped, to my surprise, then mumbled, "We're going to scrub floors and wash walls."

Scrub floors? No car? Was she joshing with me? She sure didn't look joshed. What was going on? What was next? A hog slop supper? If I saw a little man with a beard dancing around with wooden feet, then I would know I was still on the train. Dreaming. But that cold wind gnawing my face and fingers let me know I was wide awake.

Finally we came to a monstrous building with a million stone steps. I groaned. Like climbing one of Big Willie's mountains! But Aunt Valentina hurried us around in the dark to a back door, and knocked.

A man opened it. "You keep coming and going like this and I'll get somebody else," he said.

"I'm sorry, Mr. Hartwig," my aunt said meekly. "It won't happen again. I've brought my niece here to help."

"All right, but it's two for the price of one. Get it?"

What did that mean? Aunt Valentina said, "Yes, sir," and motioned for me to follow her. We entered a small, dimly lit lobby. My aunt removed her coat and hat, set them on a bench, and told me to set my things there, too. I hesitated. "It's all right. It's just us here and the doors are locked. Now, let's get to work."

"Can we sit down for a minute?" I begged.

"No. Well, for one minute." She sat down, rubbing her back and making a face. I set my schoolbag and my violin down, then placed her coat on top of them. I had hardly sat down when she eased back up. "Mr. Hartwig's the head janitor, and my boss," she whispered. She nodded toward a short White man standing by some double doors. He smiled a little when we passed through.

I gasped. Rows of seats stretched before me to a massive stage, where gold brocade curtains cascaded down on each side. Ornate balcony seats were suspended above both ends of the stage.

Marble pillars decorated with carved figures of fat babies toting harps, bows, and arrows lined the walls. Chandeliers with hundreds of yellow electric lightbulbs glittered from the ceiling. I reckoned the room was five times as big as our capitol's rotunda, and the capitol was the biggest building I'd ever been in. Mouth open, I turned to Aunt Valentina.

"Yes, isn't it fabulous?" she said without smiling. "You're in the Abyssinian Theater. Fabulous productions in a fabulous place, for Harlem."

I still tried to see her in furs and jewels on the stage singing grand songs. "And where you work?" I asked hopefully.

"Yes, scrubbing floors. Right now."

"Oh." My vision collapsed. I followed her into a small room. She picked out scrub brushes, soap, water buckets, and long stained aprons, and gave one of each to me. We tucked bunches of dry rags into the apron pockets. "I scrub and you rinse, then we both dry."

"But, Aunt Valentina —"

"Shush your mouth and come on."

I hated to admit it, but Aunt Society was right about one thing: Aunt Valentina was going to work me to death. When we began our trek to the stage, I tripped on my apron, and the heavy water bucket I carried struck my leg. Water splashed onto the velvety red carpet. Aunt Valentina set down her bucket and quickly dropped rags on the wet spots. Squatting, I patted the carpet with my rags, too. "It's all right, we got it up," she called to Mr. Hartwig, who was watching from back at the doors. "Be more careful, Celeste!" she snapped at me under her breath.

Holding up my apron with one hand, I carried the heavy

bucket with the other. It didn't have quite as much water in it now. Even so, struggling up the steps to the stage with that bucket was like climbing the Statue of Liberty with her torch in my hands.

We began the awful job of scrubbing, rinsing, and drying the enormous stage floor. Down on my tender knees, I trailed after Aunt Valentina. After the first hour I was as wet as the floor. The sweet voice that cheered me so when she came to Raleigh and that she'd greeted me with at the train station now snarled, "Go faster! Don't let water sit on the floor. It'll stain the wood. Girl, you missed all that soap!"

My tears mingled with the rinse water. My back and knees throbbed. I'd scrubbed floors back home but not like this. Now I knew why Aunt Valentina walked bent over. I reckoned that I would, too, pretty soon. Just like in that book of fairy tales I loved to read at school, I felt like I was poor overworked Cinderella and Aunt Valentina was *both* mean stepsisters. She had changed from the beauty to the beast with her ugly ways almost in an instant. But this wasn't a fairy tale. This was real!

After a while I lost track of the time. I vaguely remember leaving the building and staggering in damp clothes through icy air and black streets with my schoolbag and Dede. I stumbled a lot. Seems the last time, I fell and didn't get back up.

A warm hand touched my cheek. Familiar perfume tickled my nose. Momma? When I opened my eyes, the face I saw was Aunt Valentina's. Harlem, New York. No clothes. No Poppa. Where was Dede? I saw my violin at the foot of the bed I lay in, by my schoolbag, praise the Lord.

"Good morning, sweetheart," said my aunt in her regular calm, soothing voice. "I'm sorry you had such a hard introduction to New York. Have these poached eggs and toast." She held out a tray.

"Thank you," I whispered back. I took the small tray of food and set it on my lap, careful not to let it touch my sore knees and legs. I told myself not to drop anything on the quilt covering me, either. It looked just like the one we had at home. My fingers were so full of water blisters that the fork slipped and fell into an egg. The yolk broke and poured into the white. Now, I knew about eating scrambled, fried, and boiled eggs. But did New York folks eat them raw? Not wanting to hurt Aunt Valentina's feelings, I sopped at the egg with a piece of burnt toast and nibbled at it. It wasn't too nasty.

My aunt sat at a small table against the wall, drinking coffee from a large green cup, watching me eat. She still looked like how I had imagined her when I was on the train. At least that part hadn't changed.

I tried to think of something friendly to say. "Do you mind if I start calling you Auntie Val, for short?"

She smiled, nodding. "Sure. But with an 'i'— not 'ie.' Makes me think it's fancier."

Encouraged, I continued. "Can we go to Easter service? We most always go back home, and I'm usually in the Sunday school program."

"It's this Sunday, isn't it? We'll see. You'll need to find something to wear."

"Oh, that's right." Damn that robber! "Maybe I can keep my coat on."

She nodded like she was sympathetic, but didn't say anything else. Not knowing what else to say, either, I glanced around the room. It was tiny, for one thing. A small icebox and sink stood by the table, where a hot plate set. The four-poster bed I was in filled the whole end of the room. Bags, hatboxes, sacks, and shoes were piled on the floor along the walls. Dresses, coats, and other clothes swung from hooks and nails stuck in the walls. One white dress with a white head rag made me wonder if she was a nurse. Or was it a costume? A red, black, and green flag draped over the back of the front door. What country was that from?

I tried to think of something else simple to say, because I was afraid to ask about the serious stuff. "Your coffee sure smells good."

"Oh, here." When she poured a cup from the pot on the hot plate and brought it to me, I froze. Neither my parents nor Aunt Society allowed me to drink coffee. Aunt Society, who was always on the lookout for things that would make me darker-skinned than I was, said drinking coffee could make me black. I didn't believe coffee could make anybody black, because Poppa and the old bat drank it and they stayed the same color. Momma hadn't drunk it at all.

Being this far from home and Aunt Society, I decided to give it a try, just to see. But before I could wrap my fingers around the handle, Aunt Valentina took the cup away. "I forgot. You're too young to drink that. I'll fix you some mint tea."

As she filled the pot with water at the little sink, she said, "We need to have a good girl talk and catch up on everything. But right now I have to go out for a bit. While your clothes dry, you can wear that blue waist and skirt hanging from that hook. Oh, wait! I meant to ask earlier. How was Taylor when you left?"

"Fine," I said around a mouthful of raw egg.

Wrong answer. She frowned up. "He couldn't be fine. He has consumption. When does he go into that sanitarium? Or do you not know?"

"No, ma'am, he's not fine, but he's still stirring. I don't know when he goes in, but Mr. Hodges said it should be sooner and not later." I smoothed out the quilt on the bed. "We have a quilt just like this at home."

Her frown disappeared. "Momma — your Grandma Lassiter — made one for me and one for your momma when we were little bitty girls. Momma was one of the best seamstresses in Raleigh. She taught your mother how to sew, but I managed to avoid learning. It's a Seven Sisters quilt. See the seven points? This yellow's from an old tablecloth, this white's from old sheets, and this green's from a skirt she had. I forget now where the burgundy cloth is from."

She rinsed out her cup at the sink, then gathered up her coat, hat, and purse. "I've got to go out for a little bit. I'll be —"

"Oh, but can't I go with you? What if there's a fire, or a terrible storm, or somebody tries to break in? What if —"

"Oh, girl, you'll be safe. You can always go next door to Mrs. Dillahunt's, in Nine-A." She pointed to the wall beside the bed. "She knows you're here. Now I *must* get going. Just feel right at home. What there is of it. Oh, and I keep a chamber pot under the bed, and you can wash up at the sink. You can take your bath and do your other business in the lavatory. It's the door by that pretty fern plant in the hallway. Mrs. Dillahunt and I are the only ones on the third floor of this boardinghouse, so we have the lavatory to ourselves. Bye now."

Then the door closed and the room was as quiet as a coffin. I was by myself in big old hog slop, poached-egg-and-burnt-toast-eating, sweatshop-working, floor-scrubbing New York City. My new home.

Chapter Six

As soon as Aunt Valentina left, I propped the chair she'd been sitting in against the door. That helped me feel more secure, since I saw a hole where a key could go, but she hadn't left me one. On the way back to the bed, I noticed a framed photograph on the wall. Two women in pretty dresses — one standing, the other in a chair holding a baby — stared unsmiling at me. Behind them stood a handsome, unsmiling young man in a suit, with his hand on the seated woman's shoulder. Friends of Aunti Val's, probably. Somebody's family? Unlike my family, at least they were together. But here I was, all by myself. How could I persuade Aunt Valentina to return to Raleigh with me, so we could be a family together again, too?

"Oh my, look at me, in New York City sipping tea," I said aloud. Hey, I'd made a poem. Thinking of "Forsythia," I remembered that I'd lost our only copy of the *Brownies' Book* magazine. If only I'd placed it in my schoolbag.

Momma would say I should quit thinking sad thoughts and that I wouldn't get much done lying around. So first I'd get dressed. It might be fun wearing my aunt's clothes. These weren't fancy like hers that I'd tried on back home, and they were still too big, but this was all that I could wear, for now. Next I needed to wash my dress and stockings so I'd have something clean, too, not just dry. I could write in my journal about my trip; I could write to Poppa, Aunt Society, and to my Butterflies friends. I might play Dede. Maybe I'd even go meet that lady next door. I set my cup on the night table by the bed. Things might not be so bad up here in New York, if I worked at it.

With the tray in my hands, I slid out of bed. But my right foot tangled in the quilt, and I hit the floor. A yellow stream of slimy egg rose into the air and splattered on the quilt.

"Oh, my heavenly Father!" *Quick, soap, rags!* With the quilt still snarled around my ankle, I crawled across the floor and scrounged around in the drawers for rags and soap, but couldn't find anything. We sure had had enough last night.

Besides runny eggs, the toast had also hit the quilt, but at least not butter-side down. I scraped the eggs off with my fingers, then ate the egg and bread. If Aunt Valentina kicked me out for destroying her quilt, at least I'd have some food in my gut.

Hurry, girl, hurry! She might return any minute. I wet the toe of one of my stockings and rubbed at the remaining egg. That only spread the yellow stain. Maybe the lady in 9A would know what to do. Quickly I dressed in Aunti's clothes, smoothed down my hair that was sticking out like porcupine quills all over my head, and rinsed my mouth with the last of the tea.

When 9A's door opened at my knock, I jumped back. A monster head draped with wet brown and green strips peered at me through small oval slits. The skin on its face was a gooey white. A thin twig dangled from the red gash that probably was its mouth.

"I — I —"

"You must be Valentina's niece, enty?" the thing said, waving rubbery hands, which I saw were actually rubber gloves. "I'm Miz Dillahunt, but call me Miss D. Don't I look a sight? My head pain me so bad I got to use this home cure."

"Hello," I squeaked. Suddenly a miniature monster stuck its white face around Mrs. Dillahunt's hip. I did my back-away dance again.

"And this is Gertie, my grandbaby." Mrs. Dillahunt pushed the little monster toward me. "I babysit her now and then. Say hello to Celeste, Gertie. She's eight. That's why I got the head-hurt. My beauty mask fights off wrinkles. Gertie likes to wear it, too."

Gertie made a face at me. Or was she smiling? I didn't see any teeth in her mouth. Mrs. Dillahunt pulled the brown strips from her head. "They say paper and collard greens soaked in vinegar and wrapped around the head like this draw out the hurt, see."

Now I knew that drinking everlasting life tea or inhaling smoke from burning pine tar knots cured headaches, but I kept that to myself. Grown folks sometimes didn't like someone young telling them things they didn't know.

"So you come aknocking on my door. What you want?"

"Yes, ma'am, I need to clean some egg off something."

Her white eyebrows rose high on her forehead. "Like off a pan been scorched?"

"No, ma'am, like off a quilt."

"Oh, blessed assurance, not that Seven Sisters quilt!" She pushed past me into Aunti's room.

Gertie followed. "Your aunt's gonna beat your butt," she said.

"No, she won't," I replied. "It was an accident." Or would she?

"Where t'is? Oh, here t'is." Miss D held up the quilt and eyed it carefully. "Well, this won't be your death, nor the quilt's, either." She carried it to the sink and splashed water over the stains. Opening a cupboard above the sink, she removed a bar of lye soap and rubbed it over the quilt. I frowned. Why hadn't I thought to look up there?

"Some better." She studied the wet quilt. "I'll sling it over these chairs to dry. How did egg jump to quilt, Miss Celeste?"

I told her what happened. "Wouldn't it dry faster if we hung it out the window?"

"Where you see a window, Celeste?" Gertie asked.

I looked around in surprise. No windows! No wonder Aunti kept the lights on all the time. I sat back down on the bed and rested my chin in my hands. "Thank you for cleaning it up, Miss D. I was afraid Aunti would kick me to the curb for this."

"I doubt that, being as she just left the curb herself. See how thrown together this room is, boxes and such everywhere? I just got through helping her get this place. Where *is* she, anyway?"

"I don't know. She said she had to go out."

"You the one whose momma be dead?" Gertie asked.

My mouth opened and closed. How did she know that? "Yes, her momma's passed on, but we don't talk about that, you hear?" Miss D scolded. She draped the quilt over the chairs, with newspapers beneath it to catch the drips. Then she headed for the door. "Time to wash off this mess, Gertie. Mine's itching. Celeste, do come over whenever you want. Gertie needs to be around young folks like you who have good manners, and I'll enjoy your company."

I thanked her again but I wasn't ready to deal with Gertie yet. And what did she mean about my aunt just getting off the curb?

I carefully inspected the wet quilt. The egg stain was gone. At least that part wasn't ready for the curb.

A few hours later Aunt Valentina returned. When I started to explain about her quilt, she just shrugged. "It's all right. Miss D told me downstairs." She set a large straw basket on the table. A skinny loaf of bread stuck up from it. "We'll eat, then we got to go out."

"Where? To the theater?" I asked hopefully. "Or to scrub floors again? My hands and knees still hurt. And I was wondering, when will I get paid?"

"I'll explain later. Get some bowls, and spoon out this oxtail soup, honey. It's delicious with this French bread. Then put this sweater on under your coat. That waist and skirt are thin." She handed me her blue sweater while I pinned my lips together, then I set the table. The soup was good, but I wanted to talk! When I opened my mouth to speak, she frowned slightly and kept chunking food into her mouth, so I did the same. Afterward, she pumped at her thick braided hair and batted her eyes in the mirror over the dresser a couple of times. "Ready?" She headed for the door. After throwing on her sweater and my coat, I followed her downstairs.

Aunt Valentina didn't walk bent over now, so this time I really had to move my dogs to keep up. Pickin' 'em up and puttin' 'em down! We flew along One Hundred Thirty-sixth Street and past its crowds. I wouldn't have thought it was possible for so many people to be on one street at the same time. I wondered where Madam C. J. Walker's building was, but I didn't dare ask. Clothes flopped from windows and lines strung overhead between brick and brownstone buildings.

The sunny day lifted my spirits a little. Now and then I saw girls my age playing hopscotch in dresses and Buster Browns and coats like mine, and twirling jump ropes. If I hadn't been so mousey, I'd have asked Aunti if I could join them for a few minutes.

Several ladies snuggled in coats sat on the stoops of buildings talking, sewing baskets in their laps. Men stood in grocery store and pawnshop doorways, laughing and spitting. A black-and-white gooch-eyed dog barked at us when I walked too close. A couple of boys stood by with shoe-shine kits. Seeing them look at me made me think of Big Willie. Had he reached the coal camps yet? Would he return to Eagle Rock, and would I see him again? I hoped so. I didn't know exactly why, though. Maybe it was because he was moving from one home to another, like I was. And those long eyelashes!

When Aunt Valentina stopped to allow a Dodge touring car and a Model T to pass, I spoke up with something I thought would be safe. "Miss D and Gertie put white wrinkle cream on their faces, and Miss D put collard greens on her head."

"Yes, for her head-hurts. Did she use her Gullah talk? Like 'enty' means 'doesn't it' or 'isn't it' or 'is it' or 'don't you think so'? Sometimes I don't know what she's saying. She's from around Charleston, and she believes in that make-do medicine, too, like my sister did. But Elizabeth never did that collard-green thing."

Praise God, she was talking! Anxious to keep her going, I asked, "Does Gertie live with her? I don't want to have to put up with her mouth every time I turn around."

"She just babysits Gertie whenever her momma wants to run around. Seems like that's been happening more and more lately.

Miss D's a sweet woman, but her daughter-in-law takes advantage of her."

Eager to unravel another mystery, I went on flapping my lips. "What did Miss D mean when she said you just got off the curb?"

"It means that Miss D talks too much," she snapped. She took off walking fast again. Oops. After that I couldn't even get a grunt out of her.

After a while I noticed Colored doormen in green and black fancy uniforms help Colored ladies in expensive-looking furs and Colored men in stylish suits into and out of new motorcars, then in and out of their swanky buildings. I'd seen people dolled up in fit-to-kill outfits at the Stackhouse Hotel but not like *these* Harlem folks. Aunt Valentina had dressed like this when she'd visited us in the past. I didn't see many clothes like that in her room, though.

Finally we stopped at a wooden one-story building where the marquee read IMPERIAL CLUB. Aunt Valentina smoothed my hair. "I have a job interview here, so just sit down in the lobby, take your coat off if you get hot, and stay put."

Hesitant to ask what *kind* of job, I only nodded, and trailed her inside to the lobby. Aunt Valentina introduced herself to a light-skinned, gray-haired woman behind the counter. The woman looked down her long nose at Aunt Valentina, then swept out of the room, my aunt behind her. The lobby was furnished with red upholstered Queen Anne chairs, matching thick carpeting, and red and emerald wallpaper. An enormous, lush Boston fern sat regally in front of the bay windows that looked out onto the street. I carefully crossed my legs at the ankles and settled my hands in my lap as I had learned to do in our etiquette class at school. But even so, in my old coat and my greasy hair, I was out of place there. I hoped that woman wouldn't come back and give me the evil eye like she had my aunt.

Just then a young Colored woman in a tall pompadour hairstyle and carrying a smart black coat walked past. A black glove fell from her coat. "Oh, miss," I called, quickly grabbing up the glove. "Miss!"

"Yes?" She turned around uncertainly, then spied the glove I held out. "Why, thank you. I'd have never even known where I'd misplaced it."

She smiled in such a friendly way that I got over some of my shyness. "You're welcome. I'm waiting for my aunt. She's a famous — uh, my favorite aunt."

"Oh, does she give lessons here?"

"No, ma'am, she had to talk with someone."

"I see. My name's Caterina Jarboro. I'm studying voice and piano, to be a concert singer. I just finished a lesson. You may have heard me singing."

"Oh, my." I stared at her until I remembered my manners. "My name is Celeste Lassiter Massey, and I'm from Raleigh, North Carolina. I've never met a concert singer before. I play the violin and I call it Dede."

"After the violinist in New Orleans? How creative! I'm from Wilmington, North Carolina, but I live in Brooklyn now with my aunt. Small world, Celeste." She reached into her bag, removed a small card, and gave it to me. "Call me sometime. We North Carolinians have to stick together. All right, I must run."

On the cream-colored card in elegant writing it said, CATERINA JARBORO, CONCERT SINGER, with an address and telephone number. I tucked the card into my sweater pocket to show to Aunt Valentina. Perhaps a new friend already. What a blessing!

I was daydreaming about eating at a fine Harlem restaurant and eating the good food Mr. Smithfield talked about when the long-nosed woman returned. Aunt Valentina followed, frowning, her lips pressed tight together. "Come along, come along" was all she said to me.

Outside, the air had grown chillier. As we walked, I kept peeking at her, but she stayed quiet so I did, too. We walked and walked till night arrived. I was freezing, and my dogs howled. We entered a side door of a building, and like before, she handed me a long apron and a bucket. But this time I wouldn't take them. "Why've we got to be doing this?" I fumed, unable to keep frustration from my voice. "You said you were a famous singer and dancer."

"I thought I was, too, but it doesn't look that way now, does it? So let's get to work."

"No! I'm tired!"

"Do as I say," she said calmly.

"No, I want to go home!"

"Go home, then. I got work to do." She picked up a bucket and a bundle of rags and left the other things on the floor. I balled up my fists as she walked down the long aisle and then turned a corner without looking back. As soon as she did, my heart took a leap. I couldn't stay there by myself. What if some ruffian came up behind me and grabbed me? I didn't even know the way out of the building, let alone back to the boarding-house.

She had truly brought me there to work me to death. I would

have been better off being worked to death by the Hugel-burgers. At least I'd still be in North Carolina. I snatched up the apron and trudged after her, the heavy water bucket, apron, and rags flapping and sloshing against my coat. Again. When we staggered back to my aunt's tiny room, I think my back was bent as low as hers had been.

We both fell into bed angry. "Well, just exactly when are you going to pay me after all this work?" I hissed into the dark.

"Sure won't be tonight," she hissed back. "And we won't be going to Easter service. I'll be too tired even then. Now close your mouth and get some sleep."

"And what about school?" I held my breath.

"It's too late in the year. Now go to sleep, I said!"

Tears rolled out the sides of my eyes and soaked the pillow. I should have known. Aunt Society was right. And sure as sugar, I reckoned that things would only get worse.

Chapter
Seven

I paused from drawing a picture of our forsythia bush in my journal, with a cardinal singing on a branch. Praise God for my good health. April arrived in Harlem still so chilly I fixed echinacea and goldenseal teas each morning to ward off colds, pneumonia, and croup, after walking home every night in wet clothes. After three weeks here I hadn't seen a single show in New York, but I did know that Harlem must have the dirtiest theater floors in New York.

Most days Aunt Valentina's eyes seemed so sad I thought she forgot she even saw me. And whatever had made me think that Aunt Valentina could help me keep our family together? That was why I had wanted her to come to Raleigh, so I could stay home and we could take care of Poppa — or at least see him. But here we just staggered from one awful night of scrubbing to another.

I closed my journal, tired of drawing and writing. Momma would say I should pray for the Lord to turn my burdens into blessings. If I could do that, maybe I could lift my aunt's spirits, as well as my own.

Aunt Valentina had gone out again somewhere. I hoped she'd return with food. She usually brought back small tin buckets of soup, beef bones that we gnawed and sucked until they turned shiny, the heels of bread loaves, a baked potato or two, and tiny fancy squares of cake. From where, she never said. So good, but never enough. *Dear Lord, please don't let it be from hog slop troughs!*

I opened my journal again and wrote, "Dear Poppa, I miss you so!" with hearts drawn around the word *Poppa.* When I wrote him last week, I didn't say what I was going through. Now that he was in Coopers sanitarium, I knew he had enough to deal with. He'd sent us an official letter from the sanitarium that said only that he was there, nothing else. I wondered what Coopers was like. I hoped he would write and tell me. But I also didn't share my problems with him because I was afraid he'd tell Aunt Society, who'd be pleased as punch that I was suffering.

Our dark little room made me feel like I lived in a cave. Or was down in a coal mine like Big Willie was. What were my friends Swan and Angel Mae and Evalina doing? Nobody but Poppa had written to me. I missed Raleigh!

I glanced at the broom in the corner. Our dirty dishes from yesterday still sat in the sink. The bed was unmade. More work! As I pulled Dede from under the bed, I wished I could play downstairs in the lobby beside a sunny window or on the porch, even if it was cold. When I opened the case, inside was Miss Pinetar. All this time I'd forgot about her. I screwed the stick into her back and placed the paddle on my knee. First I tried singing "Over There," Poppa's favorite war tune, then "Lift Every Voice and Sing," our national Negro anthem that we sang in church and school all the time. And then my own "Forsythia."

"Hey, Cece, that you?" Gertie stood in our doorway gawking, with her thumb in her almost toothless mouth. "Grandma sent me over here to see what you doin'."

"I'm trying to enjoy myself," I said, irritated at her interruption, and reminded myself to ask Aunt Valentina how to lock that door. "Go away. I'm busy."

"No, you ain't. You're just singing and thumpin' on that doll thing." She strutted right into our room, and flopped onto the bed beside me. "Lemme see her."

"Keep back or you'll wind up with a nub at the end of your arm." I raised the paddle to smack her hand. "But since you're in here, be quiet and listen."

"Just let me touch her."

"Not with those saliva-coated germy fingers."

"Then let's go buy a bag of candy. You got some money?"

"I can't leave the house, all right? I got to clean the room, so you need to go back over to Nine-A. Now."

"Ole stingy thing." She flounced out the door, adding, "And you don't do *nothin'* fun!"

She was right, but sharing my things with her wouldn't change that. Still, I felt a bit guilty for being so mean. She was probably lonely, too, with just her grandmother to play with. Too bad! After closing our door, I set down Miss Pinetar and lifted Dede to my chin.

A few hours later Aunti breezed in, humming and smiling. Still in her fine coat and hat, she sat down on the bed. "How's your day been?" she asked. Before I could answer, she said, "I'm sure you want to know why we've been working so hard." I nodded, listening carefully. She breathed in deeply, making her chest heave. "Before you came up here, I ran into some bad luck — long story. But your helping me work has kept a roof over our heads. And I can pay you. Hold out your hand and close your eyes."

The Lord had heard my prayers, I thought. I shot out my hand and pinched my eyes shut so tight I saw little red dots. I felt something hard drop into my palm. Silver dollars? Slowly I opened my eyes and counted five nickels in my hand. Twenty-five cents? I tried not to frown, but my eyebrows squeezed together anyway. Sweatshop money, for true! I got more for scrubbing the Smithfields' three front porch steps.

"I know it's not much," she said, "but things are really hard and I want to give you something."

"I don't mean to sound sassy, Aunt Valentina, but I don't understand. You'd come down home in your fancy clothes and bring us presents and spend money left and right." I paused, and when she stood up I leaned back out of slapping distance. "You talked about traveling around and going to musicals and singing and dancing in them. Now you're half killing my hands and knees and back with this sweatshop work, just like Aunt Society said you would."

"What? What?" She crossed her arms, frowned up so hard the powder almost flaked off her cheeks. Then she sighed. "All right. Look. You're right and you're wrong. Let's go for a walk — not to scrub floors, just walk — and we'll eat, and I'll explain."

I nodded, wondering if she was going to trick me and we'd end up hauling lumber or something. I slipped on her sweater and my coat, and we left the room. For once the day was warm. And for once we walked slower. I noticed buds on the few trees we passed. Aunt Valentina wrapped her arm around mine, and that was a good sign, too.

"I truly *was* a singer and dancer, until a couple of months ago," she began. "I mean, I still am! For years I was the personal maid of

Madame Mercifal Gutness, the German opera singer. I had my own room in her mansion. She let me drive her car. I ate the same exquisite foods she ate. Those seal and even real mink furs, the hats, the clothes, oh, I had some fine things! I traveled wherever she went. You got postcards from Chicago, San Francisco, Saint Louis, Atlanta. Madame said I was indispensable to her, and I thought so, too. And I was in musicals, twice as a maid and once as a — uh — servant — well, slave. Mostly, though, I helped her backstage. But that ought to account for something, shouldn't it?

"Anyway, one day Madame heard me singing to myself, and from that time on, things went downhill. I was singing 'Go Down, Moses' and ironing her slips. Yes, I had to iron her slips, too, girl."

"Did you sing better than Madame Mercifal?"

"Oh my, yes, always, and she knew it. But I wasn't an opera singer. I couldn't compete with her, even if I'd wanted to. We hardly had any Colored opera stars, besides the Black Patti and the Hyers Sisters. So very few, and far between. Anyway, some-time later, she heard I had won the leading role in a little ole five-cent Colored musical. Why, you'd have thought I'd got the starring role in *Romeo and Juliet*! She had such a hissy fit she was strangling on her own spit."

"Which musical was it?"

"One nobody heard of. *Aunt Susie Honeysuckle*. I was supposed to be the kindhearted Colored washerwoman. But she contacted the producers and threatened them till they gave the part to her — get this — wearing brown skin makeup and a head rag. The clothes basket she was supposed to balance on her head kept falling off, and she was trying to sing Colored woman Southern with a German accent — oh, she was terrible. Whites play most big roles of Colored people, see. They don't think we can portray ourselves in theater the way *they* want to portray us. That's how minstrels got started with Whites wearing burnt cork on their faces and big white lips, and raggedy clothes, you know. Making fun of Colored people. Rich, mean-spirited Whites do stuff like that in the theater business all the time. They're in charge of everything, or try to be. New York has its own brand of prejudice, just like North Carolina does, Celeste."

I just said "Oh" to the part about prejudice. I was surprised — and not surprised — at her words. From the stories I read in newspapers, New York and Chicago and the north were supposed to be the promised land for us Colored. But from listening to Poppa and the Smithfields talk, I had heard about terrible things happening to Colored people in the north, too.

The play closed after only two performances. Madame Mercifal told Aunt Valentina that she'd fix things so she'd never get a job in a musical again, then fired her and kicked her out of the Gutness mansion.

Aunt Valentina sat down heavily at a trolley car bench to rest, and I plunked down beside her. "She was so jealous of my talent — well, of everybody else's talents. I hear she has a young singer from Italy working as her maid now, and the girl's about gone crazy. Madame should help aspiring artists, not hinder them."

"She's nothing like her name, is she?" My heart twisted for my aunt. To go from being so high on the hog to so low at the trough.

"In public she's so gracious, but away from admirers she's a witch. She was also jealous of my straight white teeth — she wore false teeth — my shapely legs, and my thick long hair. She hardly had any hair and wore wigs all the time."

Aunti laid her hand on mine. "When I heard about your situation, I couldn't let you go sharecrop for the Hugelburger sisters, but I couldn't move to Raleigh penniless, either. I took a big chance, so here we are, in Harlem."

"So that's what happened," was all I could say. We watched the trolleys pass us. Did that mean that if she got a better job she could save her money and move back home? Which was what I wanted, of course. "Aunti, the way you got treated was sort of how Aunt Society liked to treat me," I said instead. "And she said so many mean things about you, like how you're gonna go to the Devil's Pit of —"

"Excuse me, please, honey, that's enough." She held up her hand. "I don't want to hitchhike down to Raleigh and wring Society's scrawny yellow neck over her gossip." She stood up. "Let's celebrate! I will find a better job, Cece, I promise you. I've been applying for all kinds of jobs at theaters, cabarets, restaurants. With you here I've an added incentive to find something better."

I pulled Caterina Jarboro's visiting card out of the sweater pocket and handed it to her. "She seemed very nice. She's studying voice and piano and lives in Brooklyn, but she's from Wilmington. Maybe she can help you." Saying nothing, Aunti tucked the card into her purse. I stood up from the bench and we began walking again. I had another worrisome thought. "If you do get a job, wouldn't ole Madame try to have you fired again?"

"I'll worry about that after I get the job." She tucked a loose braid back under her hat.

That gave me a chance to move to a safer subject. "I love your hair, so thick and pretty. Wish mine was again." My dirty hair needed to be washed really bad. It hadn't been since January, and I knew it smelled awful. Aunt Society didn't like to wash hair in the winter. She said having a wet head in the winter gave you pneumonia.

"Thanks, doll. I've worn it like this since — since I left Raleigh. I'll never cut it again, not for anything. Long hair runs in our family. We'll get yours back up to snuff."

At that good news, I grabbed her hand. We bounced along, swinging our arms. Aunti said we were going to eat at Café Noir Le Grande right around the corner on Lenox Avenue, which was one of her favorite streets. "This is where I pick up those delicious little cakes and oxtail soup, visit with friends, and hope to get job leads. Almost everybody who eats here is an artist, actor, writer, something in the arts."

I'd never noticed this tiny café before, tucked back among the taller buildings, but I'd only been on Lenox Avenue at night. Going into this strange place full of folks should have made my tummy do a pretzel dance, but the smell of good food wouldn't let it. A tall brown-skinned man in a shiny yellow shirt, black neck scarf, and black suit buzzed over to Aunti and whirled her around. "Mademoiselle Valentina! I'm so fortunate that your beauty has again graced my presence." He leaned over her hands and kissed each one, like I had seen stars do on the Royal Theater movie screen back home. I giggled behind my hands.

Aunt Valentina curtsied. "Monsieur, you are too kind," she said, and kissed him quickly on both cheeks.

"And who's this *jeune fille* with you?"

Flustered, I stepped behind my aunt, but she kept moving. I took a deep breath and glanced at him sideways. Those foreign words sounded like French ones I'd heard in songs on the Westrand. He had green eyes! A green-eyed Colored Frenchman? Was I supposed to curtsy, too?

"My lovely niece, Celeste Lassiter Massey," Aunti said. "Celeste, this is Monsieur Jacques Le Grande, noted playwright, a good friend, and owner of this fabulous establishment."

When Monsieur Le Grande took my left hand, bowed over it, and kissed it, I almost fainted. *"Enchanté,"* he said. "Welcome to the Café Noir Le Grande, the center of Harlem, where true artists gather."

"Especially those like me, who have no money," Aunt Valentina added.

Heart pounding, with the feel of his warm lips still on my hand, I squeaked out, "Hello, moan — moan sewer."

"Monsieur is one of my very best friends, Celeste, from *waaay* back," Aunti said, pronouncing "monsieur" slowly and precisely.

"Mademoiselle, I would give you the rings of Saturn and the moons of Mars if I could. But food'll have to suffice for now." He snapped his fingers and a man in a white apron hurried over. "Please bring my beautiful guests anything they wish," he told the man. "And prepare a take-home plate of today's desserts."

Monsieur Le Grande pulled out our chairs and, after planting another kiss on Aunti, strutted away. In his yellow and black clothes, he flew around like a bumblebee the size of an airship. "He kissed my hand!" I whispered to my aunt. "Is he really from France?"

"Lordie, no. His real name's Roy Lee Estill, from the cotton fields of Hampton County, South Carolina." Aunt Valentina laughed over the voices, laughter, and music around us. "But that's a big secret. After the Klan ran him out of South Carolina, he popped up in New Orleans and learned how to cook Creole. He pretends to be French to draw in business. It works, too."

"He acts like he's sweet on you."

"No, baby, he's sweet on himself. That's just how he is, and I'm grateful. Hear the music? Look there, where it's coming from." She pointed to a raised platform in the corner of the room, where a man in a white tuxedo plucked out songs on a gold harp. A white and gold piano sat behind him. "That's Andre. He plays that piano, too. Doesn't he sound grand?"

"Now that's *really* grand," I whispered. I knew Momma would have loved to play on that piano. When Aunti picked up the menu, I did, too, but I couldn't read it because it was in French. Aunti smiled and ordered our lunches, which turned out to be roast chicken, glazed sweet potatoes, buttery cathead biscuits, gravy, green beans with almonds, sweet tea, and my favorite, pecan pie. Now I knew two words connected with chicken and eggs — *poulet* and poached!

I concentrated on eating. It seemed to taste better here than in our little room at the boardinghouse. As we ate, a woman in a white uniform and head wrap, with an armful of newspapers, headed for our table. Tiny red, black, and green flags stuck out of her uniform pocket. Was the woman a Red Cross nurse about to ask us to give blood? "One God, One Aim, One Destiny," the woman said as she handed Aunti a newspaper called *Negro World*.

"She's a Garvey-ite, a follower of the Honorable Marcus Garvey," Aunti told me. "A famous man," she added when my face remained blank. Before I had a chance to ask what Marcus Garvey had done to become famous, a handsome man in a ritzy blue serge suit stopped by our table. "Celeste, this is Mr. James Weldon Johnson, a famous writer." She beamed. "James, my niece, Celeste Lassiter Massey, from North Carolina."

"I've heard of you," I gasped. "You wrote 'Lift Every Voice and Sing.' We read your poem at school and sing it in church."

"He's also the head of the National Association for the Advancement of Colored People. That's the group that publishes the *Brownies' Book* magazine, you know," Aunti continued, showing her beautiful white teeth at him.

Speak up, Celeste, speak up! "Mr. Johnson, sir, I love to read your magazine. We sent in our poems for the student writing contest, but I don't know how we did." My heart beat so fast I could hear it thump through my words. "I brought one of your magazines with me so —" I stopped. My precious magazine was gone forever. "But I lost it," I finished.

"I'm sorry to hear that," Mr. Johnson said. "Come by our office and pick up any copies you want. Dr. W.E.B. DuBois actually founded the magazine, and Miss Jessie Fausett's the editor. I'll pass on your remarks. They'll be pleased. Valentina, I just wanted to tell you that I met with the city's employment commissioner the other day. I put in a good word for you."

"Thank you, James. You know how much I appreciate everything you do."

After he left, I softly clapped my hands. "Oh goody, I can get more magazines!" I exclaimed. "Aunti, you know everybody. But James Weldon Johnson!"

"His group tries to help us Colored, and tries to stop lynchings and such. The famous Booker T. Washington ate here a few times before he died," Aunt Valentina said. "I saw him myself. And a singer and actor named Bert Williams has dropped in. Roy Lee's been around a long time. He's much older than he looks. It's certainly a place where good folks can meet. I just wish more people who hire would come, too."

I ate, and looked at and listened to the snatches of conversation around me until I couldn't hold any more of anything. After the afternoon darkened into evening, we walked back home with our arms full of food. My brain buzzed with having met and heard about so many famous people. I couldn't wait to write to Angel Mae, Swan, and Evalina. Why, my letter could end up being ten pages long! Aunti's explanation about how she got kicked to the curb helped a lot. I still didn't care for so much hard work, but I couldn't tell my friends about that.

We stopped in front of a brick building on One Hundred Thirty-sixth Street. The sign read MADAM C. J. WALKER COLLEGE OF HAIR CULTURE. Her salon was in there, too. "Her daughter A'Lelia and her people are in charge now. A'Lelia's townhouse is right there." She pointed to an upper-story window. "It's fabulous inside. Kings, queens, and princes from all over the world fight to be invited to her dinner parties. She has a mansion in another part of New York that's the size of the North Carolina capitol building."

"Have you ever been to her parties?" I wondered if her castle had a rotunda, too.

Aunti resumed walking. "When I was still with Madame Mercifal, I got invited many times, and of course I went. When I lost favor with Mercifal, I lost favor with a lot of people, including

A'Lelia. We still speak, but I haven't stopped by lately. When my money gets better, I'll take you in for a treatment."

A thousand questions jumped into my head about Madam Walker, her daughter, and those parties, but suddenly Aunti seemed sad again. I guess she was thinking about her old life when she was eating high off that hog. I thought fast to say something positive. "When you do get another job, you don't have to use your real name, do you? So Mercifal won't know it's you?"

Aunti snapped her fingers. "You're absolutely right. I'll just give the boss another name and later tell the truth. What a blessing in disguise you are, Celeste. Why didn't I think of that?" My face burned at her compliment. If I'd been light-skinned, my cheeks would have turned red.

We'd have skipped like we did when she visited in Raleigh, too, if we hadn't been carrying Monsieur's food. I reckoned Aunti would have skipped because she had finally told me the truth. I would have skipped because if she got a good job and saved her money, we both could go back home. But maybe it was good that we didn't skip. We still had to go to work that night, and we needed to save our strength.

Chapter Eight

I awoke to Aunt Valentina washing clothes at the sink and singing. I hadn't heard her do that since I'd come to New York. "No wonder Madame was so jealous," I said, yawning. "You could sing a newspaper advertisement and make it sound pretty. What is it?"

"Aren't you sweet? It's the title song from *Aunt Susie Honeysuckle.* Say, I haven't heard you play your little violin since you been here. Why don't you try with me?" She shook out a wet waist and hung it on a hanger to drip above the sink. "I mean, if you feel up to it."

"Be ready in a second!" I hurried out into the chilly hallway to the lavatory and back, then reached for Dede. "But first Miss Pinetar must dance while you sing." She hadn't seen my puppet, either. I explained where I got her from and she said the doll was cute. Miss Pinetar jumped and clacked her little wooden feet on the paddle to Aunt Valentina's singing, and I hummed, familiarizing myself with the catchy song. "Aunt Susie Honeysuckle" was a complicated tune, but by using the doll I was able to pick up the rhythm. Then I set her down, tucked Dede under my chin, tuned it quickly, and off we went! Then Aunti took me into fairly simple songs: "Balm in Gilead," "Camptown Races," and "Yankee

Doodle Dandy." Suddenly she twirled about, and with a wink returned to singing "Aunt Susie." I was ready. When she stopped, I kicked into that sassy ragtime piece "Maple Leaf Rag."

"Oh, my, I'm impressed!" she said, raising her eyebrows. "You've really progressed."

Miss D stood in our open doorway, clapping. "I declare, this child's got talent. Do 'Swing Low' for me."

When I lit into a fast "Swing Low, Sweet Chariot," Miss D's alto joined Aunti's soprano. We paraded around the room, singing, playing, humming, and clapping. I added some riffs I had learned from listening to the new blues music at Café Noir Le Grande. Blues on a violin! I must have overdone it because Aunti held up both hands. "That's enough. I got to get back to my washing."

"Celeste sure ain't whispery when it comes to that fiddle." Miss D smiled wide at me. "Playing and humming at the same time. Now that's unusual. Do you know 'Jook Joint Jump'?"

"No, she doesn't." Aunt Valentina slipped her arm around my shoulders, and at the same time gently nudged the violin from under my chin. She cleared her throat. "She's a marvel, isn't she?"

"Well, I was on my way to work anyway," said Miss D. "We'll have to do this again. Cece, you keep playing like that and you'll be onstage with your aunt, won't she, Val?"

Aunti didn't say anything but went back to washing. I sat down with Dede in my lap. "Thank you, Aunti, for sharing your music with me. Playing really sparks my spirits."

"Mine too. You know, you talk like a little ole woman sometimes, instead of a thirteen-year-old. I guess that comes from being around Society so long."

"Oh, she says I talk sassy and that I'm impudent." I blew out my breath. "And not good for anything but digging dirt out of corners and scrubbing floors." I stopped. That's what I'd been doing with Aunti Val.

"Society has a lot of nerve. She and Taylor, their two brothers, and their parents, God rest their souls, were some very poor people for a very long time. I bet she didn't tell you that." I shook my head, surprised again. "Fishermen don't make much money if they've not got their own boat. Of course you knew Society set fire to their house when they were kids, didn't you, because of her awful cooking? And that their parents died in that fire?" I knew about that. My folks had told me, though Aunt Society never brought it up. "Well, I bet you didn't know that afterward Society and her brothers lived for years in a tiny lean-to they built, until they managed to buy a little pitiful boat and do their fishing. Did you know that your father met your mother while traveling back and forth from Morehead to Raleigh, selling fish?"

"Momma told me they first met at the Stackhouse," I said, trying not to frown. Aunti Val was wrong about that. "Poppa always talked about how much he loved living in Morehead City, and telling fishing stories, and stuff. He never talked about him being poor. Momma always said I shouldn't look down on poor people, anyway — poorer than us, I mean."

Aunti Val grunted but let that go. "Well, grown folks don't tell children everything, you know, especially if it involves sin or tragedy. Plus, it just ain't your business. But I'll tell it, as long as it's not about me." She grinned. "Anyway, your folks got married and Taylor moved to Raleigh, but he'd still go back and forth. He smelled like fish all the time! But a few years later his brothers drowned when their boat capsized. That ended the business. Society stayed down there by herself, up to her elbows in fish guts and blood every day and half the night for other fishermen. I'd rather scrub floors any day." She snapped her camisole so hard it popped twice. "Though not like this, of course."

"Me too." I'd never cleaned fish, but I'd killed and gutted a chicken and hated that worse than anything. "I thought Aunt Society lived in Raleigh for years and years," I said, "and was a seamstress."

"Not until your mother took sick after Emmanuel was born. Taylor asked her to move to Raleigh to help. She sold her More-head City property and bought that house in Raleigh that's around the corner from you-all. Your Grammaw Lassiter taught her how to sew. You knew that Grampa Lassiter worked for the governor, landscaping. Anyway, we were all glad when Society took to sewing. Your momma couldn't let Society come visiting up in *her* house smelling like croaker and spot."

When I giggled, Aunti said she went with Momma and Poppa to Morehead once when they still had the fish business, when my uncles and Aunt Society lived in that place near Calico Creek. "Funky, stale, fried hogfish stink stuck in every inch of that house so bad I had to go outside. I liked standing in the backyard looking at the creek, but the yard crawled with so many flies and maggots from where she cleaned fish that I nearly passed out."

I shivered and squeezed my eyes shut. "I used to like to eat fish, but I don't know now."

She laughed. "Anyway, your momma and I scrubbed many a floor to help when we were young, and we were proud of it."

"You and Momma?"

"Sure did. Plus, we gave recitals at St. Paul AME, in school, all over Raleigh. I sang and she played piano. We even performed at the Negro State Fair."

"Think of that! Momma never said a word about all this. How old were you?"

"Oh, from around four and six years old until when we got grown. Until I moved to New York. I'm sure she told you and you forgot. Kids do forget things, you know."

"And now you and I are doing the same things, scrubbing, singing, playing. Maybe we can be a team, like Miss D said."

"Well, we're scrubbing floors."

"But maybe one of these days we'll be on the stage of the Abyssinian, performing, not scrubbing, huh?"

"You'd be too shy for that." She scrubbed hard on her red nightgown. "I'll be ready for you to start washing your things in a few minutes."

"I've been meaning to ask you who those people are in that picture." I pointed to the one of the man, two women, and baby.

"Oh, that one." Smiling, sighing, and frowning at the same time, Aunti lifted the photograph from the wall and brought it to me. She tapped the glass over the woman standing. "Your mother," she said.

"Momma looks so young." I ran my fingers over the glass. "And so pretty."

"I'm in the chair holding you. You were six months old."

I clapped my hand to my mouth. "Bald-headed and fat, with chipmunk cheeks and chunky arms."

"You were a quiet baby, like you are now," she said softly, and smiled. "You had the sweetest little grin, and you knocked us out with your big hazel eyes."

"And is this Poppa?"

"No, that . . . that was a friend, a kind and dear friend. You . . . would have loved him. He's gone now." She turned away so I couldn't see her face.

"You mean he moved?"

"No, I mean he's — he's deceased. He passed right after that picture was taken."

"What was his name?"

"Chavis," she said softly. "Nathaniel Chavis. Now no more questions."

"Sorry. Didn't mean to pry." Maybe he was an old flame. I returned the picture to the wall, but I kept glancing back. No wonder I had been drawn to it. I was looking at myself. "You know, I miss Momma and Poppa so, and now I don't even have our family picture anymore, because of that thief stealing it," I told Aunti. I scrubbed on my slip. "But I can look at this one here. So when one door closes, another one opens, doesn't it?"

Aunti spun around and stared at me, then her lip curled down. She flopped onto the bed, covered her face with her hands, and burst into tears. Seeing her cry for the first time ever, and missing my folks and my home, I sat down beside her and cried, too, rubbing my eyes with my soapy hands. Just as quickly, Aunti clapped her hands like she was slapping off dust and stood back up. "Enough blubbering. Now let's get back to work."

I nodded and wiped my face with my skirt. I decided not to mention the picture to her again, not if she was going to break down like that. And I was glad she had told me so much good juicy gossip about Aunt Society.

After we finished our clothes, I wrote a short, polite letter to Aunt Society at her Raleigh address — which I'd never done before, I realized with a start — requesting some more clothes. I also inquired about her health, how she liked living in her old home round the corner from us again, and said that I missed her, which was true. I didn't ask if she missed cleaning fish, though. Finally I wrote a group letter to Swan, Angel Mae, and Evalina. I'd planned to sooner than this. Seemed like I really hadn't felt like it, though. I gave them highlights of the train ride; meeting folks like Big Willie and Mr. James Weldon Johnson; eating at Café Noir Le Grande; and getting Miss Pinetar. I didn't mention scrubbing floors or living in that tiny room, though.

After several days passed but neither Poppa nor Aunt Society sent me any clothes, Aunti said we couldn't wait any longer. "Let's go shopping. What would you like?"

At first I pictured myself with a whole new wardrobe, then I trashed those dreams. Where would Aunti get the money to buy so much? "If I could have some more stockings, drawers, another waist, and another skirt or two, that'd be fine," I said.

"Oh, more than that. I know a fabulous little place called the Twice As Nice store, where I get lots of beautiful things dirt cheap. What're you frowning about? You object to secondhand clothes?"

"But you said you got your clothes from Madame Mercifal, didn't you?"

"The Twice As Nice is very well known, Celeste. No cooties, lice, fleas, bedbugs, ticks, or other moving, biting vermin. Costume people go there all the time to buy period clothes for productions." She smiled, then her face turned sharp. "I've no need to lie to you, honey. Madame gave me things, and I bought things, all right?"

"Yes, ma'am. Momma bought me secondhand things and we altered them. It's not that. But when Aunt Society took over, she'd buy the ugliest clothes and alter them so bad I'd have darts going every which way, and the hems would be crooked. She was a seamstress, but not a good one."

"Oh, you poor baby. Miss D alters my clothes. I never got the hang of it like your Grammaw and Elizabeth did. Stuck my fingers with the needles too much. She'll do yours."

She handed me a skeleton key on a string. "I've been meaning to give you one. I hardly ever lock the door, but maybe I should."

We dressed quickly and soon were outside in the warm air. Was spring here at last? When we passed Madam C. J. Walker's shop, I saw ladies with bibs sitting in chairs, hair all over their heads or wrapped in towels. We walked and walked *and* walked, but I hadn't got tired and my dogs weren't barking yet so I guess I was getting stronger. We turned a corner and suddenly we were in the middle of a burst of stores, honking cars, tall buildings, and people.

We wandered in and out of shoe stores, tailor shops, men's and women's clothing stores. Some folks sold shirts, shoes, and ties out of sacks right on the sidewalk. A man in a large, crowded stall shouted and fussed at people eating grapes out of his baskets and squeezing mangoes. Spicy pork rinds and sweet potato odors from open-air carts mingled with the fragrance of baked bread and beer from restaurants. Signs swayed everywhere: CABBAGE, HAM HOCKS, AND POTATO PLATE SERVED FRESH DAILY. GERMAN BEER HERE. HOT GARLIC BREAD AND SPAGHETTI LUNCH SPECIAL. CURRY GOAT AND FRIED RICE JUST LIKE HOME IN JAMAICA. Cooked goat? Who'd want to eat a billy goat?

A woman cooking pig's feet, corn on the cob, and other food at a small, steaming cart waved at my aunt. "How're you doin' on this pretty day that the Lord has made?" she said to us.

"I'm about as fine as frog hair." Aunti laughed.

"Since a frog ain't got hair, least not any you can see, then you got to be awfully fine," the woman said, and laughed. She nodded at me. "Who's this?"

"My niece, Celeste, from North Carolina. Celeste, this is Pig Foot Mary, one of our fine Harlem entrepreneurs," Aunti told me.

"Have an ear on me," Miss Pig Foot Mary said, and handed me an ear of corn. What a funny name! I thanked her and munched while she and Aunti talked. It tasted as good as our North Carolina corn.

"Miss Mary owns whole buildings that she bought with money she made selling food right here in the street," my aunt said.

"With all the money you got now, you could stop cooking." Aunti slapped Miss Pig Foot playfully on the arm.

"Not quite. I got my eye on another place to buy and fix up here on Lenox before I quit my pots." They jabbered some more, than we walked on.

Aunti said that Lenox Avenue was one of her favorite streets in Harlem. "You can see and buy or trade anything you want here. And just look at Pig Foot Mary! Buying buildings! You wouldn't know it to look at her, but she's rich. She's an example of what a Colored woman can do."

I clucked and marveled aloud, but inside I was thinking that it seemed like almost everybody but Aunti Val was making money. That was why I was saving the money that Poppa had given me, and trying to save the little bit I received from Aunti. Today, though, I planned to buy some licorice! I hadn't got hold of licorice since I bought some at the pharmacy back home, seemed like months ago.

We edged around a grinning man in a red vest and hat, playing an accordion. A real monkey perched on his shoulder. It was brown and about as big as my shoe, with tiny paws and a wizened face. The monkey wore a matching vest and cap. It chattered and held out a tin cup to me, watching me with its beady black eyes.

"Can that monkey dance?" I asked my aunt. "I saw one dance at our fair back home."

"Only if you put money in its cup first."

Considering how hard I'd had to work to get those nickels, giving one to a monkey would be a waste of good money. Across the street three boys danced the ham bone, slapping their legs and chests with their hands. A man walking by threw some pennies to them. One boy stopped long enough to snatch up the coins.

Soon we reached the Twice As Nice shop. We were the first customers of the day. Aunti was right about the beautiful clothes! Thick otter, raccoon, and fox furs sprawled on tables, their tiny glassy-eyed heads and clawed paws still attached. Red, green, orange, and blue feather boas coiled like fuzzy snakes on shelves. High- and low-heeled women's shoes and pumps, children's high-top, black patent leather, and Buster Brown shoes, and men's boots, brogans, and moccasins lined more shelves. Boys' and girls' blue sailor suits, boys' knickerbocker knee-pants suits like the one Big Willie wore, dresses, floor-length hobble skirts, fancy embroidered middy blouses and other waists, and coats, sweaters, and jackets hung on hangers and on dress dummies. My mouth watered. I wanted them all.

"Pick out what you want," Aunti told me, "and then we'll sort through them and buy what I can afford. This'll be my welcome to Harlem gift to you, even though I'm late."

Loaded down with four skirts, underclothes, a dressy red waist with a lace collar, three fancy white embroidered waists, a white crinoline dress, and a yellow dress similar to the one I had lost, we finally left the Twice As Nice. "Is that better?" Aunti asked.

"Thank you, thank you! Better than my birthday and Christmas both," I said happily. "I can't wait to try them on." On the way back we stopped by a little grocery and bought some food fixings, and my favorites, red licorice and lemon drops. We ended up at the Café Noir Le Grande for our main meal. Monsieur Le

Grande kissed our hands again, fed us bread and oxtail soup, and gave us more food to carry home.

We passed a big building with a sign that read UNIVERSAL NEGRO IMPROVEMENT ASSOCIATION. Men in military uniforms stood outside the doors, and red, black, and green flags fluttered from the windows. "This is the headquarters of the Honorable Marcus Garvey," Aunti said. She sounded excited. "He's from Jamaica, working on being king of the Colored world. He travels all around the world, when he's not in jail."

"Is he a criminal?"

"Well, he has these plans and dreams, see, but the government doesn't like him or his plans. He's trying to buy boats the size of Noah's ark so Colored people can take what we make in our factories to sell everywhere. I bought shares of stock when I still lived with Madame Mercifal." She stopped. "Wonder what I did with those things? They're supposed to make us rich. Hope I didn't throw them away. See those red, black, and green flags flapping all over Harlem? Like my flag hanging on my door at home? That's his flag. People love King Garvey."

"I see," I said, but I didn't. I didn't know whether to smile or frown. And how could he sell pieces of boats — Aunti called them "shares of stock" — to people and make money? How could she forget where she'd put stuff that was supposed to make her rich?

As we walked along, I thought about the Colored people I knew who owned businesses. Mr. Stackhouse, of course. The Bivenses with their wagon and herbs. Mr. Lightner. Mr. Berry O'Kelly, the mayor of nearby Method. He had his own high school, and was in charge of the Negro State Fair. We had

Colored lawyers, and doctors like Dr. Pope, and teachers. Bishop Henry Delany was in charge of Saint Augustine's School, and all his children were professionals. There was Shaw University. Over in nearby Durham was Dr. James Shepard, who started up a college for Negroes, too. I met him one time in the pharmacy. Poppa paid premiums to North Carolina Mutual Life Insurance Company every month. It was the biggest Colored insurance company in the world, right in Durham.

But I didn't know anybody Colored anywhere who owned big boats or huge factories. In fact, the only big boats I had ever heard of were the *Titanic* and the *Lusitania*, and both of them sank. But maybe Mr. Garvey's boats wouldn't.

Once we reached home and rested, I modeled my new clothes and admired myself in the mirror. Aunti said I looked just like Momma, which made me stand even straighter.

"You got your glad rags today. You got coins jingling in your pocket. What else do you need to have to be a Harlem Queen of Sheba?" Aunti said, shaking her shoulders and slapping her hip.

I touched my greasy hair. "Can we —"

"Oh, my, yes, let's get to that hair!"

At last! Her fingers massaged my scalp in sudsy Madam Walker shampoo she had on hand. She washed it the same way Momma had. My chest ached with remembering. I didn't want her to stop.

"Don't feel bad that you have short hair," she was saying. "You're right in line with that new 'bob' style. Lean your head back so I can rinse it with this rosemary and lavender water. That'll make it smell really nice. After you dry it good, I'll oil it with Walker's pomade. I can't imagine anybody smearing nasty lard in a child's hair nowadays the way Society did. We'll get your hair pretty again, and it'll grow, too."

"Just like Momma used to do." Tears stung my eyes, but it wasn't from the rinse.

"Just like Elizabeth would do." She patted my cheek. "Don't worry, Cece. Living with me in New York won't be so bad. I promise you."

Chapter Nine

Now that the days were warmer, people paraded up and down One Hundred Thirty-sixth Street every Saturday and Sunday in their best clothes, just strolling! If we weren't too tired, we strolled along with them, smiling and exchanging greetings. When we could afford it, we stopped at little restaurants and sampled their foods. One Sunday, Aunti persuaded me to try something purple at a Japanese place. It was kind of rubbery but tolerable — until she told me it was baby octopus. I imagined little arms wiggling all down my throat. I held that thing in my mouth until she turned her head. Then I spit it out in my napkin.

These days, when Aunti asked me if I liked being in New York, I'd say, "Oh, yes!" I wasn't falsifying. Now that it was warmer, I *did* like New York more than when I had first arrived. But I surely hadn't expected to come here without Poppa.

I wrote Aunt Society that we lived on the third floor in the middle of Harlem, to make her think we had a fabulous view. But you have to have a window to have a view. I still didn't like scrubbing New York floors. I also remembered thinking about how I'd wished to get away from Aunt Society. I should have been more careful back home about what I wished for.

One night after we had wearily hoisted our backsides up the

stairs into our mouse hole of a room, Aunti pulled a letter from her skirt pocket as she eased down to the bed. "I meant to give you this earlier. It came yesterday, but I forgot."

From Poppa! "How is my girlio?" his letter began. I read his letter aloud while Aunti listened and rubbed her small, shapely feet. "'I eat plenty of beef, oatmeal, and boiled eggs to build up my strength. The azaleas are blooming, and everything is green. I feel pretty good.'"

"That's wonderful," Aunti murmured.

"'I sleep in a large room with three other men, but I don't mind. We each have a corner for ourselves, and lots of windows. I get up at five thirty every morning to milk four cows. I was a fisherman, not a farmer, so I'm all thumbs with these cows. By the time I finish milking one cow, the milk in the bucket of another one's turned sour.' Oh, Poppa!" I giggled. I hoped a cow wouldn't kick him.

"Taylor, Taylor." Aunti chuckled, shaking her head.

"Listen, Aunti. 'I got your letter and talked with Aunt Society on the phone. I told her about your clothes problem. She hasn't come to see me yet. You know how she hates to travel by car, and she refuses to go anywhere in the Bivenses' wagon.'"

"She never moved fast if she didn't want to." Aunti smeared face cream on her cheeks and forehead. "She's so old-fashioned."

"But so slow she can't write to me or send me clothes? I wrote to her, too." I sighed with a little bit of frustration, then read on. "'I don't know how long I'll be here, but I couldn't have stood it at all if you'd had to be with those Hugelburger women out in the sticks. Talk loud when you speak, girlio. Say your prayers. I feel bad that your things were stole, but the Lord'll make a way for you to keep on without them. Love to Valentina. Mind what she says. With more love than ever before, your dear Poppa.' "

"My dear Poppa. I miss you so much!" I wiped tears off my face so they wouldn't wet up Poppa's letter, and sighed again.

"I'm glad your father feels better," Aunti said. "And see? Time's flying by. You'll be back home before you know it."

"And maybe you can come back with me," I said, still sniffling.

"But don't you like it here?" She laughed. "Eating all that octopus?"

We talked some more about Poppa's letter as we got ready for bed. I picked up my brush and began giving my hair one hundred strokes. Ever since Aunti and Madam C. J. Walker took over my hair, I'd made brushing it a habit, no matter how tired I was. I wanted to grow hair! I think it was growing, a little. It was a lot smoother, and smelled like lavender now. I wrapped a silk scarf around my head to keep my hair neat, and snuggled in by my aunt.

"Aunti, did you call Miss Jarboro?"

"I forgot where I put her card," she mumbled.

"Right on the table, propped up against the sugar bowl. Want me to get it?"

"I can't do anything with it now. Maybe next week."

Next week? I swan! Why hadn't Aunti called her? Talk about not moving fast. She might have already missed an opportunity. Poppa told me that the Lord would turn your burdens into blessings if you told him your specific needs. Well, I'd been telling him and telling him. Maybe he needed for me to *do* something specific, too. I listened to Aunti's breathing gradually ease to her regular sleep snore.

All righty, Lord, here I go. Back out of bed, I dressed quickly, and with my shoes and Miss Jarboro's card in my hands, I tiptoed out of the room and hurried downstairs to the house telephone on the front desk. I gave one of my precious nickels to the night clerk, who told me what to do. Worried that Aunti would appear and force me to hang up — since she hadn't given me permission to call or leave the room — I kept one eye on the stairs.

"Hello?"

I swallowed and cleared my throat. "Miss Jarboro, please, is that you?"

"What? Who's this?" a sleepy-sounding woman said.

"Miss Jarboro, this is Celeste, Celeste Lassiter Massey, from North Carolina," I yelled, remembering Poppa's advice to talk loud. "Please don't hang up."

"Oh, yes, the girl in the lobby. This is Caterina Jarboro. Are you all right?"

"Yes, ma'am. Pardon me for calling so late, but I wanted to ask if you'd please help my Aunt Valentina. She needs a better job. She sings and dances, but right now we're scrubbing floors." I spoke quickly so she would hear everything and not lose patience and hang up.

"I don't own a theater, and I'm not a producer or director, you know. Where are you?"

"At our boardinghouse. See, my Aunti lost her job being a maid for Madame Mercifal Gutness, so that's why we got to scrub so much."

When Miss Jarboro didn't say anything, I got scared that she'd hung up. "Hello?"

"I'm listening. I've heard of Madame Gutness. She was in that *Aunt Susie Honeysuckle* play. Ha! May I speak to your aunt?"

"She's asleep, upstairs. She doesn't know I'm calling. She's a — a — fabulous singer and dancer. She says she sings 'Aunt Susie Honeysuckle' much better than Madame. She had that part until Madame made her give it up, then she fired my aunt. I don't know who else to ask for help, ma'am." I held my breath.

"Hmmm. If I could talk with your aunt, maybe we could come up with something. You go get her, or have her call me back right quick."

"All right, thank you, good-bye." I hung up, slid on my shoes, and took those stairs two at a time. I had only used a telephone once before, back home, and had lost my nickel then. But I'd done it right this time! I paused at the top of the stairs and squeezed my eyes shut. "I will lift up mine eyes unto the hills, from which cometh all my help." *Help us, Lord, please. If it be thy will. Amen. And please give me a sign, so I'll know for sure.*

When I opened my eyes, Aunti was frowning in the hallway, tapping her bare foot, braids bouncing under her scarf with each angry foot-slap. This wasn't the sign from God that I was looking for. My blood drained from my brain to my toes.

"Where in tarnation have you been?" she demanded. Miss D — and, oh no, snaggletoothed Gertie, too — stood by her in their white anti-wrinkle cream and their nightgowns.

"I — I — was on the telephone, talking to Miss Jarboro," I stuttered. "She wants you to call her right now."

"Why?"

"To talk to you." Hand shaking, I held out the card to her. But she leaned away from the card like it was covered with influenza germs.

"I told you I didn't care to chat with that girl tonight. I need to get my sleep, and you do, too, instead of sneaking off like this! We got to go to work soon."

"Wait now, Val," said Miss D. "Cece must have a good reason for calling this girl. What does she do, Cece?" After I filled her in, Miss D raised her mushy white eyebrows. She looked like a chocolate cupcake with white icing on the top. "Val, she's gone to all this trouble to run down this Miss Jarboro for you. The least you can do is ring her back, enty?"

"Ain't no enty about it. I'm not gonna do it. She was just being polite, anyway, with Cece calling her so late."

"Cece, you're in trouble again," Gertie said around her thumb.

"Hush, Gertie," said her grandmother. "Val, she might can give you a name to contact or help some kind of way."

"But I told Cece I might phone her next week. I'm not ready tonight!"

"How ready do you have to be to make a phone call?" I tried to give her one of my nickels.

"Excuse me?" Aunti snapped, and slapped her hands to her hips. "Who gave you permission to tell me what to do?"

"Nobody," I said aloud, but inside I thought, *The Lord.*

Aunti stared at me. Then she sighed and released her hold on her shapely hips. "Oh, I know you mean well, but you don't understand how horrible it is for me to keep being rejected. I didn't mean to snap at you. Come on." She moved toward our room.

"Valentina Lassiter, ain't you got any gumption anymore?"

Miss D broke in. "Do I need to sprinkle 'Get Right' powder in your shoes to set you on the right road? Go ring this girl *now*."

"Let me be, Ripsey Dillahunt." She went into our room. I heard the bed creak when she got in again.

Miss D took my nickel and the card. "You've done all you can," she told me softly. "Now leave it to me. C'mon, Gertie."

Behind her back Gertie shook her finger at me as if to say, "Shame, shame."

"Keep doing that and you'll have a nub yet," I hissed. Back inside our room, I undressed again and eased into bed. "Aunti, I'm sorry for butting into your business."

"Things aren't as easy as you think they are. So many important, high-up folks have already told me they can't help. Somebody as far down as her won't be able to do a lot of good."

"Momma always said nothing beats a failure like a try," I said, and added, "I didn't mean that to be sassy," when she opened her mouth. *Don't get your hackles up with me again!*

"Miss Goody Two-shoes, let me be," she said. Then she laughed. "I see I have to make my Pitiful Promenade by myself tonight. You're sure not gonna help me feel sorry for myself."

I just grunted. When I was sure my aunt was asleep, I crept out of bed, got my packet of goldenseal powder from my schoolbag, and dropped a pinch into her work shoes. The Aunt Valentina that I used to know back in Raleigh wouldn't have been too tired to call anybody or too scared to do anything. I didn't have any of Miss D's "Get Right" powder, but maybe my goldenseal would do the trick.

The next morning I received a picture postcard from Mr. Smalls. One side showed him sitting stiffly in a chair with Mr. USA on his knee. On the other side he wrote, "A young fella named Richard S. Roberts in Columbia, S.C., yearned to take our picture, so we let him." He asked about my family, and hoped I was having fun with my aunt and Miss Pinetar in New York. He planned to be in our Great Negro State Fair again and hoped he'd see me there.

"Aunti, you think Poppa'll be well enough to go to our state fair? It's in October."

"Let's pray he will. You know, I haven't been to that fair myself in years. That's where I met —" She paused. "That's where you meet so many fine people and see such great sights and learn about accomplishments that our people have made."

"Maybe we can go back in time for it," I hinted, but she didn't reply.

"Yoo-hoo, Valentina! Cece!" Miss D called from our doorway, dolled up in a beige crinoline dress and a floppy white hat with red and yellow flowers, green ribbons, and blue plumes. She looked like a plump bouquet. "Stir your stumps and get dressed, ladies, we got places to go."

"Where're we going, with you decked out so grand?" Aunti asked through a mouthful of toast and raw New York poached eggs. "Where's Gertie?"

"Gertie's momma got her early this morning. C'mon. We're going out, I said. Wear that pretty emerald two-piece suit, the one with the fringe, and that beige cloche hat, and your beige dancing shoes." Miss D slapped her white gloves across her right palm. "Celeste, you throw on something nice, too."

"What've you got up your stylish sleeve, Ripsey Dillahunt?" Aunti didn't budge. "Why do you keep looking at Celeste?

Celeste, have you been on the telephone again? Somebody, speak to me!"

"I called that Jarboro girl last night," Miss D said. "She's very nice, Val, just like Cece said. She wants you to come by today to this new musical *Shuffle Along* that she's rehearsing with. Listen. She said, and I'm repeating her words, 'If Miss Lassiter's as good as her niece says,' and I declared you were, then she thought maybe you could get on as somebody's understudy, or even get a real part before they put this show on the road, before they open it on Broadway."

I clapped my hands. Praise God and Miss D! "Broadway!"

But Aunti snorted and flapped her hands at Miss D. "A Colored show on Broadway? Oh, please. All we Colored ever get are minstrel shows and washerwoman plays. You and that girl's been sipping on something to pickle your brains. No full Colored show's ever been on Broadway before."

"There's always a first time, Val." Miss D glanced around. "So much junk in here! Cece, can you find her green suit in all this mess? Val, get up!"

While they fussed at each other, I pushed around dusty boxes and bags under the bed, and finally found the beige shoes. After fumbling and twisting around on the walls through her clothes, I reappeared with a mouthful of boa feathers and her green suit.

I put on the most pitiful face I could think of as I held the suit out to my aunt. She stared at me, then at Miss D. "Cece, you should see your face! You look like the sad mask we see on the theater marquees. Oh, Ripsey, all right, I'll go. But don't you expect much. I know I won't."

But still I thought I saw a spark of excitement on her face as we dressed. My face was lit up, for sure. Maybe this was Aunti's big break! And mine!

Out on the street Aunti kept jerking up on her skirt. Miss D stopped. "What in the world's wrong with you?"

"I feel like I'm wearing one of my great-great-grandmomma's old-fashioned long skirts, with this ugly fringe around the waist." Aunti tried to roll up the skirt around the belt.

I pulled down on my new secondhand yellow dress. Miss D had hemmed it too short! "This makes me feel like everything from my ankles to my thighs is naked. Aunt Society said decent young ladies don't let their knees be seen in public."

"Well, that cuts me from her list, doesn't it?" Aunti muttered. "If Society's legs were as fine as mine, she'd want to show hers, too."

Miss D snorted. "Mirror turn its face from you two upstairs so you couldn't see these things before you left? I reckon you'll snatch everything off and get bare right here on One Hundred Thirty-sixth Street! Ole country gals, tugging and wrenching right in front of Madam Walker's shop, with everybody gawking."

I glanced around and sure enough, women in chairs inside the salon stared at us. My face burned. I saw Aunti peer up at the third-story windows like she suspicioned that Miss A'Lelia was up there watching and scorning us. "Cece, behave." Aunti smoothed her suit.

We fell in behind Miss D where she couldn't see us, and wiggled on up the street.

Aunti pointed to a large building we passed on the right. "This is the One Hundred Thirty-fifth Street branch library. Much as you love to read, I'll have to take you in sometime. It's the Colored branch. New York has bunches of libraries." I craned my neck, staring. I couldn't think of a Colored library anywhere in Raleigh, except maybe at Shaw University or Saint Augustine's, but I couldn't go to them. I just had our little library at school.

Aunti stopped again. "I don't plan to ruin my good shoes walking in all this dust. Let's take the subway."

"Only if you promise not to embarrass me," Miss D grumbled.

Was a subway ride like a trolley? Momma and I rode in a trolley in Raleigh a long time ago. The Colored section in the back was so crowded that we had to stand up, even when I saw empty seats in the White section up front. Momma said those seats were reserved for White people. My face was pressed up against people's behinds, and I had to shove bags and sacks from pushing against my head.

But before I could ask, Miss D and Aunti went down some steps, and I had to follow. We were going to take a ride underground! Aunti paid our fares and we stood on a platform with a crowd of people, and a long train sped up. Folks hurried out of the doors, then a rush of people — and us — got on. We sat down together and rolled away, so fast I think I left my stomach back at the platform. We were like moles moving lightning-fast around in the ground. I pressed against Aunti, trying to remain calm.

I noticed, too, that we were sitting with White folks. Had Miss D and Aunti made a mistake and got on the wrong part of the train? We had to sit separately on Raleigh's trolleys. But quickly looking around, I realized that White and Colored were sitting together. All righty now! I smiled at Aunti and leaned back to enjoy my first subway ride. I didn't much care for it because I couldn't see anything but bored-looking people. I was glad when the train stopped and we came back up into the sunshine.

A steady honking, backfiring, and yelling parade of cars, trucks, buses, bicycles, carts, and people passed us. It seemed like the buildings must be as tall as the sky, but Aunti explained that there were buildings even taller in other parts of New York.

Eventually we reached a dilapidated one-story building that looked like a single good breeze could blow it down. We entered a large chilly, dim room. Another windowless place! Maybe New York ran out of glass when these neighborhoods were being built.

A group of folks in one corner kicked up their legs and danced, while another group sang, and a third worked over their lines. All the ladies, I noticed, had short bob hairstyles — like mine! Aunti tucked her braids farther under her hat. I hoped her long hair wouldn't be a strike against her.

Before I could worry about how to find Miss Jarboro, I saw her walk toward us. Remembering my manners, I curtsied, pulling at my skirt at the same time, until Miss D poked me with her elbow. "Hello, Miss Jarboro, ma'am." I took Aunti's hand. "This is my Aunt Valentina Lassiter. Aunti Valentina, this is Miss Caterina Jarboro, of Wilmington, North Carolina."

"Pleased, I'm sure." Aunti stiffly jerked her head at Miss Jarboro.

"Celeste talked so much about you, I feel I know you," Miss Jarboro said. She extended her hand to Aunti and smiled broadly.

I knew how Aunti loved to show her pretty white teeth. Where were they now?

"And I'm Mrs. Ripsey Dillahunt, who called you last night," said Miss D, introducing herself before I could. "And do you have a leading role?"

"Oh, no," said Miss Jarboro. "I'm in the chorus line, but I'm understudying for other parts, too. I thought Miss Lassiter could audition for the chorus line and understudy. Sometimes a girl who can't travel away from town drops out, so she'd have a chance to get that spot. We go on the road to Washington, D.C., and Philadelphia before we open here on Broadway. See, we're all praying that *Shuffle Along* will truly make it to a real Broadway theater. This place here is just our practice hall; you know how that goes, Miss Lassiter." She smiled warmly. When Aunti didn't say anything, she added, "If you're interested."

When Aunti still didn't say anything, she raised an eyebrow at me. "Or perhaps you'd like to audition, Celeste, if you like to dance."

"Me?" I could barely do the two-step, let alone dance in a musical! "I —"

"No, she's still a child," Aunti burst out, like she'd been trying to get a word in all along. "She doesn't care to perform. I'm the one who's the performer in the family. Of course I'm interested."

"That's what I thought." Miss Jarboro smiled. "I was just teasing."

"Oh, good," I said, relieved. "I —"

"You see I'm here, so I'm ready," Aunti said. "When do we get started?"

"You all just take seats near the front here, then I'll come back and get you, Miss Lassiter."

After Miss Jarboro walked away, Miss D chuckled. "She knew you'd wake up if she offered the part to your niece."

"Be quiet, Ripsey. Celeste, did you tell her you wanted to be in theater?" Aunti wore this slightly embarrassed, slightly angry expression.

"No." I shook my head hard, bewildered by her question. "I couldn't even —"

"Val, you should have been talking to Miss Jarboro," Miss D interrupted. "How're you gonna audition for the chorus if you don't talk?"

"Ripsey, I was hoping for something higher than the chorus line," Aunti whispered. "Oh, look — Gertrude Saunders, Adelaide Hall, and Lottie Gee! I know them, and I wager they've got the starring roles. Shoot, I'm as good as they are. Look, there's Miller and Lyles, the fabulous vaudeville comics." She nudged me and pointed to some men with papers in their hands by the musicians' section. "And Eubie Blake and Noble Sissle, the composers, are over there with them!"

"Go speak to them," I whispered, "since you know them."

Aunti fingered the fringe on her skirt. When she headed toward the musicians' section, I crossed my fingers. But instead she spun off for some seats and sat down. I sighed and followed. Like Miss D had said, seemed like the only time Aunti got excited was when Miss Jarboro joked about me auditioning. I hoped Miss Jarboro wouldn't get fed up with her moodiness and not put in a good word to the producers about her.

We watched people do some dance kicks, then I got up my courage. I didn't want Aunti to keep snapping at me. "Have you decided on another name yet?" I asked carefully. "To keep Madame Gutness off your trail?"

"Not gave it a thought," she murmured, watching the dancers.

"How about Val, from Valentina, and Chavis, for that man in the picture who you said was your good friend?"

She glanced at me sharply, but only said, "Hmmmm."

When a man hurried to the front of the room and issued orders, the musicians began tuning their instruments. Miss Jarboro and the other people took positions. With a drumroll and a cymbal crash, the musicians set off and the folks began to sing and do a dance that Miss D whispered to me was the Charleston.

"I can do that better than most of them," Aunti said under her breath. She swung her shoulders to the music. "Look at that girl with that white dress on, stumbling all over the place."

The girl danced all right to me, but I didn't tell that to my aunt. "What if you got out there?" I whispered. "Dancing in your chair won't get you noticed."

"Say what?" Aunti slipped off her jacket and dropped it into my lap. She ripped the fringe off her skirt, roped it around her neck, and mashed her hat more firmly onto her head. She practically flew onto the chorus line, the fringe flapping around her neck like butterfly wings. "Go, Aunti, go!" I whispered.

When the dance ended, the man who had called folks up pointed to Aunti. Aunti's and the man's lips moved, then they left the other dancers and went to a corner. "You think he got mad and made her leave?" I whispered to Miss D. I surely didn't want her to blame me for that.

"The way he was showing all thirty-two teeth, he's either gonna hire her or ask her for a date," Miss D replied.

Aunti sashayed back to us, smiling and shaking her fringe. "They hired me!" she bubbled. "I'll only be in the chorus, but it's a start. I can't leave with them for Washington, D.C., because I got to get my traveling money together first. But I can join them there later, and then open with them in Philadelphia. He also wants me to be an understudy for Adelaide, Lottie, and Gertrude. Isn't that fabulous?"

"Praise God and pass the biscuits!" I said. Some of the other people heard me and laughed. But my plan was finally moving ahead again. She'd open on Broadway, make money, and then we could go back home! "When do we leave for Washington? I could help you with your wardrobe and your hair and food, like you did with —"

"Oh no, the road's no place for a child," Aunti exclaimed, sounding surprised. "You'll stay with Miss D till I get back. If that's all right with you," she added to Miss D. Miss D nodded.

"But I thought — well, all right," I whispered. Now I was going to be separated from even the one relative I had here in New York. What if Aunti didn't come back?

Chapter Ten

From the way Aunti interrupted me I knew she didn't want me flapping my lips in front of her new friends. I guessed she couldn't afford to have me tagging behind her on the road, either: I'd just be another mouth to gobble up scarce food. Maybe she wanted a spell away from me. Still, being left behind was a calamitous letdown.

"Um, after you become a big star with lots of money, we can return to Raleigh for the fair," I said to cover up my distress at not being able to travel with her. "By then Poppa'll be home and you can live with us, and —"

"Whoa, this little filly's just galloping! She went from hardly saying a word when she moved here to making more noise than a Victrola! Excuse me." Laughing, Aunti took me by the arm and steered me to a corner. Miss D followed. "Just when my career's rising off the ground again, what makes you think I want to go back to Raleigh?" she whispered.

That was something else I shouldn't have flapped my lips about. "Well, no, you wouldn't, not with a new job, I guess." My stomach knotted up. But if she didn't go back, I really couldn't, either, at least not until Poppa was well. The law wouldn't allow me to live in the house by myself because I was too young, and Aunt Society wouldn't stay with me because she said I was too —

sassy? Too something! Bowing my head, I studied patterns in the linoleum floor so Aunti Val couldn't see the disappointment in my eyes.

"Oh, now you're drooping. Celeste, I didn't say I *wouldn't* go back." Aunti flashed her toothy smile. "Isn't that right, Miss D?" She playfully flicked the fringe at Miss D, but Miss D took it and tucked it into her purse.

She and Miss D had a five-second staring contest, then Aunti looked back to me. "We got lots of water to cross between now and then," she finished.

While I fretted, the lady named Lottie Gee walked over to us. "My, my, it's been a long time since I've seen you, Valentina. Welcome to *Shuffle Along*," she said. "And who's this? Your daughter?"

"Now, you know I'm too young to have a girl this old! She's thirteen." Aunti's smile didn't reach her eyes. I knew she wasn't pleased with Miss Lottie's assumption. "This is my niece Celeste, from North Carolina. And my friend, Mrs. Dillahunt. They came to offer support."

Miss Gee spoke to us and we spoke back. "So, Valentina, how's Madame Mercifal? Is she giving you time off to work with us?"

"She's freed me up, that's for sure," Aunti said, glancing at me meaningfully when I breathed in sharply. "Tell me more about the costumes. Or do we wear our own clothes? I hear this show has a tight budget."

"Sitting so pretty with Madame Mercifal Gutness, you needn't worry about a little thing like a tight budget." Miss Gee lowered her voice. "But I'm sure you're already aware the show doesn't have any money. We won't get paid until after we've come back from Washington and Philadelphia and open here May twenty-third. But everything'll work out."

Not get paid? Miss D pulled me off to the side while Aunti and Miss Lottie kept talking. "Don't you say anything," she whispered. "I heard what Lottie said. Cece," she said louder, "I know you must be getting hungry. You like chitlins? There's a barbecue joint not far from here."

I shook my head, knowing what she meant. "I can't stand anything that's pork, not after having to use pig grease on my head," I said softly.

Rehearsal ended. Miss D and I had to hurry to keep up with my aunt flying back to the subway. "Aunti, how can you have a job and not be paid?" I panted.

"Oh, she meant no money in my hand *just yet*," Aunti said as we tromped down the stairs to the subway platform again. "That's not unusual. We'll just keep doing what we've been doing until my new money rolls in." We pushed through the subway doors and found seats.

"But I don't want to keep on!" I said so loud an old White man across the aisle peered over at me. Money was supposed to roll in immediately!

"What did the man who hired you say about salary?" Miss D asked. "After all, Lottie could be wrong. And when does the show open in D.C.?"

"He told me that he couldn't pay me right away. We'll open in D.C. in a few weeks, in early May. That'll give me enough time to raise money to get there. All these questions! I thought you two'd be happy. *I* am."

"Val, you know good and well that if I don't ask, I won't know, 'cause you won't say," said Miss D, slapping her gloves against her purse again. Their voices got so low I couldn't hear them over the subway's rumble. Then I heard Miss D say, "You better straighten up and fly right, girl. Don't be so wishy-washy. You know Cece wants to go back home and she wants you there, too."

At least Miss D understood how I felt. Aunti didn't seem to. The least she could have done was thank Miss D and me for helping her get this job, but she didn't. I was just too outdone with her to even bring it up.

Back at the boardinghouse Aunti fixed a big vegetable salad as she sang lines from *Shuffle Along* songs. I sure didn't feel like singing, or even playing Dede. How could good news be so bad at the same time? I wished Evalina, Angel Mae, or Swan were around to talk to. I hadn't even heard from them yet. Had they forgotten about me, too?

After supper I got into bed feeling lower than the rug on the floor. But Aunti was still bubbling. "I told Mr. Blake about Madame Mercifal. He said he and Mr. Sissle weren't afraid of her. If they decide to put my name on the program, he'll bill me as Val Chavis, the name you suggested. Ain't that cute?"

"Yes, ma'am, cute," was all I said. Seemed like anything I tried to do to get back home was like grabbing fog with my fingers: I could see it and feel it, and it stayed within my reach, but I still couldn't hold it in my hands. Why couldn't I make her want to go back to Raleigh as much as I did? I hadn't come to New York because I wanted to, like she had. I'd been here long enough. It was time for me to get ready to go back — even if it wasn't possible, I added sadly to myself.

I began going to the *Shuffle Along* rehearsals with Aunti, but since I didn't have anything to do there, I took Miss Pinetar along. When Miss Lottie, who played the rich girl named Jessie, practiced "I'm Just Wild About Harry," I danced my puppet around on my lap. Aunti sat down by me to take a break. "Seems like if you're wild about somebody you'd want to show you had some fire," I told her. "Like this." I jerked Miss Pinetar's arms and legs around while I softly sang the song faster.

"I'll be sure to tell Lottie to follow the bouncing wooden doll next time." Aunti chuckled. "You got a point, Cece, but don't ever tell stars how to sing their songs. I know from personal experience that they don't like it." She returned to the chorus.

Aunti had also asked me to come along to help her unravel the complicated plot, since she didn't seem to understand it any more than I did. As far as I could figure it, a Mr. Jenkins (played by Mr. Miller) and a Mr. Peck (played by Mr. Lyles) were part-ners of a grocery store in some town down South called Jimtown. When the partners decided to run against each other for mayor, they both secretly swiped money from their own cash register to buy votes, then each accused the other of stealing. Jenkins on the sly hired a private detective to catch Peck, while Peck hired one to catch Jenkins. Lo and behold, unbeknownst to each other, they hired the same detective, named Keen-Eye.

Now. The fellow named Harry (played by Roger Matthews) that Jessie (Miss Lottie) was so wild about was a good guy who wanted to become mayor, too, but unlike Peck and Jenkins, Harry wanted to run an honest campaign and refused to buy votes, since that was illegal. He didn't have any money anyway, but fortunately Jessie was so much in love with him that she was willing to help him finance his campaign. Harry and Jessie's campaign and their love hit some snags, though, when Jessie's daddy refused to give them any money unless he knew for sure that Harry'd win the election. Worse yet, if he *didn't* win, Jessie's daddy wouldn't let him marry Jessie, either! Mr. Peck won the election, and a string of other calamities sprang up, which convinced me never to enter politics.

Just when everything seemed hopeless, Keen-Eye the detective exposed the crooks, particularly Mr. Peck and Mr. Jenkins. Mr. Harry became the new mayor and won Miss Jessie's hand, *and* her daddy's money. Everybody sang, danced, and lived happily ever after.

By the time the show went on the road, I figured I'd know as much about it as Aunti did. Maybe I could be Aunti's understudy, just in case she got sick. That thought made me laugh. Aunti'd go on the road even if she had to crawl. Humming low, I imagined that Miss Pinetar was a real girl, and she and I were dancing with the chorus.

"What in the world are you doing?"

I jumped. Miss Lottie stood in front of me, pointing at Miss Pinetar. I hid my doll among the folds of my comfortable old long skirt. "Nothing, ma'am."

"You were performing my song. I like how you did it, fast and snappy. Little doll just jumping! You gave me a good idea. Watch."

She went back to the stage area singing "I'm Just Wild About Harry" and danced like she really was wild about her man. She lit up that whole room! Everybody applauded when she finished, including Aunti. "That girl Celeste is the reason for all of that." Miss Lottie waved at me. "I plan to do it this way from now on. Thanks, Celeste."

I scooched down in the seat, my cheeks burning, as folks nodded and smiled at me. Clapping, Miss Lottie came over to me. So did Aunti, but she didn't say anything. "Do you have musical theater in your veins, too?" Miss Lottie asked.

So I can end up scrubbing floors all night? No, indeedy! "I want to be a doctor, ma'am."

"Oh, I see. Most young ladies say they want to be in the movies, or be teachers, nurses — and mothers, of course."

"Celeste's very ambitious," Aunti said. "You know we young women today have our goals set high. But she doesn't want to be an actress." She pursed her lips.

As we walked back home, Aunti was quiet. She didn't mention how I had helped Miss Lottie, so I didn't, either. Did Aunti think I was butting into a leading lady's business? I was pleased, though, that Miss Lottie liked my idea.

When we reached the boardinghouse, I checked the mailbox. A letter from Angel Mae! I tore open the large brown envelope, and inside were also letters from Evalina and Swan. About time! I began reading Angel Mae's letter right then on the stairs. "Dear Cece," her letter began. "May this letter find you in the best of health and the purest in mind, thought, and deed. I am the same. If you wondered why you haven't heard from us, we wondered about you, too. Neighbors from blocks around had wrote on your envelope 'wrong address' before it finally got to me."

I fanned myself with my hand in relief. Well, no wonder! I must have been in a big hurry — or tired — to have written it wrong. I read on. Did I eat caviar all the time? How did I like living in a mansion? Both questions made me snort. *How about octopus instead of caviar, Angel Mae?* Had I heard from the *Brownies' Book* magazine people yet about our stuff? I kept forgetting. Maybe Aunti could take me to the NAACP office and check on our poems like Mr. Johnson had suggested. I carefully refolded and replaced Angel Mae's letter in the envelope.

Swan's letter was about the Great Negro State Fair, October 25 through 29. Mrs. Bracy planned to hold cooking classes this summer for girls our age, so they could enter the fair's exhibits. Swan said Mrs. Bracy wanted to know if I'd seen the Statue of Liberty yet. "Evalina yearns to rear a pig to show at the fair, but her folks say no, so she's having spasms about it. Nobody else is. We have to smell and dodge enough mule, dog, cat, duck, and guinea hen poop already around here. Pig poop, too?"

Evalina's was the shortest. Her handwriting looked like worm trails in the dust. She mainly wanted to know about Big Willie. "Has he got to the coal mining camps yet? My my, you wrote a lot about him. Is he gonna be your beau? Those coal mines are dangerous places. They're always caving in or blowing up and lots of men get killed. Men also get into big fights with each other and sometimes the state or the president has to call in troops to break things up."

She wrote that she hadn't seen Poppa or Aunt Society since I left. "I miss you and wish you were here so I could give you a thousand hugs and kisses. Love, Evalina. P.S. Momma won't let me raise a pig for the fair."

I missed her, too. I missed everybody. Would I never get back home to see them? Would I ever see Big Willie? Would he and his triplet brothers and sister return to Eagle Rock in time to come to the fair? I tried not to think about coal mine disasters and the fights.

Aunti, who hadn't said much to me since coming home, asked about the letters. I offered to show them to her, but she declined. "Maybe you'll get one directly from your aunt. That'd be one I'd like to see." She winked at me, picked up her tortoiseshell comb, and began loosening her thick black braids. I wondered why she'd want to see a letter from Aunt Society, who was her sister-in-law. To see if Aunt Society had written about her? Or did she mean that the old bat would never write to me?

Each day in April was busier than the day before. After rehearsal we went on to scrub floors almost every night. Sometimes after rehearsal or scrubbing we stopped at Café Noir Le Grande, where Aunti whispered with Monsieur and we picked up food. All that walking and working made my arms and legs more muscular, but I was so tired I'd still fall asleep at the table.

On the rare days we didn't work, Aunti would let me stay home from rehearsal, too. But then I washed and ironed our clothes, cleaned our room, and slept. When I could, I wrote in my journal, studied my textbooks, or played Dede downstairs on the front porch in the fresh spring air. I was disappointed about not being in school, but how could I have gone to school all day and worked half the night?

I longed to go to that branch library Aunti had pointed out, but I hadn't because I was afraid I'd get lost. Though I felt a little more comfortable here, this little part of Harlem was still bigger than all of Raleigh, it seemed.

If I didn't keep our door locked when Gertie was visiting her grandmother, she'd barge right into our room. "Lemme play that fiddle," she'd begin. I'd tell her no, and rush around the room snatching things out of her hands, like my brush, my violin, Aunti's hats and furs, and so on. "Well, ain't you got nothing I can play with?"

"No. Go read a book or something." I'd stand in front of the bed so she couldn't jump up and down on it.

"I can't read. Gimme a nickel for some candy."

"You eat too much candy as it is. That's why you don't have any teeth. You should eat fresh fruits and vegetables."

"Vegetables is weeds and I ain't eating no weeds. I ain't got good teeth because a hant comes along at night, gets on my back, twists my head backwards, and pulls 'em out as soon as they grow in."

"Now, that's a falsity if ever I heard one. Sit down in that chair there and behave or else go home."

Gertie'd sit down for a minute and start picking at her nose, or her braids, which was why her hair usually stood straight out on her head, no matter how many times her grandmother rebraided it. Finally she'd clump back out the door. "Do, Lord, remember me," I'd breathe.

When Aunti got home, I'd tell her whatever Gertie had said or done. "Gertie's momma is a real dumb Dora," she said. "She fills that child's head full of tales about witches and voodoo and stuff. I truly believe Gertie has a vitamin deficiency that causes her teeth to be so rotten. I don't know why they don't take her to a dentist or a doctor."

"If Miss D made her eat those greens instead of playing with them, she'd get more calcium and her teeth would stay in her head," I said.

"Probably so, but she's got her grandmomma wrapped around her little bossy finger. Miss D lets Gertie do anything, partly to spite her daughter-in-law." Aunti slapped her mouth gently. "Hush, Valentina. You didn't hear me say a word of this, Celeste."

"Yes, ma'am. I mean, no, ma'am." I laughed.

The closer May neared, the slower *Shuffle Along* seemed to shuffle. The producers were still trying to find a Broadway theater to premiere it in on May 23. In a couple of weeks the cast was supposed to hit the road for Washington and Philadelphia, but folks were still trying to finish hammering the sets and to piece together costumes. I heard Miss Lottie tell Miss Jarboro that some costumes were leftovers donated from other musicals. When Aunti and some other ladies were given Oriental-looking dresses to wear, they were puzzled as to how Asia was part of the play. So Mr. Blake and Mr. Sissle composed a song with an Asian flavor, added it to the show, and told Aunti and the ladies to perform it in their kimonos. They did, and the rehearsals went on.

But worse for me, the closer the time came, the sooner Aunti would leave me. I'd be an orphan in New York!

May arrived. I thought up dozens of reasons why I should go on the road with Aunti and why I shouldn't stay behind, but none of them worked. She started to sound irritated with me. On the afternoon she was to leave for Washington, I waited, nervous and full of dread, for her to return from rehearsal. And then be gone.

Aunti sailed in the door. "We got to hurry and get me packed 'cause Jim's downstairs waiting. He's rounding up folks to take them to the train station."

When she swept off her hat, I threw my hands to my mouth. Some awful thing had happened to her head. Half of her hair was missing!

"I know, I know, I said I'd never do it," she told me when she saw me gawking at her head covered with short ringlets. "But they told me if I wanted to stay in the show I'd have to cut off my braids. Short hair is all the rage anyway now, so I had Lottie whack 'em off."

After setting several bags on the table, she pulled three braids from her purse. They wrapped around her arm like black ropes. "I'll have somebody make us hair brooches from these."

I touched the short hairs clinging around her neck. I remembered how lost I'd felt when my own hair broke off, thanks to Aunt Society. "I bet you miss them already. It'll grow back, won't it?"

"I'll be praying every day that it will," she said. "It's all right. Well, no, it's not all right, but sometimes you got to sacrifice to get what you want, Celeste."

Eyes shiny, Aunti stroked her shorn braids.

"Hey, Miss Valentina!" Gertie yelled from the hallway. I closed our door before Gertie could come or peep in. "Grandmomma wants to know when Cece's coming over, and when you leaving."

"In just a few minutes," Aunti told her through the door.

"Cece gonna bring that doll?" Gertie wanted to know.

"Maybe," I said. Aunti charged about grabbing up and dropping shoes, picking up and setting down cosmetics and soaps.

She rummaged through boxes on the floor and through dresses on the wall.

"You got some candy over there, you bring that, too," Gertie went on.

"We're trying to get me packed," Aunti yelled. "Go home."

After she left, I touched Aunti's braids again. "Gertie's gonna drive me into hysterics every moment you're gone."

"You're a big girl, Cece. You know how to deal with her. Where's my blue cloche hat? The one with the three peacock feathers?" She had me rummaging with her until we finally situated in four suitcases what she thought she wanted to take. Packing in advance would have made so much more sense, but that wasn't Aunti's way.

"Look, when you get tired of Gertie, come back over here during the day and lock the door so she can't get in. But sleep over there at night. I hardly ever lock things when we're home, but you never know who might wander in uninvited from the street."

"All right." I wanted to say one more time that it'd be even better if she'd let me go with her, but I knew it was useless to say that now. As nervous as she was, it might upset her. I packed up my sack of licorice, my new secondhand brush and comb, my toothbrush, and a few other things in one of Aunti's smaller bags. "You know, if Gertie's too bad, maybe I could turn Miss Pinetar into one of those voodoo dolls Miss D talks about, and put a spell on her."

"Ha! Wouldn't that be something? But don't say that around Miss D." Aunti's muffled voice came from her last forage among her clothes. "She believes in that stuff."

"I know. It's a blasphemous thought. But exciting." I shoved

Miss Pinetar and her dancing stick and paddle into the bag. Since she was made of wood, I couldn't stick her full of pins, anyway, but maybe her dancing might keep Gertie calm. "Lord, please don't make me have to sleep by Gertie tonight," I said aloud. "She probably still wets the bed."

We set Aunti's bags in the hallway, then turned toward Miss D's open door just as she came toward us. She saw me first and started to smile, but then she saw Aunti's bare head. "No, no, you didn't!" she shrieked, throwing her arms up in the air, then pressing her hands to her chest. She fell back in a chair.

"Ripsey, that's too much drama. It'll grow back. My people's got *good* hair." Aunti handed Miss D a piece of paper. "Look, here's the address of the theater where we'll be performing. I don't know where I'll be sleeping until we get there and find a place. I'll leave a message with Mrs. Tartleton."

We helped carry Aunti's bags down to the lobby and out to a rickety truck where Mr. Jim stood smoking a cigarette and tapping his foot. "Shake a leg, girl!" He snatched up the bags. "Whoa, woman! You must have packed every piece of clothes you got!"

Aunti hugged me. "Will you be back in time for Mother's Day?" I asked. "It's next Sunday."

"It depends on how the show's coming along. You be good. Bye!" She hugged Miss D, then climbed into the truck and they rattled away.

"Well, there she goes," I said sadly. I hated to see people leave me behind.

Miss D nodded. "She was sure glad to go, enty?"

We headed back upstairs. I dropped down in an overstuffed

chair near the door with my bag, swinging my foot, looking around, while Miss D gathered up combs, hair oil, and her other tools to do battle with Gertie's hair. Her apartment was L-shaped, much bigger than Aunti's mouse hole, and was neat and homey, with a window. All I could see out the window was a brick wall of the building next door, but at least a little sunshine came in.

One end of the L was where we were in her front room, with enough space for a couple straight-back chairs, a divan, and small tables covered with pretty crocheted doilies. The middle part of the L held her sink, an icebox, a stove, and cupboards. The bottom part of the L was where her bed, closet, and dresser were located. She even had a tiny lavatory space where she kept her chamber pot and a bowl and table for washing up.

Well, here I was in somebody else's place. Just call me Leap Frog, hopping from one lily pad to another. Would I ever return to my own lily pad back home?

Fuzz, lint, dust balls — Gertie, did you roll your head around on that dirty floor under your momma's bed again? My goodness!" Miss D had locked Gertie between her knees. Gertie squirmed worse than a worm impaled on a hook. "See how pretty Cece's hair is, and how nice and quiet she sits, like a lady? Cece, your hair's growing good now, enty."

I wanted to tell Miss D I'd rather be back in our room. Instead, I said, "Yes, ma'am. Aunti uses Madam Walker products on it, and I brush it every day."

"Why'd your Aunti cut her hair?" Gertie asked between twists. "She got head mange or ringworm? Or lice?"

"None of 'em, Gertie," I said patiently. This was going to be a long three or four days for me with ole nosy Gertie here.

"She had to cut it, to stay in the show," Miss D told her. "She took the path of least resistance."

I stiffened a little. "I pray I don't sound sassy, but what does *that* mean?"

"Rather than stand her ground and fight for what she believes in, she just changes her tune to satisfy the other fella."

"Did she do something wrong?"

"No, she did right. Her boss said she had to cut it, so. And to have you stay with me while she's on the road was right, though you may not think so. The road's rough enough for grown women, let alone young girls like you, still wet behind the ears."

My ears are quite dry, thank you. You think I'm still a baby. But I kept all that to myself.

Miss D glared down at Gertie. "Girl, I'm warning you! Jerk away from me one more time and I'll pull every strand of hair out your hard little head!" I held my hand over my mouth and coughed, but actually I was hiding my smile while Gertie and her grandmother tangled. After a while Gertie quieted down a little and that ended the show.

"Miss D, do you go to church on Mother's Day?"

"Oh, I used to go every Mother's Day, every Easter, every Watch Night, Women's and Men's days all the time in South Carolina. I work some Sundays now, you know, but I go when I can. My son down in Carolina sends me a Mother's Day card sometimes. But back to Val — except for a wedding or a funeral, she's not been inside a church up here once, and I've known her for over fifteen years."

"She went with us to St. Paul," I said softly. That was while Momma was still alive. We hadn't been to church since I'd been here with Aunti. She was always too tired come Sunday.

Miss D leaned toward me a little. I thought I saw sympathy in her eyes. "One thing I think she did do wrong, though, was to tell you she'd be back in three or four days. She won't be back that quick, not in time for Mother's Day."

"Oh. But she said she would." I stopped. Maybe Miss D knew something that I didn't. "So was she telling another falsity?"

"No, she means to be back, but she just won't be." She shrugged. "I've waited on her time and time over the years to follow through on one thing or another, but half the time she don't. She means to, but she don't." Her mouth pulled down. "I hate to be telling you these things, but I want you to know the truth. It'll work out, honey. But now tell me how I can get this child's teeth to grow. Short of taking her to a doctor or a dentist. I ain't got that kind of money."

"Drinking milk and eating green vegetables are always good," I said, still chewing over what she'd said about Aunti.

"No! Milk is nasty and'll give you tapeworms," Gertie said with her face squinched up.

"There she goes again with that tapeworm stuff. Cece, her momma loves to tease her with such tales."

"Down home, folks get tapeworm, hookworm, and such when they don't wash their hands after using the outhouse, or when they walk barefoot around outhouses and pig poop," I told Gertie. When Miss D nodded, I went on. "Gertie might like milk more if you put something in it to sweeten it up. Or maybe it's the cow milk. Folks would tell Mr. Hodges and Poppa all the time how cow milk hurt their stomachs."

"That's true." Miss D waved her comb at me. "I never drunk cow milk when I was a child. We always drunk goat milk. Folks don't drink goat milk much anymore. Everybody wants bottled milk from a cow. Except this child. Well, tomorrow I'll carry us over to Marley's grocery. That's a Jamaican store. You'll like Marley's. It's got herbs and spices for most anything that ails you and for cooking, and food like goat milk, and —"

"I ain't drinking no billy goat milk!" Gertie shouted.

"But you got to grow teeth! Thank you, Cece. I clean forgot about sweetening the milk. You'll make a good root worker."

"Yes, ma'am. But I'm gonna be a doctor, not a root worker. Momma said 'root worker' sounded too much like we used voodoo."

Miss D waved her hand at me. "Root worker, voodoo doctor, hoodoo doctor, doctor — whatever works is fine with me. 'Cause I'm a Baptist, anyway. Where can a Colored girl get doctor training down in Carolina?"

"Maybe I could go to medical school up here in New York," I replied.

Gertie broke free of Miss D's knees and, jumping up and down, swung her little hips. "Lemme see that doll do some hoochie coochie!"

Miss D dropped the comb into her lap and blew out her breath. "I need a break. Cece, would you please get out that doll?"

I assembled Miss Pinetar and began singing. We had Gertie bouncing up a storm with Miss Pinetar until she got so tired she had to take a nap. While she slept, Miss D finished braiding her hair, and wrapped string around each braid to make it harder for Gertie to pick apart.

That night after I'd brushed my hair and said my prayers, I lay on one side of Miss D in her big lumpy bed, thinking. Gertie lay on the other. Had Aunti reached Washington yet? Was she drinking champagne and eating caviar or octopus at a party? Was she rehearsing? I knew one thing she *wasn't* doing: she wasn't scrubbing floors, and praise the Lord neither was I. I grinned in the dark.

One thought caused my smile to fade. Why would Aunti be so nonchalant about Mother's Day? She didn't understand that this was an important day to me. When Momma was living, I'd give her flowers, and draw Mother's Day cards to give her. Momma, Poppa, and I would get spruced up and go to church. We'd eat a big dinner at church afterward or at home, and sometimes have the Smithfields over. Then Momma and I'd take dinners to the sick and shut-ins.

After Momma passed, Poppa, Aunt Society, and I went to church on Mother's Day, but it was terribly wrenching. Poppa and I cried and cried, and even Aunt Society sniffled. Then we laid our cards and sprigs of white azaleas from our bushes on Momma's grave and cried again. Last Mother's Day, Poppa felt too sad and sick to go anywhere, but Aunt Society and I did. After church I put our cards and flowers on her grave. I spent the rest of the day lying on the couch with Poppa and listening to the Westrand. For once Aunt Society didn't complain about using too much electricity. But now, so far away from Momma's grave, what could I do in her memory? I decided to think warm thoughts about her and keep her memory strong in my mind and in my heart. I'd give thanks to the Lord that I had had such a kind, sweet Momma.

Nobody teased me back home for being motherless; Evalina and Angel Mae would have beat them up. Thinking about my momma and my friends, I cried in the dark without making a sound.

The next morning as soon as we left the boardinghouse for Marley's grocery store, Gertie fell down on her back in the street and rolled around. "Oh Lordamercy not today," Miss D moaned. "Gertie, stand up and walk like you got good sense."

Gertie screamed. Her white sailor suit was brown with dirt. I bent over her writhing about like she was having a spasm. "Is she having a fit?"

"No, but I'm gonna give her one," Miss D growled. She grabbed Gertie under both arms, lifted her to her feet, and shook her a little. "Gal, you better straighten up and fly right before I smack your braids loose. Why you got to act so silly? I declare!"

As Miss D dragged Gertie up the street, she told me that when Gertie was a toddler, Gertie's mother had carried her whenever she got even a little bit tired. "Gertie learned early that if she fell out, her momma would pick her up. So she did and still does. And her momma still does! Her momma's about as smart as a sack of rocks. Cece, some children get raised up, some get hauled up. Gertie gets hauled. I wish I could keep my darling grandbaby with me all the time. I'd straighten her out."

We all three knew Miss D wouldn't hit Gertie, no matter what she did. Right off, her darling set off such a pitiful whimpering and whining that Miss D half carried, half dragged her the rest of the way. Aunt Society would have left Gertie on the ground to get run over by a motor car. I would have, too.

When we reached the store, Gertie stood up straight as a lamppost and started talking like she had good sense. "Grammaw, buy me some chocolate cookies and some peppermint balls, please."

"You'll not get a thing, acting like a fool," Miss D snapped. At that Gertie screeched like she'd truly been smacked upside the jaw — which was what I yearned to do. People edged away from us while Gertie bawled. Like Miss D said, the store shelves were stocked full with bags and strings and bottles of herbs, but I didn't get a chance to look around much with that gal's mouth going off like a fire alarm.

I hurried around the store to buy my little bag of red licorice, and in one herbs and spices section I grabbed up a bunch of fresh lambs'-quarter leaves to make a spring tonic. Miss D and I quickly paid for our purchases and left. Gertie was madder than a wet cat now because she didn't get any treats. She screamed and snotted, fell out, and picked her braids, with Miss D yanking her along by the arm and fussing. But as soon as we entered our boardinghouse, Gertie shut up and walked normally again.

"She's scared her little narrow behind's gonna get smacked now," Miss D told me in the lobby, "now that she's home, enty."

"I love you, Grammaw," Gertie whimpered, blinking her big brown eyes at Mrs. Tartleton, who ran the boardinghouse, while hugging her grandmother around the waist.

"Oh, Gertie, aren't you a sweet little thing?" said Mrs. Tartleton. I spoke to Mrs. Tartleton, but grunted when Miss D melted. Gertie was a better actress than Aunti sometimes.

Upstairs in her room Miss D poured out a cup of goat milk, handed it to Gertie, and began putting the other food away. She told me to get some milk, too. I'd drunk goat milk before. As long as I didn't smell it, the taste was tolerable. I hadn't drunk any kind of milk since I'd left Raleigh — Aunti Val never bought it — so even goat milk was a treat.

I watched Gertie suck up a mouthful of milk and let it dribble from the corners of her mouth. Miss D turned to see Gertie blow bubbles in the cup, which made her sneeze. Goat milk splashed all over her face. "Stop that!" her grandmother hissed. She took away the cup and wiped Gertie's face.

"You drink that stuff you'll get a tapeworm in your gut," Gertie told me. I examined the milk to see if anything moved in the cup. "My momma said tapeworms in the milk make my stomach hurt." She picked at a braid.

"Not in New York," her grandmother said. "Leave that braid alone and drink that milk, Gertie!"

Gertie's momma isn't very bright, I thought, *to tell her child such falsities.* Aunti had said that Gertie's poppa wasn't too bright, either. No wonder Gertie was so goofy. I swirled a stick of licorice around in my milk and sipped some through the candy.

"Why'd you do that?" said Gertie, eyeballing my licorice.

"To make it taste sweet. You gonna drink your milk?"

"Through the licorice," she said with her hand out. When her grandmother said she had to drink more milk first, Gertie took a sip, then drank almost all of it. I gave her a small piece. She popped it into her mouth, sucked on it, and waggled her head back and forth, smiling.

"Praise be to the Glory," Miss D exclaimed. "We spent all morning getting one cup of milk down this child. Now I got to go clean Mrs. Manowitz's house. You want to go with us, Cece, or you want to stay?"

"Stay," I said. I didn't want her to be tempted to have me scrub Mrs. Manowitz's floors for her.

"Then Gertie can stay here with you."

"Oh please, no, Miss D. I can't handle Gertie. And — and I need to go back over to Aunti's so I can, uh, wash out my clothes and dust the furniture, you know, and —"

"Miz Manowitz's got a dog from Mexico that looks like a rat. Gertie's scared to death of it. I hate to take her. But I know my grandbaby's a handful. C'mon, Gertie, put on your clean waist so we can go. Here's my house key, Cece. We'll be back before night."

She had a million precautions for me to follow — keep the doors locked, don't turn on her stove or Aunti's hot plate, don't wander around outside, and so on and so on. I just "yes, ma'amed" her. She must have forgotten that I had stayed by myself many times when Aunti was gone. As soon as they left, I returned to Aunti's room and sang, "Aunti's comin' with loads of dough, she'll be a star, we'll go to Raleigh, don't you know!"

As I filled the sink with hot water to wash my stockings and other garments, I daydreamed about us returning to Raleigh draped in furs and throwing money into the air. How would Aunt Society get along with her now? Probably like an old cat whose space got invaded by a young one. I laughed. But why wouldn't Aunt Society write to me? I frowned and slapped my sudsy skirt on the washboard. I was tired of getting upset because I hadn't heard from her. I paused. Maybe she was sick. Maybe she'd contracted tuberculosis, too. I shook my head and scrubbed harder. Aunt Society never got sick. Even cold germs were too scared to cross her path. Old bat.

After rinsing my clothes, I hung them around the room to dry and started to sweep the floor, but stopped. I wanted to be outside in the warm May sun! Taking Dede and both house keys, I locked both doors and skipped down the stairs.

"Morning, Celeste," Mrs. Tartleton called out from behind the counter as I reached the lobby. I was glad to see her. She was nice. She was so thin I could almost see clear through her arms. Her veins crisscrossed her hands under her skin like little brown worms. One day I'd ask Miss D how much she weighed.

"Morning, ma'am." I thought I'd test the waters. "I'm gonna take a walk, just down the street and back, to get a little sun."

"Did Miss D say you could leave the boardinghouse?"

"No, but — but — she didn't say I couldn't," I stuttered. "I mean, not exactly."

"Listen to me, Miss Saucy Cece. You're not fooling me. You know Miss D doesn't want you in these streets by yourself, not even in the daytime. But at least I can sit with you on the porch."

I smiled. "All right." I hadn't really figured I'd get any farther than there anyway.

We sat in the warm shade, and I played "Forsythia," some ragtime, and, of course, some songs from *Shuffle Along*. "You can sure make that fiddle sing," Mrs. Tartleton said. "Harlem's the right place for you."

"I don't want to sound sassy, but I might like Harlem better if I could see more than water buckets and soapy rags at nighttime. I don't talk with any girls my age —"

"Or young men, either?" Mrs. Tartleton arched an eyebrow.

"Oh, I'm not thinking about any boys," I said, and suddenly saw Big Willie's face. "But I imagine going to that branch library and to Mr. James Weldon Johnson's office where the *Brownies' Book* magazine's published would be nice." I explained about the *Brownies' Book* and how much my Butterflies Club friends were depending on me to see about our poems. She promised to take me to some places when she had a day off.

"Oh, wonderful!" I thanked her over and over, and my hopes rose. Then I played some more while the morning hustle of cars and trucks and people crowded One Hundred Thirty-sixth Street.

After that I returned to Aunti's room and cleaned, searched without success for Aunti's boat shares, wrote in my journal, and tried to study my geography book. I hadn't touched my schoolbooks since I'd been here. School down home was almost over, anyway. I looked at the United States map. Raleigh, North Carolina, sure looked far away from Harlem, New York. I was still staring at the map when Miss D and Gertie returned.

That evening Mrs. Tartleton came up to where I was with Miss D. She had a message from Aunti saying where she was staying. "And she said to tell you she'd be in Washington longer than expected."

"So that means she won't be back for Mother's Day, just like you said, Miss D." I tried to keep from frowning, but Miss D and Mrs. Tartleton saw my face.

"I'd be pleased to have you and Miss D as my guests at my church," said Mrs. Tartleton, who was a widow and lived with her brother Dexter.

"Well, that'd be fine," Miss D said, and I nodded. "Cece, I reckon your Aunti hasn't done a thing with those clothes you bought at the Twice As Nice. Bring them over here and I can hem one for you to wear." I broke into a smile and ran to get my skirts. I snatched up Aunti's pale green one, too. Maybe Mother's Day would work out for me after all.

In the middle of the night I woke up to see Miss D place a sleeping Gertie into a woman's arms.

"It would've been nice to take my grandchild to church with me, for once," Miss D was saying, sounding disappointed.

Come Sunday morning we gathered in the lobby. I wore Aunti's green skirt that Miss D had hemmed, my white embroidered waist, and Aunti's green, flowery silk shawl. We discovered at the last minute that an old pair of Aunti's white fancy pumps fit me, too. They were way too small for her anyway because Aunti had a substantial foot — "country gal footses," Miss D called them. We were able to twist my hair into a tiny bun and tie a white ribbon around it. Miss D wore a white linen dress covered with pink carnations, and her big white floppy hat. Mrs. Tartleton wore a yellow organdy dress patterned with tiny white morning glories, and a big blue hat.

"Am I presentable?" I asked, nervously patting my hair. I'd never walked in pumps before. What if I twisted my ankle and fell on my face right in front of the altar? My heart thumped rapidly and my tummy had looped itself into pretzels again.

"You look perfect," Mrs. Tartleton replied. She reached into her purse, pulled out her rouge box, and touched my cheeks. She squinted at me, then smiled in approval. "Everybody'll be looking at you because they'll be wondering who this pretty young lady and this older, dignified, handsome lady are. I wish I could've got Dexter to come with us and see you, Ripsey."

"Oh, how you talk, Etrulia," Miss D said, smiling. "And look at you, Cece! Grown enough to have your cheeks painted! You look so pretty! I wish I could've had Gertie to take, too. Her momma came and got her last night."

I lowered my head, smiling, cheeks burning, feeling bashful at their words. Grown enough! I looked up at myself in the lobby mirror and almost didn't recognize myself. I looked just like Momma! Aunt Society would say I was surely going to the Devil's Pit of Never-Ending Fire for having rouge on my cheeks, but I reckoned Momma would be pleased. I wished she could have been there, too. Or Aunti Val.

We set out for All Saints Heavenly Deliverance Church a few blocks away, looking like a bouquet of spring flowers. We strolled in, Mrs. Tartleton in the lead, me, then Miss D. I greeted everyone like Mrs. Tartleton and Miss D did, but was relieved when we sat down in the visitors' pew. My dogs were barking!

By the time the preacher began shouting about the grace of God and motherhood, two women had caught the spirit and passed out, and a man had jumped a pew. The mother of the church offered up a Motherless Child prayer that touched me so that I had to cry. Miss D handed me her handkerchief. But at least I'd *had* a good mother, I told myself, thinking about Gertie, and that made me feel good all day long.

A couple of days later Gertie popped back up at her grandmomma's. I'd been looking for my licorice ever since. "It's not nice to take other people's stuff without asking," I told her for the tenth time. Ole thing didn't say a mumbling word. "Gertie, you took my candy and I want it back!" Surprising myself, I made a fist.

When she saw my fist, Gertie sat up in her grandmother's bed and screeched. That brought Miss D in from the kitchen area. "Chile, why you got to holler so early in the day? What's wrong, Cece?"

"I keep asking her about my candy." Before I could say anything else, Gertie jumped out of the bed and ran to the chamber pot.

Miss D folded her arms, shaking her head. "She ate your candy and drunk all that goat milk. Now she's got the stomach flood, enty!"

I broke into giggles. Goat milk and licorice were running right through her like a flood, all right. "What a waste of good candy, my last two sticks."

"She'd had to ate a lot more than that to make her sick. Maybe it *is* the milk. I better feed her some bread to cut the flow, and make her drink lots of water to clean her out," said Miss D. "One thing after another."

I grunted. I got the stomach flood once, after eating green apples. Momma and I'd been looking for lambs'-quarter plants to cook with our other spring greens. My stomach pained me so bad from those apples I could barely walk home. Momma fixed a drink from blackberry roots to cure me. I doubted Miss D had any, though.

"And I got to clean Miz Sheehan's today." Miss D tapped her nose with her forefinger, frowning. "Gertie'll have to stay home with you. Miz Sheehan won't let her sit on her chamber pot all day."

I looked at Gertie back in bed, doubled up. *But what about my licorice, greedy thing?* I sighed. "Yes, ma'am. Miss D, if you have some chamomile tea, that might —"

"Yes, yes! Chamomile can bring peace to anybody's innards, at least till we can get something better. I'll put water on to boil." Miss D patted Gertie on the cheek, set the teakettle on the stove, then started ironing an ugly Happy Home Apron dress for work. Old folks sure liked those dresses.

As soon as her grandmomma's back was turned, Gertie crawled out of bed again, this time toward a wad of paper on the floor. I saw it, too, and beat her to it. An Ex-Lax wrapper! I raised one eyebrow at Gertie, who had scrambled back into bed and peeked at me from under the blanket. Ex-Lax looked and tasted like chocolate but its job was to loosen your bowels. So! Ex-Lax — not goat milk or licorice — had caused Gertie's stomach flood. "You ate the wrong kind of candy this time," I said quietly.

Gertie held out her hand. "Gimme that paper, and don't you tell Grammaw," she whispered. "Do, she'll box my ears."

"Huh!"

When Miss D was ready to leave, I waved the wrapper behind my back so only Gertie could see it. "I'm gonna do my best to take good care of Gertie," I said. "But she's gonna have to mind me. Else I'll tell you, Miss D. You gonna mind me, Gertie?"

Nodding slowly, Gertie's eyes shifted from her grandmomma's face to mine to the waving wrapper. Miss D gave her the cup of warm tea and she drank it right down. A good sign, in more ways than one.

"All righty now, Gertie," Miss D said with her hand on the doorknob. "You don't mind Cece, she'll tell me, and I'll box your ears. You let me know, Cece."

"Yes, ma'am," I said, smiling, and slid the wrapper into my skirt pocket.

I'm hungry!" Gertie sat up in bed with her face so hangdog that I softened some crackers and mashed up bits of cheese in a little warm water and made a soup for her. Cheese eased stomach flood, too. She sucked it right down. "Don't tell Grammaw I ate her candy," she said, running her finger around the bowl to get the last drops. "She won't let me stay here if you do. I like it here. Grammaw fixes soft food. Momma's food hurts my mouth."

"Don't eat any more Ex-Lax. It's medicine, not candy."

"I will if I want." She stuck out her chin.

"Your guts'll end up in the chamber pot, looking like those tapeworms," I said. I widened my eyes and tried to look innocent. "'Cause tapeworms like Ex-Lax, too."

"No, they don't. Do they really?" She squirmed a little. "All right. But see, I eat it at Momma's so I can get the stomach flood. She won't hit me when she's mad, if I'm sick."

"What? Hits you? Had you been bad?" *Spare the rod, spoil the child*, I thought.

"No! Well, sometimes. I eat it here 'cause Grammaw's so nice when I'm sick. But she ain't said nothing about tapeworms liking Ex-Lax."

I thought fast. "That's because she doesn't know you eat it."

"Oh." Gertie lay back in bed, picking at a braid. "Can you make Miss Pinetar do the hoochie coochie?"

"Only if you promise to leave my candy alone." She thought about that for a little bit, then nodded. "Say 'I promise' out loud." She did. "All righty now. Come on, Miss Pinetar."

When Miss D returned, I praised Gertie's behavior. But as soon as Gertie went to sleep, I told Miss D about the Ex-Lax. "Why, that little stinker! I won't say I heard it from you, but you can guarantee I'm going to jump salty with her if she tries it again, and get this Ex-Lax business stopped for good."

"I told her Ex-Lax could give her tapeworms."

"Ha! That'll fix her, for true." She turned somber. "Celeste. Your Aunti called me at Miss Sheehan's house. She's gone on to Philly and won't get back for a few more days."

I stamped my foot. "I'm down to my last piece of patience waitin' for her."

"I know, but you're not scrubbing floors and popping water blisters, either."

She was right about that. Yet that night I couldn't sleep. Did going to Philly mean she'd been paid and had our rent money? Or was she having such a good time she couldn't be bothered with me? I twisted and turned so much Miss D had to grunt loud to warn me to lie still.

The next morning Miss D had to go to work again. Gertie hopped around on one foot. "I'm not sick no more, Grammaw. Gimme a dime, so me and Cece can go to that store again and I can get me some candy."

Miss D cocked her eyebrow at her granddaughter. "If you feel that good, then you'll put your foot in the street with me. You leave Cece's sweets alone. And next time your stomach gets upset, maybe I'll give you Ex-Lax. Though tapeworms —"

"No, no, no more Ex-Lax," Gertie said.

Smiling, Miss D reached for her comb and for Gertie, who frowned at me but didn't say anything. I just wiggled my fingers at her.

After they left, I wrote in my journal about my successful medical treatment of Gertie, read over my schoolbooks, played Dede, combed and brushed my hair, and washed up. I checked the time. The grandfather clock's hands had only moved about half an hour. After counting out ten nickels, tying them in my handkerchief, and tucking it into my stocking, I grabbed up my violin case, slung the strap around my shoulder, locked the doors, and took off downstairs.

I skipped up to Mrs. Tartleton's desk, where she sat embroidering. "Hey, girl! Things stay slow here with my boarders away at their jobs so much," she said. She peered at me through her gold-rimmed glasses. "You planning to stand on Lenox Avenue and play for pennies this morning?"

"Yes, ma'am, with a monkey in a red jacket, holding a cup, dancing on my shoulder." I laughed. "No, I'm gonna sit on the porch. Though I'd rather go to Marley's for some licorice."

She lay down her needlework. "Tell the truth, I wouldn't mind taking a stroll myself before it gets hot. Come go with me. You can get candy at Schwartz's grocery. It's a lot closer than Marley's."

"Oh, praise God, 'cause I'm dying to get out and about."

After locking up her little cubbyhole office, she pushed her sun hat down on her head and picked up her purse. Outside in the warm May sun I wished I had brought my own raggedy straw hat from home with me, until I remembered that the thief would have stolen that, too. I breathed in the fishy rotten-vegetable car-fume smells of Harlem and twirled about in front of Mrs. Tartleton. Dede swung safely in its case against my chest. Maybe we'd see Miss Pig Foot Mary. Or Mr. James Weldon Johnson.

"Spring! This almost feels like home!" I hollered.

"Time to set out a few begonias and geraniums, spruce up the porch a little. Maybe you can help me," Mrs. Tartleton said.

"Glad to. Aunti says the Café Noir Le Grande's not far from here. Seems like it's miles away when we come home after working. Do you know the owner, Monsieur Jacques Le Grande? He's nice. He gives us food for free. And such a fancy dresser for a man."

"I've heard about his place. It's just up the street and around the corner, on Lenox. The way you two travel at night, it probably does seem like it's a smart piece off, especially when you're on foot and tired."

Ahead of us a woman pushed a wobbly cart bulging with bags, a broom, a mop, and pans. Around her several children carried armloads of clothes, while a man in the lead struggled to steer an even more rickety cart piled high with chairs, end tables, and a headboard, with a mattress on top. He had to peek from around the furniture to see where he was going. "You think they're moving out or moving in?" I asked Mrs. Tartleton.

"In, probably. More folks come to Harlem than anywhere else I know."

"I heard Aunti and Miss D talk about a place around here called Strivers Row. You think that's where they're going?"

Mrs. Tartleton raised her eyebrows. "Oh, no! Strivers Row is for rich Colored folks. It's yonder ways. Strivers Row Colored people have homes the size of our boardinghouse. What's a family of only two or three need with a house that big?"

"I wouldn't mind," I said. Strivers Row was the kind of place where I had imagined Aunti lived.

After we crossed a couple of streets lined with boardinghouses like ours, we turned onto busy Lenox Avenue, and voilá, as Monsieur would say, there was the Café Noir Le Grande! "It *is* close. Let's go in. Maybe he'll give us some chocolate squares."

"No, we can't go round begging, and I reckon his prices'll hurt my pocketbook. I'm not dressed for dining in there, anyway."

"Oh, nobody dresses fancy. And he gives food to everybody because they're all artists and performers and nobody's got much money. Please, Mrs. Tartleton, can't we just stick our heads in and say hello?"

"Well." She straightened and pulled on her dress the way I used to, and primped at her curled hair coiling out from around her hat. "For just a second, since you know him."

Mrs. Tartleton made me stick by her right inside the entrance. Monsieur Le Grande flew around gesturing to people and his waiters, with his black shirt, bright red suit, and red and white beret making him look like one of those woodpeckers who drummed holes in our roof back home. Something was missing, though. No music! Mr. Andre wasn't playing harp or piano on the raised platform. In fact, that beautiful white and gold piano was covered. The harp was gone. Maybe he didn't play at lunch.

A waiter I recognized as Mr. Victor passed us with a tray of corn bread and chicken. He smiled and said he'd free up a table for us shortly. "But stay away from Monsieur," he whispered. "He's been in a snit ever since Andre quit last weekend."

He hurried on before I could ask why. "I don't think we want to bother Monsieur if he's upset," said Mrs. Tartleton. She tugged on my arm. But when Mr. Victor pointed to a table where a man in an army uniform like Poppa's was leaving, I pulled my arm loose and headed for it. So Mrs. Tartleton had to follow.

Mr. Victor pushed in our chairs to help us sit down. "I never had a man do that for me," Mrs. Tartleton whispered afterward. She fanned herself with her sun hat, looking around at the other folks.

When Monsieur Le Grande spotted us, he came over. "*Ma chérie*, my pretty-eyed Celeste. And who is this lovely mademoiselle?" He clasped Mrs. Tartleton's hand in his, bent over it, and lightly kissed her knuckles as I introduced them.

Mrs. Tartleton stuttered, "Ch-ch-charmed," and trailed off with her mouth open.

"How's your beautiful Aunt Valentina?" he asked me.

"She's in Philadelphia with the show. They're trying it out before they open back here. Monsieur Le Grande, I don't mean to be nosy, but what happened to Mr. Andre? I loved his music."

"Oh, that Andre." He rolled his eyes toward the ceiling fans, hissed, and shook his head sharply. "We mustn't speak of him." He tapped my violin case. "And what is that adorning your person? Your violin? You must play for me, and my guests!"

I thought fast for something to say to put him off. "I will, probably sometime after Aunti gets back." Next time, when he asked me again, I could think up another excuse.

"No, right now! Let me escort you to the stage." He snapped his fingers and pointed to the piano. A man jumped up on the platform and uncovered it and the harp.

"Not yet! I couldn't! I'm not ready!"

"No, she couldn't," Mrs. Tartleton added, fingering her collar. "She should get her aunt's permission first, or Mrs. Dillahunt's, who's keeping her."

"I'm sure her aunt would approve." Monsieur Le Grande grasped my elbow. "Celeste, you promised weeks ago to play for me. This is the day!"

He clapped his hands sharply for attention. Forks and knives clinked against plates as people set them down to listen. Everything became quiet except for my heart rattling against my ribs. "Ladies and gentlemen, my violinist ingénue and child prodigy M'selle Celeste, niece of the exquisite actress Val Chavis, shall regale you with selections at this time. Kindly give her your complete attention." He gently pushed me toward the platform steps.

"But I don't know what to play," I whispered to him.

"Play songs you know, or your scales. Improvise. Just do your everyday best, Celeste." My tummy turned itself inside out. My blood swooped down to my toes and up to my head. I thought I was going to faint. Monsieur began clapping, and people joined in. With my back to the audience, I leaned against the piano to steady myself and catch my breath. I laid my violin case on the piano and lifted out Dede with shaking hands. What songs could I play? Nothing was coming to mind.

I heard Monsieur clear his throat. *Do, Lord, remember me!* I tucked Dede under my chin. I tapped keys on the piano and tuned up Dede, and that gave me a bit of confidence. When I turned around and saw all those eyes fixated up at me, I had to gulp in air to keep from tumbling off the stage. When my eye fell on another man in uniform, Poppa's favorite war song "Over There" popped into my head. So I began with that one.

I raised my bow and began to play. A woman in front started clapping and chewing in time with me. I dropped a couple of notes watching her, but I got back on track, and after that kept my eyes on the ceiling fans. When I ended, everybody applauded loudly. Before I could drop Dede back into its case and rush from the platform, Monsieur said, "More, *ma chérie*, more!"

My poor little body went through the same tummy-twisting, heart-banging, got-to-pee-pee, about-to-faint hysterics again. Had Momma and Poppa felt like this when they'd played for Stackhouse Hotel guests? Did Aunti get nervous onstage? Somehow I managed to think of "I'm Forever Blowing Bubbles," an easy, silly piece, and when people laughed, I relaxed a little. They liked what I was doing, and suddenly so did I!

"I'm Just Wild About Harry"— my way — was next. I was even able to hum a little as I played. This was starting to be fun! Was I actually cut out to be a professional musician? Folks clapped loudly, whistled, and hollered "Bravo!" Someone else yelled, "Celeste's the best!"

I stopped playing and curtsied, then stood there, wondering what else I needed to do. Monsieur bounced up to the platform. He bent low and swept off his beret toward me like men did during *Shuffle Along* rehearsals after Miss Lottie and Miss Adelaide Hall sang especially well.

"*Magnifique*," Monsieur said. He pressed a five-dollar bill into my hand. As he led me back to our table and Mrs. Tartleton, diners held out coins and dollar bills to me. "Oh, no, thank you," I said, embarrassed. "I was just —"

"Take it. That's how they're thanking you," he said. So I did.

"See how much we love her, Madame Tartleton? Celeste must come back to perform at lunch tomorrow and tomorrow and tomorrow!" he said.

"I'm not so sure," Mrs. Tartleton replied. "Her aunt —"

"Is a dear friend," Monsieur reminded her.

"But she's in Mrs. Ripsey Dillahunt's care right now, and —"

"Then I'll seek Mrs. Dillahunt's personal approval by stopping by your boardinghouse tonight at seven. I know where it is. I believe Val calls her 'Miss D'?" Monsieur patted my shoulder. "You are gifted. Gifted!"

"Th-thank you," I stammered as he skipped off to another table. I didn't know people could get paid for doing something they enjoyed for free. My heart was still pounding. I didn't even remember coming down off the platform.

Mrs. Tartleton turned to me, beaming. "I declare! That Mr. Monsieur is a Colored Rudolph Valentino. Is he an actor, too? And Cece, why, you're a celebrity! You play so well, girl! Had 'em eating out of your hand. Miss D's gonna have a spasm over what all she missed."

"I'm having one now, Mrs. Tartleton. I was so scared. And look at all this money!" I spread the bills and coins on the table.

"I can't believe I got paid so much for playing ole Dede. You'll have to help me persuade Miss D to let me come back so I can make some more."

"You bet I'll talk to her. You and your aunt don't make that much after a *week* of scrubbing floors."

Mr. Victor brought us tomato soup, a green salad, a fat chicken sandwich, green beans with almonds, and my favorite, chocolate squares. "Girl, you just stunned us," he whispered, "and put Monsieur in a much better mood."

"Thank you. I'm glad I didn't have to say anything."

"You spoke through your violin," he said. "Your words came through loud and clear."

I excused myself and hurried to the powder room, where I gave thanks to the good Lord for giving me the strength to perform. Was this what it was like? Thrilling and terrifying at the same time? Mrs. Tartleton had said Harlem was the right place for me and Dede. Could I do this for a living? Could it be more enjoyable and profitable than being a doctor in Raleigh?

I don't remember walking home. But when we got there, Miss D was on the porch with her jowls shaking and her forefinger raised to fuss. Mrs. Tartleton held up her hands to ward off that finger and those jowls. "You got to hear where we've been and what's happened, Ripsey," she exclaimed. "This chile is a star and a moneymaker and Mr. Le Grande's coming here to talk to you tonight about making her become more of both!"

Monsieur Le Grande arrived at the boardinghouse promptly at seven P.M. Miss D and Mrs. Tartleton waited in the lobby, perfumed and rouged up, with their best stockings on. It didn't take but a minute for Miss D to say yes, I could play for him, as long as she was with me. Mrs. Tartleton added that she should help chaperone me, too.

I just listened. *Little ole mousey me playing violin in Harlem, New York!* Wait until Evalina, Angel Mae, and Swan heard about this! And Poppa! And Aunt Society! And Aunti Val!

"Celeste, my guests are easy to please," Monsieur said. "You are *my* child prodigy, you hear? When you play that violin it's like you're just strollin' down a Harlem street on a fine Saturday afternoon, and we're all just strollin' with you. Now, we must be professional about this. Mrs. Dillahunt, is five dollars a performance and all tips satisfactory as Cece's pay? Until I can get a permanent musician?"

"Oh my, yes," Miss D said. I agreed. Just getting the tips would be more than I had ever earned before. "And I'll hold her money for her."

"Thank you, Miss D, but I can bring a little basket and sit it on the piano. People can drop tips in there," I said, surprising myself and her, too. I could tell because she opened her mouth and closed it.

"You sure knew how to speak up on that one, enty!" But Miss D followed that with a laugh. "That's good. You're a smart young lady. Don't let nobody be in charge of your money but you, not even a bank."

"Yes, ma'am." Aunt Society had drilled into my head long ago that a fool and her money were soon parted if somebody else had their hands on it. I didn't say that to Miss D. Not that I distrusted her. But it was sort of like that old saying, "Never leave your pocketbook on the floor," because you never know what — or who — might sneak into it.

The next day Miss D, Mrs. Tartleton, and I paraded over to Café Noir Le Grande dressed up like it was Easter and Mother's Day both. I even had a bit of rouge on my lips. I kept swallowing, because my mouth and throat were so dry from nervousness. I had to fight off my fright again, of course. Would the people like me as much today as they had yesterday? Would I play as well? This time I played "Forsythia," "Darktown Strutters' Ball," "Amazing Grace," "This Little Light of Mine," and finished with Mr. Johnson's "Lift Every Voice and Sing." Humming while I played really seemed to please people. I forgot my basket, so afterward I held out my violin case and people dropped my tips in there.

"If this keeps up, I'm going to be rich," I said to Miss D and Mrs. Tartleton. "I feel like how Aunti Val must feel when she's singing and dancing. Being here might not be so bad after all, for now, I mean." They nodded, staring at the money with their mouths full of peach cobbler.

In a little while Monsieur trotted over to us with a brown-skinned, slick-haired young man sporting a thin mustache. "You were splendid, splendid, *ma chérie*. And now I have good news. This is Monsieur Duke Ellington, a pianist from Washington, D.C."

He was so handsome I could barely say hello to him. Miss D and Mrs. Tartleton didn't have a problem pumping his hand, and smiling and speaking, though.

"I've enjoyed you so much, Celeste. You're a fine, talented young lady, just divine," said Monsieur. "Now I'm going to let

Mr. Ellington try his hand, as I'm still looking for a permanent replacement for my former musician. But if you don't satisfy my folks as well as Celeste has" — and here Monsieur shook his thick forefinger at Mr. Ellington — "then I shall come back to you, Celeste, on bended knee, and beg for your return."

I managed to smile and nod my head, but as he talked, my shoulders slumped. I'd planned for this to be my get-back-home money!

"You're an excellent violinist," Mr. Ellington said. He had deep dimples and kind eyes, and his brown skin looked as smooth as Aunti Val's. "I plan to have a full orchestra one day. When you get older, please look me up if you're still interested in music. I'll save a chair for you."

I thanked him for the invitation and thanked Monsieur again. But I didn't have much appetite for the rest of my meal this time.

"Well, you got a nice little taste of show business." Mrs. Tartleton tried to comfort me. "That's how it is — easy come, easy go. And won't your aunt be surprised."

"She'll be *something*, all right." Miss D chuckled. "Seeing as how he asked her niece but never her to perform at his place —"

"She'll laugh," I broke in. "She won't be upset about my playing Dede here." I saw Miss D and Mrs. Tartleton raise their eyebrows at each other. *Wonder what that meant?* I asked myself, but I let it go.

A few evenings later I was at Miss D's and she was telling me how a South Carolina ghost called a plat-eye chased her through a swamp outside Saint Helena, when we heard a clatter of footsteps and loud voices outside the door. "What in the world? Thieves?" Miss D grabbed her pressing comb off her table and held it like a weapon. I grabbed the broom. Cautiously we peeked out into the hallway.

Mr. Jim, the *Shuffle Along* driver, stood in the hallway holding Aunt Valentina around the waist, with one of her arms draped around his neck.

"Something in my back slipped out of kilter last night. AWWWWWW!" Her hat was slung over her right eye.

We helped Aunti into her room. Mr. Jim said he'd leave her bags in the lobby. He couldn't bring them up because he had to get back to the show. We thanked him and got Aunti settled in the bed. I rubbed Vicks salve on her back. "Aunti, what happened?"

"I'm just a little sore," Aunti kept saying, though I could see that she hurt even to take a breath. "I was doing the Charleston and something went *flink!* in the same spot in my back where I hurt it scrubbing floors."

"I'll warm you up some oxtail soup," Miss D said. "We already ate."

I told Aunti about our trip to Marley's, and Gertie's episodes with goat milk and Ex-Lax. She laughed so hard she hurt her back again and I had to rub her some more. "And I played Dede twice at Café Noir Le Grande, Aunti! I was so scared I didn't think I could do it, but I did! Miss D and Mrs. Tartleton were impressed with the food, too."

Aunti stopped laughing. "You played your violin at the Café Noir Le Grande?" She rubbed her nose two or three times, frowning, her eyes narrowed. "Twice? And he paid you? I see. Like I told Lottie, you do have ambition. Though I didn't think it'd pop up like this. Why did he have you perform? Or did you ask him to?"

"Oh, no, Aunti!" I explained quickly how I didn't want to and how he pulled me up to the platform and how Mrs. Tartleton told him I couldn't. Then I had to explain how Mrs. Tartleton and Miss D came to be there. She grilled me until I was sorry I had even mentioned it. I had thought she'd be pleased. Miss D was right. She was *something*, all right, but pleased wasn't the word.

"Congratulations, Celeste," she finally said, grumpy.

"Would you tell me about the show and everybody?" I said, to try to take that awful expression off her face.

Still sounding out of sorts, Aunti said Mr. Sissle promised that she could open with the show in New York if she felt better. "He was very impressed with me, you see. The Howard Theater in Washington, where I joined the cast, was a gorgeous place. And our shows were absolutely fabulous." She was back to her normal tones. "The Dunbar in Philadelphia was the same, and well, here I am." She stopped and her eyes narrowed again. "So why did you go to the café in the first place?"

As I was squirming under her next slew of questions, Miss D brought over the soup, and Aunti quit talking in order to eat. But when Miss D praised my violin playing at the Café Noir Le Grande, Aunti puffed up again.

"Why've you got your face all tore up? Soup not tasty enough?" Miss D asked. "Or has hearing that Celeste played her violin at the Café Noir Le Grande done stuck in your craw? Valentina, the girl's good. Quit pouting."

"Ripsey, I'm not pouting," Aunti mumbled. "My back just hurts."

Miss D cleared her throat, glanced at me, and changed the subject to Gertie. When we got Aunti talking about herself again, she brightened up. Miss D finally left, and I got ready for bed, halfway dreading being alone with Aunti. I turned down the lamp and crawled into bed carefully, so's not to disrupt her back, or her mood.

"We finally found a theater here to open in," she said. "It's the Sixty-third Street Theater. Place is so rickety they'll probably still be working on the sets come opening night. It's not exactly located in the traditional Broadway district, but Mr. Sissle says *Shuffle Along*'s a Broadway show no matter what. And did everything go all right with you and Miss D?"

"Yes, ma'am. I missed you something awful, Aunti. I missed you almost as much as I do Poppa. You know, everybody'd love to see a famous Broadway actress from Raleigh — you — back home. They might put you in the Negro State Fair parade."

"Hmmmm," she murmured. I could tell that parade angle had caught her attention. "Maybe so. But first, Broadway!"

Chapter Thirteen

May 23! Opening night! My heart beat so fast you'd have thought I was in *Shuffle Along* with Aunti and Miss Jarboro and them. Was Aunti as excited as I had been playing at Café Noir Le Grande? And would her back be all right now? In Raleigh, when Colored and White sat in the same building, we Colored folks usually had to sit so far back or so high up we couldn't see what was going on half the time. But here in the Sixty-third Street Theater, things were different. Miss D and I sat near the orchestra pit in front near the end of the row — good seats!

Trying not to gawk, I looked around at the handsome laughing Colored men in straw hats and snappy suits, and at the pretty whispering Colored ladies with silk shawls and furs around their shoulders, glittering jewelry around their necks, and ostrich and peacock feathers in their hats. Miss D wore a bright blue silky suit. She'd altered Aunti's flowery green organdy dress for me, and I wore her same white pumps from Mother's Day. I'd practiced walking in them, and now I was doing fine. I wore my hair in a bun — my new style. I had rouge on my cheeks and lips, Aunti's lemonade and cherries cologne behind my ears — oh, I was the cat's pajamas!

I saw Miss Jarboro standing with some other cast members

near a stage door not far from us, and waved at her. She saw me, too, and wiggled her fingers at me. Just then Mr. Blake appeared in the doorway, jabbed his forefinger at Miss Jarboro, then pointed to the stage. Miss Jarboro motioned for me to come over.

"What's she want?" I whispered to Miss D.

"Maybe your aunt's back went out again. Hurry up and go see."

Miss Jarboro thrust an armload of programs at me. "Oh, you look so pretty. We don't have time to pass these out. Will you do it for us? Thanks, honey." She followed Mr. Blake and the other performers through the door.

I searched for Aunti's name while straightening the programs in my arms. I didn't get much of a chance to look because people quickly crowded around to get the programs. "Hurry up, girl, show's about to start!" said a man, snatching several from my arms. "Give me a bunch and I'll pass 'em on," said another. They pushed around, almost trampling me, then hurried on to their seats. I'd never seen such grabby folks. I picked up a couple programs from the floor and nearly bumped heads with a man doing the same thing.

"I thought they were going to stamp you down to South America," he said. "Aren't you Valentina's niece? I'm James Weldon —"

"Oh, Mr. Johnson, yes, it's me, Celeste! Thank you. Please take this clean one." I leaned around folks to hand him another sheet. "Can we come by your office to see about my Butterflies Club friends' poems sometime?"

"Your what? Oh, yes, certainly. But to make it easier for you,

I'll have Miss Fausett mail you back an announcement of the results, as well as your submissions, and the current *Brownies' Book*. We have your aunt's address. How's that?"

"That'd be fabulous." Handing people programs, I followed him for a few steps. "This is my first Broadway show, and it's — it's — the cat's pajamas."

"Oh, you're speaking Harlem, are you now?" He laughed and paused. "Funny thing. This building's not located where Broadway shows are traditionally held. But the tickets cost the same as a Broadway musical, so some say it really *is* a Broadway show. Certainly Mr. Blake and Mr. Sissle believe it is. Either way, *Shuffle Along*'s going to change American theater for us Negroes, I assure you."

Just then the lights dimmed. I passed out all but two programs, for myself and Miss D, and hurried back to my seat. On with the show!

Shuffle Along rolled along. Folks laughed, applauded, or dabbed at their tearful eyes with handkerchiefs in the right places. Miss Lottie brought down the house with "I'm Just Wild About Harry" — done my way, of course. Aunti in her dazzling Oriental outfit was stunning. I thought she danced better than anyone else whenever she appeared onstage. I wished she could have sung a solo or danced by herself, but you can't have everything.

When *Shuffle Along* ended, Miss D and I and everybody else got to our feet, clapping and shouting and whistling so loud I thought the chandeliers would crash down on our heads. Aunti and the cast returned to the stage and curtsied and took deep bows. Several men in white tuxedoes with tails walked onstage and presented bouquets of roses to Miss Lottie, Miss Gertrude Saunders, and Miss Adelaide Hall, while they threw us kisses.

Folks in the audience threw flowers to them, too. When a small bouquet of yellow roses went astray and landed in the aisle near me, I scrambled over and seized it. Quickly pulling two from the bouquet for Miss D and me, I hurried to the stage and held up what was left of it to Aunti. "Val Chavis! Val Chavis!" I screamed in a loud voice I didn't know I had. In the glare of the lights and the noise, Aunti was too busy grinning, throwing kisses, and bowing to see me. I backed away toward my seat, embarrassed.

"Celeste!"

She did see me! When I rushed back and held up the roses, she snatched the bouquet from me, beaming. Pleased, I returned to Miss D, and handed her a rose.

She thanked me and sniffed the rose. "This show's making *you* bloom as much as it is your aunt, if not more. When you first landed in Harlem, you'd have been too shy to even get out of your seat tonight."

I smelled my rose, too, nodding. She was right.

Afterward, we stood around in the crowds, waiting for Aunti to come from the stage. "This is a grand night," Miss D said. "She's on her way to becoming a big cheese. That is, if somebody gives her a good role. She can't be a hoofer all her life."

I had to shout over the clamor so Miss D could hear me. I knew from *Shuffle Along* talk that "hoofer" meant dancer. "So she can make loads of money and want to come home to Raleigh in style, of course."

Miss D touched me on the nose with her flower. "But why'd she want to go back down there if she's making money up here? Hey, I'm just flapping my lips."

Of course she will, I said to myself. *She's got to. She's got to know how important it is to have a family around you. I do.*

We waited and waited and waited. Finally the crowd thinned and Aunti joined us, bubbling, doing a little dance, humming. We hugged her while she sang, "I'm just wild about — everything!"

Miss Lottie, Miss Adelaide, and their admirers swept by us. "Coming, Val?" Miss Lottie called as she passed. "The cast party's at Café Noir Le Grande. We're gonna party at that joint all night!"

"I'll be there in a flash," Aunti hollered. When she started to follow them, my shoulders drooped and Miss D grunted. We weren't going to be part of her entourage, I could see that. Aunti stopped to look back at us. "Oh, well, no," she added slowly. "Right now I'm going to celebrate with my family."

Of course her words made us smile, but as we left the theater, Aunti was silent. Why was I even a bit sad? Aunti was with us, wasn't she? Miss D must have read our thoughts. "You could have gone on to the party, Val, and Cece could have stayed with me, like before."

"I know." Aunti took our hands and began to sing, "Everything's dandy, girls, smile!" I didn't know where that song came from, but it made me feel better.

At home Miss D came into our room with us and leaned against the door while Aunti babbled on about things that had happened backstage, like Mr. Jim still hammering on a piece of the grocery store set when the curtains opened.

"What happens at a cast party?" I asked when she finally slowed down.

"Everybody gossips, talks over what to keep in a scene, what to take out, stuff like that." Aunti sat at the table still wearing her costume and makeup. "We eat, probably pop a bottle of champagne. A few of us girls might even smoke cigarettes!" She got up, rattled around in the cupboard, and brought out three glasses. "To *Shuffle Along*, and to us!" She poured water into the glasses and passed them around for a toast.

"To us!" we repeated, and then clinked glasses and pretended we were drinking champagne.

"Well, I'm gonna head on in," Miss D said. "Oh, did you like your flowers? Celeste strutted right up there through all those folks to give them to you."

"I loved them. Made me feel like a diva!" Aunti said and winked at me. I noticed just then that she had drawn a big black mole on her right cheek, and her eyelashes were twice as long as normal. Oh, Aunt Society would have a conniption to see Aunti fancied up so like a loose woman. "I must have left them backstage. I'll get them tomorrow. That was so sweet of you."

"You're welcome," I said. I doubted, though, that they'd still be there, but that was all right. I understood how excited she was.

As I brushed my hair and undressed for bed, I heard Aunti and Miss D talking in the hallway, but I didn't bother to listen. I had things to think about. What Miss D said about Raleigh and Aunti still bothered me. I got into bed. Why *would* she want to return if she became a star? Had I made it harder to get my family to-gether back home by urging Aunti to be in this musical? As I drifted away, I heard Aunti return, but she didn't come to bed. She left again. I woke up off and on all night but I didn't feel her slip in the bed until it was almost daylight.

I got up around seven A.M. like I did back home to get ready for school, and commenced my household chores while Aunti snored. She didn't get up until around noon. She didn't say where she'd been, and I didn't ask. I figured she'd gone to the Café Noir Le Grande for the cast party.

When I went with her to the show that night, I volunteered to hand out programs. Miss Jarboro was grateful. "You know how to do the right thing at the right time," she said. But this time I decided that these folks were going to *act* right when they approached me for programs.

"Everybody, take your time, don't push," I said loudly but politely. "Yes, sir, here you are." To my surprise and pleasure, people obeyed. "My aunt's a singer and a dancer. She wears an Oriental costume. She's good! Yes, ma'am, you'll love the show."

"Say, didn't I see you at Café Noir Le Grande one time?" said a woman waiting to receive a program. I nodded, blushing. "You played that violin so well! Next time I'm there, I'll tell Monsieur how much I enjoyed you."

So many people began coming to see *Shuffle Along* that week that I began running out of programs. After one show the next week Aunti took me to the Café Noir Le Grande to make up, I guess, for not taking me the first night. Some of the cast came, too. We sat with Mr. Jim, who also was a dancer, a fellow who played trombone, and a hoofer named Marcella, the one that Aunti had said early on stumbled all over when she danced.

Monsieur stopped by our table. "*Ma chérie*, I'm so glad to see you!" He kissed both of Aunti's hands. "And Celeste, my ingénue! How are you? M'selle Val, a friend stopped by the other day and mentioned how much she loved Celeste's violin playing."

Aunti's made-up face stiffened a little. "Yes, she's a little trouper." I tried to think of something to say to him to change the subject before she had a spasm.

"M'selle Val, she said Celeste extolled your *Shuffle Along* talents, too," he continued. I breathed a sigh of relief, and Aunti's face lit up. "As you may know, I'm looking for a permanent musician to replace the former one. With such fine praise, Val, I'm wondering if you'd like to accompany Mr. Duke Ellington, my new pianist, with a few songs for the rest of the summer."

Everybody at the table applauded. Aunti's mouth fell open. I was surprised, too, but glad. Maybe now she'd be happy and quit being upset that I'd played here before she did. She hugged Monsieur. "Yes, yes, yes! I'd love to."

Miss Marcella shook her shoulders. "Monsieur, you have room for a hoofer, too, at your lunch times?"

"I'll keep you in mind," Monsieur said smoothly. "Thank Celeste for bragging on you so, Val. I'd have asked you as soon as Andre left, but you were out of town, remember? I knew you wouldn't mind Celeste being your fill-in. She was perfect."

I didn't know whether to puff out my chest or feel irritated that Monsieur called me Aunti's fill-in. I thought he'd hired me because I was good. Well, maybe that was the same thing. As long as she didn't seem to mind, then I guessed I wouldn't. Her face was still beaming. Suddenly I understood what Miss D's "taking the path of least resistance" meant. Monsieur was keeping Aunti from being upset with him — and letting me off the hook, too.

"Of course, that was fine. When do I start?" She flashed him and me her wide, toothy smile. "Thanks, kiddo. I'm proud that you stood in for me."

"Well, you had bragged on me to Monsieur, so one good turn deserves another," I replied, with the biggest grin I could create. When he and Aunti began to plan, Mr. Jim, Miss Marcella, and the other man wandered off to other tables. I nibbled on my chocolate square, listening. I remembered Aunti's mean looks and her agitation whenever anybody had bragged on my musical talents. No matter what Aunti said, she was jealous of me, and jealousy was a terrible, dangerous thing. Like Aunt Society said, forgive, but don't forget.

A couple of nights later Gertie and her momma popped up at Miss D's. Gertie was coughing and feverish, sick as a dog, with her braids all picked apart. Miss D got worried sick herself, afraid that Gertie had that deadly influenza. Three years before, influenza had swept through Raleigh and around the world, killing hundreds and thousands of people. Miss D told us she fixed Gertie delicious beef stew and sugar-flavored water, but Gertie wouldn't eat the stew. She just coughed, snotted, and drank the water.

This morning Miss D came over and told us she had to go to work. "Can you and Cece look after Gertie for me?" she asked.

"Well, I've got to go to the Café Noir Le Grande to practice with Mr. Duke," Aunti said, folding her arms across her chest. "Matter of fact, I should be getting ready now."

Miss D glanced at me. "And I suppose you're going, too?"

"No, ma'am, I'm staying. I'll do it. I can fix her some chicken soup with lots of fat to make her feel better."

"That's a good idea," Aunti said, already rummaging through a pile of clothes she'd dropped on the bed. "But keep her away from me. I can't afford to get sick."

Miss D gave me some money. "Get what you think you need from Schwartz's grocery around the corner." While Miss D and Aunti got ready to go, I hurried out to Schwartz's grocery and bought chicken necks, backs, and feet, onions, white potatoes, green peas, and a stalk of celery. Back at Miss D's place I quickly put everything on to cook and dropped mint leaves into a pot of boiling water to steep for tea.

"If I didn't need the money I'd tell Miss Sheehan I couldn't come," Miss D told me, wringing her hands. She kept hanging around, watching while I prepared the soup, telling me where she kept the spices I needed.

"Cece, you're a fabulous doctor, girl," Aunti said in the door-way, about to leave.

"Yes, she is," Miss D added. "You mind Cece, you hear, Gertie?" she added. They left together.

Gertie's head was so clogged with phlegm that she couldn't breathe through her nose, and she could barely swallow. "Here, drink this." I gave her some tea and rubbed Vicks salve around her nose and throat. I wished I had a piece of flannel cloth to wrap around her neck and lay on her chest. I was surprised

Miss D didn't have a piece on her already. Flannel always helped break up a cold.

After a few minutes of sipping and snotting, Gertie lay back down. "My head still hurts and I still can't breathe."

"If you ate more fruits and vegetables and not so much rice, johnnycake, and syrup, you wouldn't be so sick. Keep drinking that tea while I get you some soup."

"Don't want no more soup." She turned her head away, wiping at her nose with a big white rag, and kicked off the covers. "I'm too hot!"

"You gotta keep those blankets on to sweat out that fever. Here, eat this. It's chicken." I held out a spoonful. She touched her tongue to a small piece of chicken on the spoon, then plucked it off the spoon and ate it. She sucked down the rest. "Gimme some more."

I handed her the bowl and watched her eat the chicken first, then the potatoes. She pushed aside the onions and celery, but drank down the liquid. "Let me tell you a story about a girl and some balloons."

"I don't wanna hear no story. Gimme some more soup," she sniffled.

"Girl almost got ate up by a giant squid."

"Well, all right. What's a squid?"

I told her the balloon story, explaining what a squid was, adding that giant squids tried to snatch the girl down from the sky with their tentacles, and that sharks — I called them giant flathead catfish so she'd understand — jumped out of the water and snapped at her legs.

"I wish I had balloons like that," Gertie said when I finished.

"Then next time Momma started to pop me, I'd grab them balloons and float right back to Grammaw."

"Your momma probably wouldn't pop you if you didn't do things to make her mad." I could think of a few things that I'd like to smack her for. Like eating my licorice. Gertie handed me the bowl. She closed her eyes, and the next thing, she was asleep. I waited for a bit, then I tiptoed next door, got Dede, returned, and softly practiced my scales and my favorite songs.

Gertie didn't wake up until her grandmother got home toward evening, and she was feeling better. Miss D was so pleased that she begged me to let her keep the rest of the soup. At my urging, she spread Vicks salve on the soles of Gertie's feet, then pulled her socks back on, and for once Gertie didn't protest.

"Aren't you going to the show?" Miss D asked as she smeared more Vicks salve on Gertie's throat and chest. "She's not coming by to get you?"

"I guess not. I don't know how to get there by myself," I said, sighing.

"You've got a funny aunt," Miss D said quietly. "I don't mean *laugh* funny but *strange* funny. She only thinks about herself."

"I know," I said softly. "I know."

I went back to our room, and wrote letters, then after performing my ablutions, went to sleep. In the middle of the night I heard Aunti's key turn in the lock. When she crawled into bed and started to snore, I smelled champagne on her breath.

I handed out programs again at the next several shows, enjoying the performances and even recognizing where some scenes changed from one night to another.

One morning Aunti asked me if I'd like to go to the Café Noir Le Grande for lunch, and to hear her and Mr. Ellington. "As long as I don't have to play," I said carefully.

"Oh no, you won't. I just want to have you hear me and get some more good food. And Monsieur misses you," she said gaily. "You stole his heart!"

I loved how Aunti and Mr. Ellington sang and played piano together. I played Dede along with them — in my head. I was also glad I wasn't up there, because I'd have to hear Aunti's cutting remarks later. Monsieur was so pleased to see me that he kissed me on both cheeks and on my knuckles. But no matter how many times the diners asked me to, I didn't play. I just ate my chicken, and listened, and hummed. Aunti didn't seem to mind it if I hummed.

"Aunti, I haven't seen any of the big New York sights that my Butterflies keep asking me about," I said casually during one of her breaks back at our table. "I haven't even gone to the library around the corner, and you promised to take me there." I bit into my chicken salad sandwich. "I don't know any girls my age up here, either. I just know old — uh, grown folks, and Gertie."

"What brought this on? You know I've been —" She stopped. "You're right. I've been selfish with my time. I think of you as my younger sister so much I forget you need your own fun," she said. "I don't know any married people with children your age, but I'll try to find some." She looked at me sideways, smiling. "I only know single folks."

"If we went to church we'd see lots of girls my age, and

married folks, too," I said. About that time a man stopped by the table, and she gave him her full attention.

When we got home, I found a letter from Poppa, and a joint letter from Evalina, Angel Mae, and Swan in our mailbox. Poppa's letter was short. The weather was so hot it was even hurting his feelings. He expected Aunt Society to come visit him any day. She'd been calling him almost every day about things going on at home, and each time he'd reminded her to send my clothes. He didn't say anything about why she hadn't written to me. The best news, though, was that he'd gained six pounds!

Angel Mae wrote that in canning class her jars exploded, splattering pickles and tomatoes everywhere. Evalina wrote that she still wanted to raise that pig. When she decided she wanted to bake a cake instead of canning, she and Mrs. Bracy had fights every class. "I don't think sifting all the dry ingredients together is important, and she does," she wrote.

Swan announced that her canned chowchow tasted so good church folks were already asking for her jars to serve with their sausages. She wrote that they saw *Darktown Jubilee* with Bert Williams for the fifth time, and parts of *The Perils of Pauline* moving picture serial again at the Royal Theater a few weeks ago. "But being in Harlem you probably see real movie stars all the time," Swan wrote.

Feeling a pinch of envy, I pulled out my journal, eager to write them back. I could tell them about Mr. Duke Ellington, and the *Shuffle Along* cast, even though they'd never heard of him or anybody in the musical. I could mention again that I'd met Mr. James Weldon Johnson and how I was still tracking down our poems at the *Brownies' Book* office. And I could certainly brag about playing my violin at the Café Noir Le Grande, where that Bert Williams sometimes stopped by. Of course, I hadn't seen him there yet. Oh, and how Monsieur kissed my knuckles! I couldn't tell them anything about any girls I'd met except Gertie, and she didn't really count. Could Big Willie Madison count as a new friend, even though I'd only met him once?

Chapter
Fourteen

The next day Miss D told us that Gertie and her momma — whose name I finally learned was Netta Lee and not "that gal" — left for South Carolina to visit Miss Netta Lee's people and Gertie's father, whose name was Pete. Miss D drooped around like a cow without its calf. "I just worry whether that gal takes good care of my Gertie," Miss D groaned. "Netta Lee gets down to Charleston and just cuts the fool, chasing after my son like she's his pet chicken. Pete needs to be around Gertie, true; she's his blood. But he can be just as addle-brained as Netta Lee. I should be down there, too."

"No, you shouldn't," Aunti said. "You'd just cause trouble. Look, you and Cece are dragging around here so much I can't get my beauty rest. Let's go see some of New York tomorrow, Cece. The show's not playing tomorrow night, you know, and I'm not at the café then. You come, Ripsey, if you like."

I jumped up, clapping my hands. "The library, too? And go shopping at a real department store with a candy section? And maybe Coney Island, where I can meet some girls?"

"You can't see New York in one day, so we got to be picky," she reminded me.

"I'll just toodle along to be sociable," Miss D said. She and I smiled so wide we nearly split our lips.

"You promised to take me to Madam Walker's, too," I threw in.

"I can't swing the cost of that right now," Aunti said, looking uncomfortable.

"I've got some money. How much will it cost? If you don't want me there because you and Miss A'Lelia aren't friends anymore, I can go by myself and not mention your name."

Miss D let out a whoop. "Celeste Lassiter Massey, you've learned the delicate Harlem art called 'tricks of the tongue.' And she learned it from you, Val! Make an appointment for the girl."

"All right, all right." Aunti looked at me with a mixture of what I interpreted to be pride and frustration. "I got to take the path of least resistance on this one, I guess. Now can I get my beauty rest?"

"Yes, ma'am," we said, laughing.

Miss D winked at me. "Come get some sweet tea for your aunt," she said. I followed her over to her place. She reached into her icebox and poured out glasses of tea for my aunt and me. "I think you won that round. We're old friends and I love her dearly, but Val likes to put things off too much. Chile gets downright lazy sometimes. But don't tell her I said that."

"All right. You sound just like how I do with my girlfriends when one of them talks about the other," I told her.

Sipping on my tea, I carried my aunt's glass to her. She took it and started talking about places I specifically wanted to see. That was a good sign. She was going along with something that I wanted to do. Was it the beginning of Aunti's change of heart — like eventually returning home?

I was up early the next morning so I could take a real bath in the lavatory down the hall. When *Aunti* wanted to go somewhere, she moved fast and didn't like to wait on anybody. That is, provided she didn't wake up with an excuse about how she couldn't go. When I came back, I could hear Miss D moving around next door, but Aunti was still asleep. I settled on my nice white waist, a pretty blue skirt that had once belonged to Aunti, and my comfortable old Buster Browns. I wanted my dogs to stand up to the hard walking I was sure we'd do.

With a deliberate clatter, I placed a fresh pot of coffee on the hot plate, and parked myself at the table to wait. Just as the coffee got hot, and I was getting that way, too, Aunti sat up, glanced at me, groaned, and flopped back down. I held my breath. Then she jumped out of bed — "Hi, Miss Thing! You ready?" — drank her coffee, dressed, and was ready to go just as Miss D came knocking on our door.

"Where you ladies flouncing off to?" asked Mrs. Tartleton when we reached the lobby. I told her. "Well, good. Tell Miss Liberty I said hello!"

Our first stop was at the One Hundred Thirty-fifth Street branch library. I walked around, my mouth open, marveling at the sight of so many stacks and stacks of books. Aunti said the main library was bigger than the capitol building in Raleigh. I got down to business and searched around for medical books. I finally chose one on women's ailments and cures, and another on healing herbs. Aunti checked them out for me.

"Who reads all those books in that place?" Miss D asked as we stepped back into the hot Harlem sun.

"I do, when I have time," Aunti replied.

I kept quiet. I'd never seen her read anything but theater and fashion sections of the *New York Amsterdam News* newspaper, movie handbills, the *Shuffle Along* script, and Monsieur's menus.

I saw lots of girls in short skirts and waists and boys in knickers and caps my age walking, running, and staring back at me. I waved at some of them. A few waved back. Other boys slouched against stores and flirted with the girls, or shined shoes for customers.

We took the subway again. I decided I liked it all right, because of the speed, but I still preferred to see what we were passing. Back up on street level, we walked some more. Soon I saw the Statue of Library in the distance, surrounded by water. "Is it sitting in the Atlantic Ocean?" I asked, pointing excitedly.

"No, no, it's on an island in New York Harbor. We take a ferry over to it," Aunti said.

"I ain't getting on no ferry," Miss D declared. "Y'all go on; I'll wait."

"But you're from South Carolina, Ripsey." Aunti laughed. "Didn't you say you waded in swamps and creeks, and cast nets for shrimp and jumping mullet with water moccasins swimming around your legs? How could you be scared of water?"

"I ain't scared of water; I'm scared of boats," Miss D huffed. "When those things sink, they trap people underwater, even folks who can swim. You remember that *Titanic*, the ship that couldn't be sunk? It dropped like a rock in the river, and all those folks drowned."

I'd been nervous about that ferry myself, so I was glad Miss D spoke up first. We were close enough anyway for me to get a good eyeballing of Miss Liberty. All around us stores sold postcards, books, statue replicas, and so many other Miss Liberty trinkets I almost passed out trying to window-shop. I wanted to buy everything, but in the end I chose a small metal Miss Liberty statue and some New York postcards to send back to friends, Aunt Society, and Poppa.

"Miss Liberty's head is over seventeen feet long, and her hand is over sixteen feet long," I read from a postcard.

"That's a bigheaded gal there," Miss D said, and laughed.

At one place a man snapped a photograph of Miss D and me standing on each side of a cardboard Statue of Liberty. Aunti flirted with a Colored policeman watching us until she persuaded him to take a photograph with her. Then all four of us had a picture taken together. Aunti promised us that she would give us each a copy of the photographs when they were ready.

We stopped at a food cart and gobbled down hot dogs and Pepsi-Colas. "Pepsi-Cola was first made in New Bern, North Carolina," Aunti said. "A man named Caleb Bradham invented it in his pharmacy there in 1898. I know because your momma and I were just wild about it. I still love it."

"That hot dog might have come from there, too," Miss D added. "North Carolina is a big pig state."

Well, ain't that the bee's knees! Here I was in New York drinking and eating food from North Cacky Lacky!

We walked and walked, and Aunti and Miss D identified different sights for me, like the Flatiron Building in the distance. I craned my neck, amazed at its size even so far away. It looked like it reached the top of the world! We didn't go any closer, though. Aunti insisted that she needed her nap. Miss D was getting tired, and I was, too. But now I'd seen with my own eyes so much of what I'd only read about before! I planned to remember how to use that fine art of "tricks of the tongue" to get more things done my way.

A few days later Aunti gave me money to go get my hair styled at Madam Walker's. I had my first real morning out in Harlem on my own! I decided to return the library books first, and found the library easily. I wanted to take out more books but I had to have Aunti Val with me to do it. I decided I'd have to come back soon and spend the day.

The hairdressers were very friendly, especially after I mentioned Miss Almadene Hardy, the agent I'd met on the train. I didn't mention Aunti Val's name, though. A sweet-faced hairdresser named Vernice gave my hair a fine shampooing, drying, and dressing, and then styled it in something called a "French braid." It was sort of like the old cornrowing, but the weave was different. Besides the bun and just plain straight back, now I could fix my hair another way. Some of the other customers complimented me on how nice I looked. Remembering Aunti's instruction, I gave Miss Vernice an extra quarter for a tip. She seemed happy to get it.

Feeling like a sophisticated Harlemite, I left the salon and looked at myself in almost every store window I passed. When I walked through packs of folks, people smiled and nodded. I heard one woman say, "Oh, I love her hair. I got to find somebody to do mine like that."

Don't you know that really made my head get big! Couldn't be anything nicer than to feel and look pretty in Harlem! I put more strut in my step and actually switched my hips more. I wished I'd worn those pumps and not my old Buster Browns! And maybe a shorter skirt! When I got back to the boardinghouse, Mrs. Tartleton clapped her appreciation.

Upstairs, Aunti turned me around and around, scrutinizing my hair and murmuring praise. "You look fabulous! Was Miss Vernice your hairdresser? She's done my hair, too. Be sure to keep wrapping that scarf around your head to keep your hair looking good, hear? You look just like me and your momma when we were your age."

Of all the words said to me that day, Aunti's were the best.

When I woke up the next morning, I discovered that the back of my nightgown was wet. Then I saw blood. I hadn't fallen! How could I have cut myself *down there*? I ran to the lavatory in the hallway with my nightgown pressed up against me. More blood dripped. Was I going to die?

Oh. Was it my womanhood that had arrived?

I duckwalked back to the room and woke up my aunt. "Welcome to the womanhood club," she said, and yawned. She put on her coffee, matter-of-factly told me what to do, and helped me get situated. Then we drank coffee and tea at the table like grown women while she explained what Aunt Society never had. Aunti Val didn't make having my womanhood sound like a frightening curse like I'd heard my girlfriends say. They'd said I couldn't take a bath or get my feet wet or be around people much. I'd been a little worried that I'd never get to do anything while I was having my monthly, except sit in the house. When I told all this to Aunti, she just laughed and said those were old wives' tales, like Gertie's getting tapeworms from milk.

But this business of wearing — and washing — thick strips of cloth four or five days a month was going to be a major inconvenience. On the other hand, I'd noticed that my bosom had started to poke out more, and my behind was a bit bigger. I'd been yearning for that to happen. So maybe there was something positive to it.

"Now listen, you ain't grown yet," Aunti warned me. "But you *can* get a baby if you let a boy do his business with you," she said. "Please don't let that happen, at least not while you're with me!"

"Oh, no! I want to get a baby, but I have to go to medical school and get married first. Aunt Society warned me ever since I could remember that after my womanhood starts to 'keep your dress down and your legs crossed!' "

"Good. Remember that. That's one piece of advice she gave you that makes sense."

I knew that a boy's "business" had something to do with *down there*, but when I asked what a boy did to give me a baby, Aunti mumbled something into her coffee and changed the subject. I reckoned I'd have to return to the library and read up on that to find out for sure.

The June days were passing, with me staying busy passing out *Shuffle Along* programs at night and going with Aunti to the Café Noir Le Grande during the day. *Shuffle Along* was getting good reviews in the important White theatrical newspapers and in the Colored press, which made the cast happy. Most important, Aunti was being paid for her *Shuffle Along* performances. She also began giving me twenty-five cents a night for passing out programs, and that was a blessing!

I'd hint that she should save her money for emergencies and

she'd agree. Then we'd go to the Twice As Nice, "just to look," and return with a bag of cute shoes and a dress for her, and a waist for me. I was hitting up Schwartz's regularly for red and black licorice, so I couldn't fuss too much with her for not saving.

July in Harlem was even hotter than July in Raleigh. Maybe that was because we lived around so much concrete and brick here. Since we didn't have windows in our room, we didn't get any breeze unless we left our door open, and then that was just hot air. While Aunti slept upstairs in the afternoon — the hottest part of the day — I sat on the porch and read, wrote in my journal, played my violin, or just watched folks pass by.

But upstairs was so hot that one afternoon Aunti dozed in the swing on the porch. I fanned myself and read an *Amsterdam* newspaper that Mrs. Tartleton kept on her desk. I could hear band music in the distance, probably coming from someone's Victrola. When I saw Miss D walking toward us from her day's work with bags of clothes from Miz Sheehan in her arms, I hurried to her and took one.

"Thanks, baby. It's hot enough to bake bread without a stove today." She sat down by Aunti and wiped her face with her apron.

I picked through the bags, hoping to find something I liked and that might fit, before Miss D fixed them up and sold them to the Twice As Nice. "Miss D, how's Gertie?"

"My boy wrote me that she's drinking goat milk now, she's discovered green beans, and she's got a front tooth coming in."

"South Carolina must be good for her. You know, I miss her." I held up a pink blouse.

"But there's more to it. He said Netta Lee and Gertie stay with *her* momma, and that that woman spanks poor little Gertie every morning, soon's she gets up. Says she wants Gertie to start her day out right. I'm gonna pray for the Lord to make a way to help my grandbaby. That ain't right." She patted her lap nervously.

Aunti and I murmured our concerns, but I couldn't help thinking that frankly Gertie could use a few more spankings to make her behave. Still, that was a strange way to do it.

"I'm going on up. I'm tired." Miss D stood up. "Oh, a Marcus Garvey parade's going down Seventh Avenue. He ain't in it, though."

Aunti stood up. "Oh, how I love a parade! C'mon, Cece! We can wear what we got on." She swung her arms and legs like she was marching, and I stood up, too. "His parades are so grand," Aunti said. "I saw him in one once. He wore this cap with plumes, rode in an open-air motorcar, and looked so stern in his uniform! I love a man in a uniform."

"Aunti, you love men no matter what they wear," I wanted to say, but I didn't. I just giggled. We got our dogs in the street quick. I saw so many Colored people along the parade route I could have been at the Negro State Fair parade back in Raleigh. A band in bright green uniforms stepping lively to a James Reese Europe tune passed by. Behind them men in black uniforms and shiny black boots rode on prancing black horses. Their banner read UNIVERSAL AFRICAN LEGION. Dozens of Colored women in white — Marcus Garvey's "Black Cross Nurses," Aunti told me — marched after them. We waved and shouted.

More bands and marchers passed, but Aunti told me she had

to get ready for *Shuffle Along*. "I got to find those stock certificates, too," she said. "Maybe by now Mr. Garvey has made me rich."

We wandered back to our boardinghouse, our clothes drenched with sweat. I couldn't wait to cool off with Miss D's sweet tea. When we entered the lobby, Mrs. Tartleton waved a piece of paper at us. "Valentina, you got a call from an Ada Smithfield in Raleigh, North Carolina," she said in a careful, slow voice that made me panic.

My heart thudded. Was Mrs. Smithfield calling to say I could come back home 'cause Poppa was home? Or had something bad happened to him? "She said Aunt Society has had an awful stroke and that Celeste needs to come home right away to take care of her. Here's the telephone number of the Stackhouse Hotel, where she's been waiting."

I gasped and looked from Mrs. Tartleton to Aunti Val. Aunt Society sick? I'd never known her to even have a cold. Might she die? I yearned to go home, yes, but not like this!

Leave it to Aunt Society to cause all this inconvenience for me, right when I was starting to get out and about in Harlem! was my first opinion. Then I quickly banished that thought. It wasn't her fault she'd had a stroke. A stroke was like a heart attack of the brain. It could even be fatal. Next a flood of guilt swept over me. Was it my fault? Did my praying for her to go away cause it? "Go away" wasn't supposed to mean *die!*

Mrs. Tartleton waved the paper again. When Aunti didn't move, I walked over on wobbly legs to get it. "You want me to call her and talk to her?" I squeaked. Aunti nodded with her eyes closed, her hand palm-side up against her forehead like she was about to swoon. "I guess I'll say we'll be back as soon as possible," I went on.

"That *you* will." Aunti suddenly recovered, moving her hand and opening one eye.

"But I can't take care of her by myself!" I flopped back on the divan beside her, wringing my hands. "I thought you could go back, at least for a little while. Can't somebody help her down there?"

"I can't leave the show or the café, even for a little while, as you say. Maybe she's just got a bad case of indigestion from eating her own awful cooking." Looking at Mrs. Tartleton and me, Aunti laughed a little. When we didn't laugh, she stopped.

"Valentina, you need to talk to Mrs. Smithfield, not Celeste." Mrs. Tartleton's thin forehead was full of frown lines.

Aunti sighed. "All right. Send the call through." She walked over to the front desk.

I couldn't think straight. I was going home! But to a very sick aunt. I'd see Poppa and my friends! But I'd be leaving Harlem just when I was getting out on my own, had my womanhood, breasts, a new hairstyle — just when I was settling in. Now I was going back, and traveling all by myself again.

"Yes, it's good to hear from you, too," Aunti was saying into the telephone, "though I wish it was under different circumstances. How is Society?" She paused, listening. "You do have your hands full, don't you? So some church ladies stay with her? Oh, not anymore. Celeste's doing really well. We're having so much fun! What a pretty young lady she's — Yes, certainly she's concerned about her aunt. How's Taylor? Good. No, I can't come; they need me in *Shuffle Along*. Oh yes, it's very successful. I'm finally where I want to be, in front of full houses at every performance, and making a nice chunk of change."

Aunti jabbered on about the show until Mrs. Tartleton cleared her throat and I stamped my foot. She said a few more things, and then hung up. She sat down beside me and took my hand. "When Mrs. Smithfield told Taylor about your aunt, he said you should come home to nurse her. Just so you know who gave the order. He's doing good otherwise. Society had a couple of little strokes earlier but didn't tell anybody, then this big one came along."

"That's how she is," I said. "I've never known her to be sick."

"Mrs. Smithfield said she's partially paralyzed but she can move around a little. Some ladies from Society's Baptist church still bring food over and have helped with laundry, things like that. But won't nobody stay with her. Society's back at your house. After you get there, Mrs. Smithfield'll still come over every day."

"But a stroke is so awful." I tried to control my voice as Aunti stood up and gestured for me to follow her up the stairs. "I don't want her to die, and I certainly don't want her to die while I'm supposed to be taking care of her. I'm not a nurse. And how can they just order me to go from one place to another, with no say-so from me?"

"Your father has the say-so, Cece. It's out of our hands. You know I don't want you to leave," Aunti told me. "Mrs. Smithfield said the church ladies took turns nursing her till Society got so contrary they refused to stay. That's why Mrs. Smithfield called. She can't take off from work anymore to be with Society, and she can't find anybody else. Taylor can't pay for a nurse, so you're the only one left."

"But when do I have to leave? I was just getting used to being here," I wailed.

"Well, she also said Mr. Smithfield's already got tickets. You leave day after tomorrow. I am *so* sorry, Cece. We were having fun, weren't we?"

Chapter Fifteen

My shoulders drooped. "I can't go that soon! I won't be able to say good-bye to —"

"Val, I need to borrow one of your valises again," Miss D said as soon as she saw us in the hallway. She held an armful of folded slips, bloomers, and apron dresses. "I got to go to Gertie. My cousin Sarah wrote that Netta Lee and Pete's down there fighting. I can't let Gertie get hurt."

"My goodness. When it rains it pours. Celeste's aunt has had a bad stroke and they need her to come back to Raleigh to help," Aunti told her.

"Oh, that's too bad," Miss D said, pausing to give me a sympathetic look. But I could tell from the noncommittal tone of her voice that her mind was on Gertie.

"Ripsey, you told us that Gertie was fine," Aunti said.

"T'was my thinking, too, till I got Cousin Sarah's letter. I always had my suspicions about that crazy Netta Lee. Sarah wrote that Netta Lee's carrying around a razor! That she's talking about cutting someone. I just got to round up some ticket money somehow."

"Miss D, you and I are in the same boat," I said, to try to make her understand my awful situation. "Can't nobody help Gertie and Aunt Society unless it's you and me."

"What?" Miss D finally comprehended. "You have to leave here now?" She put one hand up to her mouth like she was truly horrified.

"Ripsey, you got two good jobs up here. Miz Sheehan and that other lady won't keep you if you go trotting off to South Carolina! Just leave things as is. Let Netta and Pete work things out. And what about your place here and your bills?"

"My ladies know me, and so does Mrs. Tartleton, thank you," Miss D said suddenly, in the quietest voice I'd ever heard from her. "I save my money, Valentina Lassiter Chavis. Now you may care about your work over your family, but not me!"

"Aunti, can't you at least ride back on the train with me?" I spread my arms wide, practically begging, trying to get my needs heard, too. "What if a robber's at the train station again? How can I nurse Aunt Society by myself, with her criticizing and poking me morning to night? I'm —"

"Stop it, Celeste. You sound like you're six years old," Aunti snapped. "Grow up. Some girls take care of whole families by the time they're your age. Society did. Bad things happen. You got to roll with it, girl! Sacrifice! Look here, Ripsey, what did you mean about —"

"What kind of sacrifice are *you* making? You ain't goin' nowhere. You won't be cleaning up after nobody and putting up with their mischief." Miss D pointed at me with one hand. "But you're gonna let this child get on that train alone, knowing she got robbed before, and step into that mess back home by herself. Some sacrifice! You've turned your back on your family before when they needed you."

"What do you mean by that?" Aunti waggled her head angrily

at Miss D. "This show's my one big break, and I ain't about to drop it for Society. That heifer's been critical of everything me and my sister ever did. She was even mean to my sister when she was on her sickbed! I took in Celeste in March last minute, and I didn't mind, but yes, I've had to sacrifice!"

I stepped back so they couldn't see the agony on my face. Aunt Society mean to Momma? I knew they'd fussed at each other, when Momma was well. But when she was sick, too? I couldn't be mean to anybody when they suffered. Now Poppa expected me to nurse that ole bat knowing she'd still be evil to me. And when had I ever heard Miss D and Aunti Val go at each other like this? They were supposed to be friends, but they sounded like they hated each other.

"I wish you'd both please stop!" I shouted.

Aunti Val opened and closed her mouth. Miss D turned to me. "Cece, I'm sorry you have to hear grown women arguing. I've spent most of my life cleaning White women's houses. I scratch after money like a yard bird scraping for worms on a cement floor. I don't make money kicking up my heels and batting my eyes."

Lips tight, she held up her hand when Aunti puffed up to speak. "Cece, I won't let you get on that train by yourself again. Nothing I hate more than to see Colored girls get jacked around. Not Gertie, and not you, either. I help Valentina when she needs it. I'll fit my schedule to go back with you, somehow."

"You'd do that for me, Miss D?" I whispered. "You are such a nice lady. Look, I've saved up a little. I can give you some money on your ticket, if you'll take it." I wished she'd stay with me after we got to Raleigh, too, when I had to face Aunt Society.

"Bless your heart, honey, but I can't take your money. You've been so good to my little Gertie. When the Lord uses me like this, I must obey — unlike some people I know." She turned her back on us, strode into her room, and began folding more clothes.

Aunti motioned for me to come to our room. "All right, look. I'm going to buy Miss D's ticket so you can go together at least partway," she said once we got inside. "Keep your money. Ripsey's so dramatic. She didn't need to be so snippy about this. This is so sudden! We all got problems. But you understand why I can't come right now. I do care about you and Taylor and even Society, but I just can't mess up my life when it's finally getting on track."

"So you really just think of me as a sacrifice? I won't be around to disturb you anymore," I said bitterly.

Aunt Valentina folded her arms. "No, I don't think of you as a sacrifice the way *you* might define the word. But I did give up some things — willingly, Cece — to make a home for you here. It's not my fault Taylor and Society got sick. Life can be damned hard sometimes. But you've been crying about wanting to go back home. Now you are. Like you would say, the Lord answered your prayers. Things work out so strange sometimes, don't they?"

I couldn't respond to that. She was right about what I'd been saying I wanted to do. I just hadn't planned to do it so suddenly. I turned and began rummaging through my neat stacks of clothes and bags against the wall.

Aunti pulled out valises for Miss D and me. "You need at least a couple of these," she murmured. "You're leaving with a lot more than what you came with."

From that moment I was caught up in a whirlwind: helping Aunti and Miss D wash and iron clothes; having Aunti wash my hair and Miss D French braid — well, cornrow it; sweating up and down the stairs with messages for and from Mrs. Tartleton; and passing out programs at *Shuffle Along* one last time and saying good-bye to everybody, especially Miss Jarboro. The cast, including Miss Lottie and Miss Adelaide, signed one of my programs as a keepsake for me. I helped Miss D clean her apartment, too.

Aunti did keep her promise by giving Miss D some money to help on her train ticket. Mr. Smithfield had already secured mine, and Aunti made sure they were ready at the train station. She also promised to send the *Brownies' Book* package to me when it arrived in the mail. Miss D and Aunti stayed stiff with each other. They talked through me.

As I packed my things into Aunti's red and black valises, the reality that I was actually returning to Raleigh, to my friends, and to Poppa, began to sink in. Maybe what the preacher said at Easter was true. He said sometimes you had to go through hell on earth to get to heaven above. Some of my hells — suffering through that robbery, being lonely, scrubbing cold splintery floors, and aching, paining, and being disappointed — should have made me tough enough to handle Aunt Society now. But I wouldn't know that until I got there.

At least I wouldn't be on the train ride by myself the whole way, and that helped. Maybe by the time I returned home, Aunt Society would be better, and things could be back to being halfway normal again. I'd been to New York, seen and done some fabulous things, and now I was going home. When I thought about it that way, I began to get more excited.

That night in bed Aunti kept saying she was sorry I had to leave. "Just when I was settling in, I'm being unsettled again," I replied. "I'm ready to go, and I'm not, to be honest. I'll miss eating at the Café Noir and going to the library." I ticked off other things that I'd miss. "My reading about how great New York was supposed to be made me place this town on a higher pedestal than it really deserves. It's great, but people make a town what it is, I reckon. Miss D and Monsieur were probably the nicest people I met up here. And you, of course. But I want to see Poppa and my friends, so I guess it's time."

"I know. What can I give you as a special little gift of how much I've loved having you here?"

Come back with me, I thought. "That's so nice. You are — well, you're like Momma and not like Momma at the same time. You know what I mean? I guess that's why I want to be around you and have you back home, so it'll be a little bit like having Momma again. But you're not like Momma because you do so many exciting things, or you did. Being with you has been an experience that I'll never ever forget. I won't want to leave you, anyway. You're fun, now that we're not scrubbing floors. And — and so is New York. I just want to go home. I think." I stopped. "I don't know what I think." I was about to cry.

When Aunti kept quiet, I tried again. "Aunt Valentina, you've taught me so much. You — I don't know how to put what I'm feeling into the exact words."

"I know, I know," she said softly. "So much is going on right now. But we'll always have each other, even though we won't always be together. And I will try to get down there, I swear I will. I can't say exactly when right now."

"All right." I thought hard. "I wouldn't mind having some of that lemonade and cherries cologne. Wasn't that what you dabbed behind my ears when *Shuffle Along* opened? Aunt Society wouldn't ever let me wear anything that smelled good, not even real talcum powder. She didn't want boys sniffing after me. All she ever gave me was baking soda to dust under my arms."

"That woman's so country. You can have the whole bottle. It's from Paris. You don't need to dab much to make your presence known. Your momma's favorite was Tunisian Dreams. I only have a tiny bit left, so I'm saving it until I can buy some more. It's a very old Parisian perfume and hard to find." She slipped out of bed, opened a tiny bottle in her top drawer, and held it to my nose. I almost fainted. It smelled like Momma's neck. Tears came to my eyes. I wanted to wrap myself around that smell.

"I'll put some on a handkerchief for you to keep back home, and I'll get you some if I ever run across more. Society still probably won't like you wearing cologne, but she won't be able to do anything about it, in her condition."

With Tunisian Dreams dazzling my nostrils and my memories, I snuggled against Aunti one last time. It was like sleeping with Momma again, almost.

And then it was time to go. I stood in the hot late-July air of the Harlem train station with Aunti's pretty red and black valises, my schoolbag, and Dede. Miss D was by me with her bags and our food. I had tucked the Tunisian Dreams–soaked handkerchief into my blouse, and I'd put some French soap, a box of real talcum powder, my Statue of Liberty statue, the autographed *Shuffle Along* programs, and Walker hair jars into my schoolbag. Aunti wanted me to put them in a valise, but I wasn't taking another chance. Losing my valise before meant I lost my Raleigh keepsakes. I didn't want to lose my little New York treasures.

Aunti hugged and kissed me with tears standing in her eyes. She bit her lip and glanced from me to Miss D. "I told you last night I'd come down. I will, say, the last of August."

"You will? You promise?" She nodded. "Oh, good!" I hugged her again, hard. I could stand Aunt Society by myself for a month, I guessed. She and Miss D stared at each other, then they fell on each other's necks, jabbering and crying. The porter hurried us onto the train to our seats, and the next thing I knew, I was on my way back to North Carolina.

I wore my blue skirt, white waist, and good ole Buster Browns, but Miss D was dressed fit to kill. "Because a Colored woman should always dress in her best when traveling," she explained when I asked. "If you go in trifling clothes, they'll treat you in a trifling way. My, you smell good. Don't wear too much of that to church else you'll make the preacher come out the pulpit and beg forgiveness for his sinful thoughts."

I laughed until I thought about Aunt Society. "She was a mean ole bat when she was healthy. What am I gonna do with her now? I can't pop her upside the snout. I *could* get low-down right back, like not feed her or give her the wrong medicine if she makes things difficult for me."

"Celeste, behave and 'do unto others as you would have them do unto you.' She's probably scared that this same child she's been so ornery to is now supposed to keep her from death's door," said Miss D. I nodded.

The hours flew by. But when we entered Virginia, I began to dread reaching Raleigh. "Sister, your face is wrinkled up worse than a crunch of paper." Miss D must have been watching me. "What's wrong? Miss your Aunti Val and Harlem already?"

"I'm thinking about how I'm gonna miss you when you leave me in Richmond," I whispered, trying to keep my fear from seeping into my voice. All I could think about was being cooped up in the train alone and then cooped up in the house alone with a crotchety, sick aunt.

"Surprise! My ticket'll allow me to come right along into Raleigh with you. I plan to stay overnight with you-all, if that's all right, and go on to Gertie from there. Have another piece of sweet potato pie and quit fretting."

"Miss D!" I hugged her arm in grateful relief, then settled back to eat my pie.

The farther south we went, the sunnier everything seemed. Virginia tobacco and cotton spreads stretched wider and wider on both sides of the train tracks. I saw workers bent over in the fields, where I knew it had to be over one hundred degrees. We chugged into North Carolina, then Wake County, and finally into Raleigh! Home!

Every street, house, building, and tree looked like an old friend. Miss D didn't have to remind me to get my things ready when we pulled into the train station. Maybe I could call Mr. Bivens at the Stackhouse to carry us home with all our bags. He and ole white Lissa hung around there sometimes. After all, I knew how to use a telephone now, and I had some money.

"Welcome home, welcome home!" Mr. Smithfield in his porter's uniform was on the train before it had completely stopped. "And you must be Mrs. Dillahunt. I'm Mr. Smithfield, Celeste's neighbor. Pleased to make your acquaintance, and thank you for taking such good care of this little lady."

"T'would be the same done for my own kin," Miss D said, looking him up and down like she was inspecting Aunti's quilt for more egg stain. I knew what she was thinking — *This is the man who let Celeste get robbed.*

When I got off the train, the hot, humid Raleigh air almost smacked me out of my Buster Browns. Mr. Smithfield made sure we had all our bags and valises. Mr. Shepperson, one of Mr. Stackhouse's dapper employees, sat in Mr. Stackhouse's Model T parked nearby. He'd drive us home, Mr. Smithfield said. "Your poppa thought you'd like that."

Miss D told him that she was staying the night and wouldn't need a ride back to the station this evening. "T'would be nice to stretch my legs a bit and meet Aunt Society and your lovely wife. I'll leave in the morning."

"Well, good! I'll be free in the morning, so I can drive you back to the station." Mr. Smithfield touched her elbow.

Miss D's ostrich plumes swayed as she looked down at his hand. "I'd be much obliged if you talk to that driver man there about him picking me up. I can't let you take time away from your wife, since Cece says you travel so much and don't get to see her often, enty." Mr. Smithfield kept smiling, but he let loose of Miss D's arm.

We sat in the back of that Model T like two queens. As we drove through Raleigh, I pointed out St. Paul AME Church, the capitol building, Saint Augustine's School, and Shaw University. "This next part is our Colored business district. Coloreds own most of these businesses. There's Hamlin's Drug," I told her proudly.

Lightner's Office Building had doctors' and dentists' offices, real estate offices, shoe-shine shops, and a North Carolina Mutual Life Insurance Company branch. There was our Odd Fellows Building, and the *Independent* newspaper, one of our Colored newspapers. "And here, of course, is the Stackhouse Hotel, where Poppa, Mr. Shepperson, and I work. It's the biggest Colored hotel in the state. This car belongs to Mr. Stackhouse, the hotel owner."

"You're a little historian," Miss D said. "Down home you'd be what the old folks call a griot. A griot over in Africa calls down history from way back. Most people today just gossip."

I leaned out the window as we passed the metal fence and tombstones of the City Cemetery. "My momma and baby brother's buried here." I sniffed down toward my blouse where I'd stuck my handkerchief scented with Momma's perfume. As soon as I could, I'd visit their graves. Probably nobody'd cleaned them off on Decoration Day in May.

"Miss D, just so you'll know, Aunt Society can be really cranky sometimes," I said as we neared my house. "She might say some awful things."

"You won't have to worry about her saying anything," Mr.

Shepperson broke in. "She hasn't been able to speak a word since she had that last stroke."

What? I was tempted to shout, "Praise God for another blessing," but "Oh, my goodness gracious" is what came out. On one hand, she wouldn't be able to criticize. On the other, how could I tell when she needed help? Pass messages back and forth? But with her being paralyzed, she probably couldn't write.

Mr. Shepperson, who looked like Mr. Ellington and who was around Poppa's age, pulled up in front of our house. Though the grass was high, the house otherwise looked the same. Home, sweet home! And there was Mrs. Smithfield first sitting in the porch swing, then standing up, smiling.

She met us at the car, crying, "Cece, welcome home! My, you've grown!" She hugged me as I got out of the car. I introduced her to Miss D and they exchanged pleasantries.

"We moved her into your house because the church ladies said going into hers was like walking into a spider's lair," Mrs. Smithfield said. Her warm gray eyes held mine. "They thought they'd get bit, or ate up, it was so dark in there. Well, it's been hard on her, not able to get around. She can be, uh, irritable. Her apoplexy took away her speech, but she can make sounds that you'll come to recognize."

"She was grumpy and irritable when she *could* talk and get around," I said. "That's all I need, to have her grunting at me, too."

Mrs. Smithfield gasped. "Listen to you! Gone to New York and got loud and mouthy!"

"You make her turn those sour grumpy grunts into sweet ones," Miss D told me as we came into my house. Other than a slightly moldy fragrance, it smelled just like home. I went straight to my room and bounced on my bed, enjoying the familiar squeaks. It looked just as neat as when I'd left it.

Miss D and Mrs. Smithfield followed. "So this is where you write your poems, play your violin, and lay your head," said Miss D, glancing around. "It feels and looks just like you."

"I'll sure be glad to be back in my bed," I said. "You can sleep in here. I —" The loud clangs of a cowbell made me stop. "What in the world was that?"

"I meant to tell you about her bell." Mrs. Smithfield seemed embarrassed. "The church ladies didn't care for it, either."

The bell clanged again. "T'were me living here, I'd hide that thing first chance I got," Miss D murmured.

"Grumpy and clanging and grunts, oh joy," I whispered to Miss D and Mrs. Smithfield, and my shoulders sagged. "Where'd she get it from?"

"Alton. He found it someplace and thought it'd help. Of course it didn't. Let's go," said Mrs. Smithfield, and headed for my parents' room.

Slumped forward in her wheelchair — the chair she hadn't needed to use till now — Aunt Society sat by my parents' bed, smiling. When I saw her right arm lying crooked on a pillow in her lap, I realized she wasn't smiling at all. The stroke had twisted her mouth and her arm. She was skinnier, more wrinkled, and completely white-haired. I'd never seen her look so frail, so ancient, so silent. Poor Aunt Society!

"Here's your niece Celeste, back to take care of you," said Mrs. Smithfield loudly.

Was she deaf, too? I sat down on the bed. "Hello, Aunt Society."
I tried to keep my voice from quivering as she gazed at me
with piercing eyes. "You're wearing your favorite apron dress,
aren't you?"

"And this is Mrs. Dillahunt from New York, who came with
her. Wasn't that nice? She's going on to South Carolina. She's
one of your sister-in-law Valentina's friends."

At the mention of Aunt Valentina's name, Aunt Society, who'd
been staring at Miss D, swung her eyes back to me, frowning
fiercely. I pulled back. Uh-oh.

"Hello, Miss Massey," said Miss D. "You're blessed to have
Celeste here. Miss Massey? You can hear me, can't you?" Aunt
Society's eyes shot over to Miss D. "Yes, I thought you could.
Celeste has said so much about you. You've raised her well."

Aunt Society's streetlight glower softened a notch after
Miss D's compliment. She raised her good left hand and let it
hang in the air, waving at Miss D. But then she pointed her forefinger at me, grunted twice loudly, and slapped the bed! Bewildered, I jumped up. "What does she want, Mrs. Smithfield?
What'd I do?"

"I don't know, Cece. Society, you want water? Hungry? Need
to use the lavatory?"

"Celeste was sitting on her bed," Miss D said. "Some old people don't like folks on their bed without permission."

"It's Poppa's bed, not hers." I sat back down. Aunt Society
smacked the bed again, but I didn't move. She could have slept
on the daybed in the hallway, where she'd slept after Momma
was sick and where she'd slept when she first moved in.

"But *she* sleeps in it now," Mrs. Smithfield reminded me. "So to keep the peace, why don't you get up."

Folding my arms over my bosom, I left the bed and leaned against the wall, staring at the floor so I wouldn't have to look at anybody. If that ole bat was going to have spasms and ring that thing every time she disapproved of something, I faced terrible times.

Chapter
Sixteen

Y̶ou-all must be thirsty," Mrs. Smithfield said quickly. "Let's sit
in the parlor, where it's cooler. I'll bring you some sweet tea.
Society, you want to come, too? No? Well, ring if you need
anything."

Miss D settled herself on the parlor divan, then whispered,
"Cece, don't let your ole aunt make you hang your head ever
again. The shoe's on the other foot now."

"I know," I whispered back, settling into Momma's rocking
chair and sighing. "She's mean as ever."

"She'd knock her food to the floor just to watch the church
ladies and me clean it up," Mrs. Smithfield whispered.

Memories of my water-blistered fingers and scratched-up
knees flashed through my head. I sat up straighter. "If she does
that to me, I'll clean it up the first time," I said loudly. "But after
that she'll go hungry. Aunti Val made me scrub floors in New
York City most every night, but I ain't about to scrub my own
every day just because of *her* hysterics."

"Look out now!" Miss D whooped.

"Celeste!" Mrs. Smithfield slapped her hand over her mouth.
"You've come back full of fire and sass, hair growing, filling out,
speaking up. New York was good for you."

"Cece being in charge's gonna be hard for Society to swallow," Miss D said softly again. "Be stern, honey, or she'll run you over. You *could* remind her that this is better than her being put in the poor farm."

I thought that over. Poppa wouldn't ever go for that. "Aunti Val said she was coming down the last of August," I told Mrs. Smithfield. "That'll help me a lot. Didn't she, Miss D?"

"That's what she said," Miss D replied.

"It'll be so good to see her again," Mrs. Smithfield said politely.

I pursed my lips at both of them. "You don't think she'll keep her promise, do you?"

Mrs. Smithfield stayed quiet, but Miss D said, "Don't get me to lyin'."

"Well, we'll see." I stood up. "Can I go over to the Stackhouse and call Poppa? I know how to use the telephone and can pay for the call. And I can read up on apoplexy in Mr. Hodges's books."

"Read up on common sense, too," Miss D said, "and how to knock some into both your aunts' heads."

Mrs. Smithfield burst out laughing. "Miss D, if you lived down here, you'd have me howling all the time. Go ahead, Cece."

"Ada — can I call you Miss Ada?" Miss D said, sipping on her tea. "I hear you bake a mean Lady Baltimore cake. I do one myself that I'm not too 'shamed of."

While they talked, I slipped off to my room and transferred things from my schoolbag and valises to my secret places. Even though Aunt Society was partly paralyzed, I bet she could still get around in that wheelchair if she wanted to, and poke about.

Just before I left, I stuck my head into her room. She sat in her chair, eyes closed. I knocked on the wall to get her attention. When I told her where I was going, she opened her eyes and shook her finger "no." I reminded her that Mrs. Smithfield and Miss D were here, but she kept frowning and finger shaking. I left anyway.

Out in the hot sun, I danced, twirled, waved at folks in passing motorcars, and sang "I'm Just Wild About Raleigh" up Hargett Street. Back home! I paused when I reached City Cemetery, debating whether to visit Momma's grave. I decided I needed a longer time for that. When I entered the hotel, Mr. Toodlums welcomed me back. In a few seconds, I was hearing, "Celeste! How's my girlio?"

"Poppa, I'm home! Can I come see you? You feeling better?" His voice warmed me from the inside out. "What's a apoplexy?"

"Girlio, just hearing your voice makes me better already. You've seen Aunt Society, right? She's kind of bad off. Apoplexy is when a vein breaks in your brain. They call it a stroke, too. One could have killed her. She had three. But she's still with us, praise the Lord. I'm counting on you to help pull her through and get her back on her feet, if you can. Try to be patient with her. She's glad you're back."

"No, she's not. She made me get off your bed, she grunts left and right, rings that —"

"You be the head of the family for me. Honey, you happened to call in the middle of dinner. They only let me come to the phone because they knew you were arriving today. I was hopin' you'd call, but I got to cut out 'cause they're real strict about making sure I eat. I'm still gaining a little. By the way, me and the cows are on good terms now. Honey, they're calling me for dinner. Best time to call is midmorning or early afternoon."

We said a few other things, then we got off. His voice sounded so good! I wanted to see him *now!* I thanked Mr. Toodlums for making the call. "I wonder could Mr. Shepperson take me out to Poppa this week?" I asked. "I wanna see him!"

"I'll check. Oh, tell your guest that he or Mr. Smithfield'll pick her up at eight A.M. And I won't charge you for the call. Welcome back."

Over at the apothecary, Mr. Hodges welcomed me back, too, and inquired about Poppa. His medical book said people who had light strokes often thought they'd had a bad headache. People who had severe strokes sometimes forgot who they were, or ended up with twisted muscles like Aunt Society's mouth and arm. Sometimes one eye got bigger than the other. If they didn't die right away, some people got depressed or were as helpless as babies. Though she was close to it, Aunt Society wasn't completely helpless. She was too mean for that.

"How's she making out today?" Mr. Hodges asked when I returned the book to the shelf near him.

"Well, she was sitting in her wheelchair when I left. It's hard to understand what she wants, since she can't talk. Poppa and Mrs. Smithfield said she's glad I'm back, but she doesn't act like it. What if she won't take her medicine or let me help her? What if I make mistakes?"

"She knows what she needs to do if she wants to get better," Mr. Hodges told me. "Just do your best, Celeste. Won't nobody fault you for your mistakes."

Next I swung by Evalina's house behind me, but nobody was

there. Angel Mae lived over on South Street, which was a ways away. I'd have stopped at Swan's, since she lived behind me, too, but I was afraid of her uncle's slobbery dog and those evil cats. I knocked my own dogs on home.

The aroma of oxtails and navy beans, Miss D's sweet potato pie, greens, small red potatoes, and Mrs. Smithfield's buttery cornbread drifted through the screen door when I reached our porch. I could have ate the air! In the kitchen Miss D and Mrs. Smithfield were chattering like old friends. "I wanted to cook a little something for you to remember me by," said Miss D. "I love this stove. It heats up so quick that —"

Clang! Clang! Clang!

"It hasn't rung since you left," said Mrs. Smithfield, "so it must be for you."

"All right." I replaced my frown with a smile and, taking a deep breath, went to my aunt, heart pounding like one of those Garvey parade band drums. Aunt Society laid the cowbell on the bed and pointed to her stomach. "You ready to eat? Food smells good, doesn't it? I'll tell Mrs. Smithfield." She frowned and pointed again. "What? I don't understand you!" I rushed back to the kitchen and told Mrs. Smithfield.

"She needs to go do her business. I'll show you how we handle that." Oh, joy. I dragged after Mrs. Smithfield. She pushed Aunt Society in her wheelchair to our lavatory. She half lifted her up out of the chair and inside. After a few grunts and whispers, they maneuvered back out.

"You're doing much better, aren't you, Society?" Mrs. Smithfield panted. She removed Aunt Society's glasses and patted her face dry. "Want some supper now?"

Aunt Society grunted and lifted her hand. Mrs. Smithfield wheeled her into the kitchen. Miss D had set the table and stood by, waiting. I trailed in, feeling helpless. How would I ever learn to do all this? I couldn't even please her when she was well! Aunt Society wouldn't look at us at supper. She'd point to what she wanted, and we'd put it on her plate. She used a fork and spoon well enough with her left hand, and did she ever eat. That hadn't changed. She didn't throw any food on the floor, either.

She didn't want to sit in the parlor with us after supper, so I wheeled her to her room. I noticed a little bald spot at the back of her head. Maybe I could wash her hair with Walker shampoo and get it to grow back. If she'd let me. "You want anything?" Silence. I took that to mean no and escaped to the parlor, where Miss D and Mrs. Smithfield were eating sweet potato pie. They'd set my plate on my chair.

Mrs. Smithfield was saying, "I'd happened to go by her house to ask about Taylor and found her sitting on the front porch, just staring. She couldn't move, couldn't talk. She'd been feeling poorly the last few months, you know. Oh, you didn't? The Bivenses carried her to Saint Agnes Hospital."

Since Aunt Society hated the Bivenses, their wagon, and Lissa, that could practically have given her another stroke, I thought. Mrs. Smithfield asked ladies from my aunt's church to sit with her after she left the hospital. "They were wonderful. A couple were even practical nurses. But even as sick as she was, Society kept getting meaner until she ran them off. And she knew those ladies, too!" She pointed her fork at me. "That's when I talked with Taylor, and he said to call for you. He thought that maybe she'd pay attention to you."

Thanks, Poppa. I liked that he trusted me to nurse his sister, and it did get me back home. But what a way to have to get here.

At nightfall the cowbell rang. "She's probably ready for bed. C'mon, Cece." After another lavatory visit, Mrs. Smithfield helped Aunt Society slip on her gown while I stayed by the wall and tried not to watch. She had always been thin, but now she was a bony bag of wrinkles drooping everywhere. I didn't want my bosom and behind to hang like that when I got old.

"Make sure she swallows these pills at bedtime." Mrs. Smithfield picked up a yellow glass bottle from the nightstand. "Sometimes she hides them, then spits them out. Open your mouth, Society, so I can see. All right, dear."

Aunt Society looked at me. We both knew she'd never let me look in her mouth.

In the kitchen Mrs. Smithfield said she'd return in the morning to see Miss D off and to check on my aunt. She added that Aunt Society wouldn't want anything tonight unless she had to do her business or was thirsty. I prayed she wouldn't need either.

Back in my room I watched Miss D smear white face cream on her neck. "You think Aunt Society'll get better?"

"I expect she will if she wants to. Ole sister's still got fire left in her."

"I don't mean to be nosy, but you said something about Aunti Val not taking care of her family. What'd you mean?" That had been bothering me ever since she'd said it back in New York.

She stopped smearing. "She got into my business about my jobs and Gertie and so forth, so I had to jump salty and get into hers. She has talked off and on in the past about coming back here to do one thing or another, but she hasn't. Still, she expects folks to help her."

"You really don't think she'll come in August, do you?" I had to ask again, now that we were alone. I wrapped my scarf around my head and waited for her answer.

Miss D returned to smearing. "She said she would. Won't know till she gets here. Maybe with you down here in this situation she might hold to her word. That gal's a butterfly flitting from one rock to another."

"What's butterflies and rocks got to do with it?"

"She's flying around with her head in the sky while scrubbers and scrapers like me and you stay here on the ground, like rocks. Us rocks wish we were like them up there with no problems or responsibilities, not have to deal with the real, you know? When the butterflies get in trouble, they head for the rocks, something solid. When it's safe, they're off again. Having you come to New York is the most responsible thing I've ever known Val to do. But she leaned on you like you were grown and she was the child, didn't she?"

"No, no, she didn't," I said, wondering if that was really the case. "Entertainers are kind of, uh, flighty, anyway."

"Val's pinning everything on *Shuffle Along*, and she only got that part because you and I pushed her. She's actually too old to still be a hoofer in a chorus line, competing with young gals like Caterina Jarboro. Val's good, but that gal's *great*."

"But Aunti Val still hasn't had her big breakthrough —"

"And I'm saying at this age she may not get it —"

"— so maybe she figures she can't come home until she *is* a star." I stopped, finally understanding what Miss D was saying. "It must be awful to work so hard so long and still not have what you want. Miss D, I'm glad you know about these things. Nobody else said anything about, well, just things, except Poppa sometimes. Aunt Society was so negative about everything, I didn't like to listen to her. Aunti Val told me about a lot, but she's not here. And now you're gonna be gone." I felt dread start to weigh down on me again.

"I know what it's like to be a motherless child," Miss D said. She looked at me so tenderly tears came to my eyes. "I felt your loneliness strong the minute you knocked on my door that first day, when you and that egg tangled with that quilt. I was a motherless child. Wasn't for my grammaw raising me, who knows where I'd be? That's why people got to keep connections with family whether you're a star or a floor scrubber. Val was married, you know. You look surprised. She was married to Nathaniel Chavis, your uncle."

My mouth flew open. "What? Aunti mentioned his name, but she didn't say they were married. Just that this Mr. Chavis had died. How come their being married had to be a mystery?"

"It wasn't to folks who knew." Miss D chuckled. "They weren't married very long. It was sad and kind of funny, too, how he died. Val told me that they were sitting on top of a piano having their picture taken. Afterward, when she gave him a big kiss, he fell off the piano, broke his neck, and died, just like that. I warned her not to ever kiss me 'cause she had the kiss of death. Girl, she got mad at me! Anyway, Nathaniel was a rock. Valentina was close to your momma, too, then *she* died. I expect that your momma was probably everybody's rock. Society's tried to be a rock, but now she's sick. Me, I love my family and I want to go home to South Carolina for good. I'm their rock, see."

My mind was reeling with all this information. "So why did you leave South Carolina?"

"I went up north to get away from the hardships that the White folks were giving us Colored. A bunch of us headed for Harlem in 1901, because we heard good jobs, nice homes, and such were supposed to be so much better for Colored up there. Harlem's the Colored capital of the world! I've enjoyed it, but I'm getting old," she said. "Things are a little better now down in South Cacky Lacky. But mostly I want to be round my kinfolks. So that when I get sick I'll have my people near to care for me."

I thought about that. It made sense. I could understand why Poppa wanted me home. Just like I wanted Aunti Val home. Miss D yawned and began wiping off the cream. "Cece, I don't know that Val'll ever make it big in New York like she wants," she confided. "She ought to come back here where people know her and care about her. That's how I see it."

"Yeah, but she doesn't seem to see it that way yet." We said good night and I peeked in on Aunt Society. She was quiet. I got myself settled on the divan in the parlor. Was I flitting back and forth, too? I was sure getting moved back and forth. Was I like Aunti Val or Aunt Society? Was I a butterfly or a rock? And which one did I want to be?

Midnight came and passed. I was still awake, listening for that bell. I eased up, tiptoed to Aunt Society's room, and glanced in. Her lamp was still lit and her eyes were open. Was she still breathing? Or had she . . . crossed the waters?

"Aunt Society, you all right?" I asked anxiously.

She let out two soft grunts that I decided was "Uh-huh," meaning yes. I told her good night and tiptoed back to the couch, relieved. Bad as the circumstance was, it was good to be home. "Thank you, Lord," I whispered.

The next thing I knew, the sun was shining in my face and Mrs. Smithfield was knocking at the door. "I knew you-all'd be tuckered out from your trip, so I brought over breakfast," she said, holding a tray full of food.

At 7:45 A.M. Miss D set her hat on her head and pulled on her gloves. I placed her bags by the curb. "You take care of yourself now, Cece. I'll write to you when I get to Charleston, and I'll keep tabs on Valentina when I'm back up there. The Lord willing, I'll move to Charleston for good. I'll be closer to you, then."

We hugged and hugged. With Miss D leaving, I was beginning to feel like an orphan again, like when I left Poppa back in March for New York. "I'm gonna miss you so," I whispered. "I just don't know about Aunt Society."

"Can't be too much worse now than before." Miss D smiled. "You can still outrun her."

When Mr. Stackhouse's auto arrived, Mr. Smithfield jumped out, waved at us, and opened the door. Miss D settled herself in the back. He started to join her, but she closed the door first. "I like to be chauffeured," I heard her say.

"Alton, you ole flirt, behave before I put my skillet on your head," Mrs. Smithfield said firmly. Mr. Shepperson drove them off, with Miss D waving at us and us waving back.

"Well, here we are," I said, wiping away tears. Mrs. Smithfield nodded.

After she checked on Aunt Society and went over instructions with me, she got ready to leave. "If you have an emergency, go to the Stackhouse and get hold of me at the governor's. Maybe your girlfriends can come by, too. They've asked me about you."

"What if she won't act right?" I whispered.

"Do what you have to do. Oh, put one teaspoon of sugar and a little milk in her oatmeal."

The cowbell rang. "Help me one more time," I pleaded, but Mrs. Smithfield said good-bye and got to stepping.

Taking a deep breath, I dragged to Aunt Society. "You ready for breakfast?" She grunted, which I took to mean yes. I hurried into the kitchen, prepared her tray, and set it on her lap. Aunt Society glared at me, and with her good hand knocked the bowl off the tray. It broke on the wood floor, splattering slimy oatmeal everywhere. Her twisted mouth resembled a smile.

Oh, joy, here we go. "Accidents happen, don't they?" I said with a fake brightness. "I'll clean it up and bring you some more. This was one of Momma's good china bowls." I took the mess back to the kitchen, got rags, and cleaned everything up while she watched me.

I brought her another bowl of oatmeal. Looking me dead in the eye, she knocked the bowl over. Oatmeal spilled across the tray and onto Momma's quilt. "All right, that did it!" I put my hands on my hips. "I ain't cleaning up no more food. You want to get well, you got to eat, but you got to behave first. I know you were mean to Momma when she was sick, but I don't *want* to be mean to you."

Well, we had a staring contest and she won because I left the room and stomped to the porch with my fists balled up. That cowbell got to clanging, but I stayed put. Ole bat! Ole heifer! After I cooled off, I went to her room. She grunted and pointed to the quilt. "Too bad. You made the mess." I went to my room, got Dede, gritted my teeth, and began to play "Forsythia" while the cowbell clanged. I played until the bell stopped. I went to her room. She'd picked some oatmeal off the quilt and thrown it against the wall!

I returned to the porch. I might as well get used to dealing with the same terrible old Aunt Society that I had left. I tapped my foot. But she wasn't dealing with the same Celeste.

Going to the parlor, I turned on the Westrand to my favorite program. That set off the cowbell, but I ignored it. I browsed the bookshelves, saying hello to my old friends. I washed the breakfast dishes. The cowbell clanged. Humming to a catchy, sassy tune on the radio, I dry mopped my bedroom floor, hung my bedclothes outside on the clothesline to air, and washed my windows inside and out while the cowbell clanged.

Around noon I came into my aunt's room to see if she needed to use the lavatory or take medication, but I didn't touch that oatmeal. I sat down on the bed away from the spilled oatmeal and took her bad hand in mine. She tried to jerk it away but I held on. I closed my eyes so I wouldn't have to look at her glaring at me. "I'm glad I'm back, Aunt Society, and I'm gonna do all I can to help you feel better." So far, so good. "You raised me right. Now you gotta help me raise you back to health. But you need to be nicer to me. Don't nobody else want to be bothered with you but me."

When I opened my eyes, I saw tears slipping down her withered yellow cheeks. With a clean edge of the quilt I wiped them away, then I kissed her cheek. "Are you hungry now?" She grunted softly and with her good hand patted mine.

Chapter Seventeen

Evalina and Swan! Standing on my front porch! Screaming, I nearly tore down the screen door getting to my friends. "Look at you!" Swan touched my thick braids and stared at my bosom. "Are those *yours*? Or are you still stuffing rags in your waist?"

"This is *me*." I inhaled so that my chest would expand. "Aunti Val used Madam Walker hair stuff on my hair. It's so good to see you! Where've you been? Where's Angel Mae?"

"She's got cramps," said Swan, "but she said to tell you hello and she can't wait to get over here and —"

Clang, clang, clang! I sighed. "Sit down. I'll be right back." Somehow I had to shut down that bell. Aunt Society was pointing toward the porch, shaking her finger "no" when I reached her. "It's just Evalina and Swan, for goodness' sakes. I've been back four days, and the only folks I see are you and the Smithfields. If I can't be having my friends over, I'm gonna take your bell." I reached for it, but she dragged it under the sheet.

"Don't ring it again, unless you need something important, you hear me?" I said. We had another staring contest, then, barely nodding, Aunt Society looked away. There! I returned to the swing and sat down between my friends, who were gawking at me.

"What in the devil was that?" Evalina asked. "You got cows in your parlor?"

"Your aunt was one reason why we hadn't got over here sooner." Swan lowered her voice. "Momma'd told me about her chasing off everybody who was trying to help her. How can somebody be sick and still act so cranky?"

"Oh, don't pay her any —"

"I can't get over how good you look," Evalina broke in. "I wanna eat that New York food, too!"

"Like octopus and squid?" I laughed when Evalina looked shocked. "All right. What've you been doing since your last letters that —"

"I can fry chicken and bake cathead biscuits without burning 'em up," Evalina bragged, "and Swan's been working on a quilt with her momma and grandma —"

"Which we're gonna enter at the fair," Swan cut in. "Maybe you could can something and enter it, too, Cece. Didn't your Aunt Society teach you?"

Or show fair folks how to scrub floors and empty chamber pots, I thought. "I could play songs from *Shuffle Along* on Dede," I said. "I went to all the rehearsals, and I —"

"I have to go pick tobacco on Granddaddy's farm in August in Oxford." Evalina interrupted me again! "You know how I hate those nasty tobacco worms."

I folded my arms over my bosom. Evalina hadn't changed. At least she didn't have a cold. "Evalina, don't make me jump salty with you for talking over me."

"Huh? I thought you were through." She sounded puzzled.

"If you'd been quiet, you'd have known," I said back, gazing at her until she dropped her eyes and squirmed around. "Well, now. What'd you do Fourth of July? Aunti and I and Miss D went to a picnic in Central Park, and watched fireworks. It was simply fabulous."

Evalina raised her eyebrows at me, sucked on her teeth, and repeated, "*Oh, sim-plee fabulous!*" to Swan. Swan smiled at me but kept quiet.

"Say something, Swan. *I* know how to listen."

"Not like how you used to," Evalina replied in her usual sassy tone.

"Evalina, behave," Swan said. Well, thank goodness Swan hadn't changed, I thought. "Cece, we stayed home at my house and had a big cookout in the back."

The cowbell clanged, once. Swan stopped, looking at me. I blew out my breath. "I *told* her not to bother me while I had company, but she's probably having a spasm in there anyway."

"I never knew you to tell your aunt anything except 'Yes, ma'am,'" Swan said. "I wanna know what you've been eating, too."

"Pepper, seems to me," Evalina said, scowling. "C'mon, Swan, Cece's got to *work*."

"Maybe we'll be back after supper." Swan stood up. "We can sit on your back porch, if the mosquitoes don't eat us up, or if she" — she jerked her head toward the house — "doesn't try to run us off."

"You just got here," I moaned, but they were already leaving the porch. When I walked in, Aunt Society was gripping that bell like it was her money purse. "What do you want? You and your ole cowbell chased off my company!" She pointed to her water glass. I'd forgot it was time for her medicine.

"Oh. I'm sorry." After giving her the pills and watching her swallow, I coaxed her into swinging her stick legs out from the bed to stand for a while, like Mrs. Smithfield said to do. I didn't look in her mouth, which she'd also said to do. If she wasn't swallowing her pills, then that was her own fault, I decided. She walked a few feet, then motioned that she wanted to lie back down. I made her sit in her wheelchair instead, and pushed her to the kitchen while I warmed up her supper of navy beans, oxtails, greens, and sweet potatoes. Then I wheeled her out to the back porch to eat, and kept her out there while I straightened up.

"You'll never get well unless you get out into fresh air every day," I said while she ate. "You gotta move around to stir up your blood." She rolled her eyes at me, but kept on chewing. After I finished, I sat down on the steps with my own plate in my lap. When the sun went down, we were still out there. She had fallen asleep, sweating, the food tray in her lap.

I got her settled in bed, then heated water and washed dishes. Afterward, I returned to the back porch and waited for the girls. A Carolina moon hung in the sky like an orange balloon. I hadn't seen a moon like that since I'd left for New York. After an hour of waiting and slapping at bugs, I went inside to my room and put on my nightgown. Then I headed to the porch again. Where were Swan and Evalina? Maybe Swan had chores to do. Maybe Evalina was still mad because I wouldn't let her hog the conversation like she was used to doing. Or were they jealous because

I'd lived in Harlem and knew stuff that they didn't? Or did they just not want to come over with Aunt Society and her cowbell lurking around?

I waited till nearly eleven o'clock. The neighborhood was so quiet I didn't even hear any dogs bark. Back in Harlem when we came home from scrubbing floors or from *Shuffle Along* at this time of night, I always heard music, car rumbles, voices, cats or dogs yowling — some kind of noise. Maybe we'd have stopped at Café Noir Le Grande and enjoyed Mr. Ellington on the piano and ate Monsieur's chocolate squares. Maybe Miss D was still up and we'd go sit and gossip with her for a spell. What a difference! I wondered how she was doing. And how Aunti was. Tears came into my eyes. I missed them. I missed Harlem, too.

After checking on my aunt — she was snoring — I went to bed, thinking over what I'd said or done that might have upset my friends.

A week passed, and washing day rolled around. When I went into Aunt Society's room to collect her dirty clothes, I found her sitting up in bed. "Ha ho," she said, flapping her good hand.

I was about knocked off my feet! "What? What? Hello, hello!" I yelled back after I found my voice. "Aunt Society, you're talking!" I dropped to the bed. I thought I'd have a stroke myself. "God be praised, you're having your breakthrough! Hello, hello!"

Her "ha ho" pepped me up with the washing. Afterward, I washed the dishes with some of the wash water and used the rest to scrub the kitchen floor. I washed myself with some of the rinse water and poured the rest onto the flower beds and the forsythia bush.

By early August, Aunt Society with my help could walk about

inside the house and on the porches. She wouldn't walk in the yard, partly because she was afraid of navigating the steps, but mostly because she still didn't want to step in duck and guinea hen poop. She could produce a crooked but real smile when I had Miss Pinetar dance for her. My singing and playing "Forsythia" on Dede made her smile, too. That was a big change because she had hated my poem before, and had declared that I made Dede squeak like a rat. Best of all, she'd gotten reconciled to my having our Westrand radio on.

This was all good for *her*, but *I* hadn't been able to visit anybody, especially Poppa, because nobody was able or willing to stay with her while I was gone. I couldn't ask Mr. Shepperson to drive me because Mr. Stackhouse's car was broken down. I wasn't sure the Bivenses' mule could make the long trip in the hot weather. I hadn't even been able to call Poppa.

Once when I was taking down clothes in the backyard, Swan waved and came over to the fence. "I'd come over more but I never see you outside," she said. "Momma wouldn't let me come back over that night. She said not to be bothering you too much because your hands are so full with your aunt. But here, I can help you take down clothes."

"Thanks, Swan. I miss you so much. Sometimes I don't have anything to do, and other times I work so hard all I can manage later is to fall into bed. I figure Evalina's gone to her granddaddy's farm like she said she would, but where's Angel Mae?" I asked.

Swan shrugged as she helped me fold a sheet. "I haven't seen her myself. With it being so hot and dusty this summer, her asthma's been kicking up bad, so that might be part of the reason," she said. "It's so hot I don't feel like walking all the way over to her house. Well, I gotta go. Come to the back porch more and wave or something, so I know when I can come over, or at least meet you at the fence."

"All right. And thanks, Swan." Watching out for the duck poop, I headed back to the porch with my arms full of clothes.

That afternoon while Aunt Society rested I was sitting on the front porch sweating and fretting when Mrs. Bivens, Lissa, and Buster swung around the corner. I hurried out into the street toward them, waving. "Great day in the morning, you sure have grown," she exclaimed when she got the mule stopped. "How've you been? How's your aunts? How's your father?"

"They're all holding on, thanks. Can you take me to the sanitarium to see Poppa one day soon? I haven't been able to get out there since I got back." I patted Buster, who was happy to see me.

She pursed her lips. "That's a long trip. I'll need a little something, you know, for Lissa's wear and tear."

"How much?" I held my breath. "Like a dollar?" I still had a little money saved from Café Noir Le Grande and scrubbing. I was trying to make it last.

"That'd be fine. I expect she'll make it if we rest a lot. You wouldn't be taking your aunt, would you?" she whispered.

"No, ma'am. I got to find somebody to sit with her before I can go."

"Well, you let me know the day before. Much as we need the rain, it'll muddy up the roads too bad."

That afternoon a lady brought us over a pot of greens. When I asked if she could sit with Aunt Society, she smiled, blessed me, said no, and kept going. When I saw Mrs. Smithfield walking home, I asked her about sitting with Aunt Society. She said she couldn't this week because the governor was having guests and she'd have to fix fancy meals. She might be able to next week, though. "And call the sanitarium to make sure they allow children. You got grown folks' responsibilities, but you got a child's age," she advised me gently. "Sometimes places like that won't let children come around."

Nobody else stopped by that whole week, not even any ladies with food. I was about to drop with the heat, and loneliness. One afternoon, after I'd snapped bushels of green beans for canning and cleaned yellow corn that Mr. Smithfield had left on the back porch, I heard a knock at the front door. I rushed out to the porch, with corn tassels hanging off the front of my dress and my face. *Praise God, Angel Mae!* We danced around, screaming.

"I'da come by sooner, but my asthma's really been bothering me," she said, "and then I caught one of those awful summer colds. But girl, you look good! I've been missing you so!" We hugged again and sat down in the porch swing. She brought me up to date on things happening in Raleigh, which wasn't much different from what I already knew. I told her some more things about what I'd done in Harlem.

"Yeah, I know all that. We got your letters and your Statue of Liberty postcard. Evalina came over before she left and told me you were bragging about everything and had your hair done up fancy and thought you were cute. You know Evalina." She wiped her plump, sweaty face.

"Can I ask you something?" I asked. She nodded. "She and Swan didn't really seem interested in what I was saying. What was wrong with them?"

"Nothing really. But Momma and them say when someone they know goes to Harlem, they always come back with the big head, bragging and carrying on. All we talked about while you were gone was that we hoped you wouldn't get the big head, too. So maybe that's why."

"The big head? Do you think I do?" Without meaning to, I touched my head.

"No. You always talked about New York, so that wasn't new. Remember when we met at the Butterflies Club how we all loved to talk about what we wanted to do? Evalina said she wanted to be a cowgirl and live in Texas after we saw that cowboy movie at the Royal. She didn't even know where Texas was!"

"Oh, and how Swan said she wanted to be a Red Cross nurse and help our wounded soldiers in France, but that was only because she loved the white uniform and the red cape!" I giggled.

"And I wanted to be a teacher and open my own school like that lady Charlotte Hawkins Brown did for us Colored over in Sedalia. I still do," she said softly. "But now we're just canning pig snouts and getting fat" — she pointed to herself — "while you're out there meeting Broadway stars, eating foreign food, and seeing fancy sights."

She nodded at my bosom. "And growing those." I looked down proudly. "Girl, Evalina's having hissy fits because you grew *those* and got your womanhood, and she hasn't." She laughed. "She just *knew* she'd grow hers before you grew yours. So don't pay that girl *no* mind." Angel Mae, who was stout, had had her bosom for years.

I got her some sweet tea. We laughed and talked some more. She even asked me about Big Willie. I felt so comfortable, finally being with her again. I wanted to show her some of my New York treasures, like the Statue of Liberty statue, and my clothes, but thought I'd wait. I didn't want to act like I had the big head, even though she said I didn't. After about an hour, she said she had to leave.

She hadn't got down the steps good before I heard, "Ha ho!" I stamped into my aunt's room. "Now what?" I snapped.

She blinked and closed her mouth. "Na-nothin'," she mumbled.

"I didn't think so. Just let me *be* for a minute, will you, please?" I slouched back to the porch and sat with my chin resting on my fists. I knew I didn't need to sound so ornery to her, but my goodness! Hearing her voice reminded me of how much work I had to do, like wash and can those beans, finish the corn, and — when was Aunti Val, or Mrs. Smithfield, or a church lady, or anybody coming to help *me*?

The sun beating down so fierce the whole month didn't help, either, even though we all prayed for rain. Almost all North Carolina was dry. I read in the paper that cotton and tobacco crops were withering in the ground. Our yard was so dry it looked like a red bald head with a few brown strands lying around. I slowed clothes washing to save water, which I didn't mind a bit. I made sure I watered the forsythia bush, though.

Dry weather didn't bother the mosquitoes. They grew so big they nearly carried Aunt Society and me off the porch. Even rag fires didn't help. But I did notice that my aunt's speaking ability was getting better, especially when she was outside, and that was good.

When Mrs. Smithfield stopped by the next day to tell me she

could get off next Thursday, I nearly jumped into her arms. I rushed to let Mrs. Bivens know. She said Thursday was all right, but did I call the sanitarium first to make sure Poppa would be available? No doctors' appointments or anything else scheduled? I'd forgotten to call about age requirements, too.

What if Poppa wouldn't be free or I'd be too young? So close to Poppa but yet so far! Well, that sent me into snapping at Aunt Society, frowning at Mrs. Smithfield, and hollering at the ducks and guinea hens doing their business right under our clothesline. And then my womanhood came on, and that didn't help at all!

The next Wednesday afternoon while Aunt Society was having her nap, I ran to the Stackhouse and called the sanitarium. The lady who answered said visitors had to be sixteen. I figured I looked mature enough now, so I told her I was. I asked to speak to Poppa so I could warn him about my new age, but she said he was out in the fields. She'd tell him I was coming.

Panting, and amazed at my little lie, I hurried to the Bivenses' house, told Mrs. Bivens things were good for tomorrow, and gave her four quarters. About to drop from running in the heat, I staggered back to our house to write a note for Mrs. Stackhouse, when the cowbell rang. I tightened my lips as I caught my breath. *Now what? Can't I leave you alone for a second?* I charged into her room and stopped, stunned.

My aunt lay on her side on the wood floor, clutching her bell. "What happened? Are you hurt?" I screamed and ran to her. She smelled like pee. I spent the next hour changing her clothes. "I'm sorry, I'm sorry," I kept saying. "But couldn't you have waited?" I knew she couldn't, though, because her kidneys were still weak.

I expected her to be angry but she ate her dinner quietly in her wheelchair. I know she wondered where I'd been. "Aunti, I've fixed things so I can visit Poppa tomorrow."

She brightened up at that. "Hi ho! Me too."

"No, it'll be too long, too hot and uncomfortable for you." She frowned up. "You don't like the Bivenses' wagon, remember? Mrs. Smithfield'll stay with you. Everything's all right."

She slowly turned her wheelchair around. I jumped up to help her, but she waved me away and rolled herself into her bedroom. At least she didn't throw her tray on the floor. The next morning when Mrs. Smithfield arrived, Aunt Society was scowling so bad I thought her whole face would go crooked.

"What's wrong, Society?" Mrs. Smithfield asked, but Aunt Society just glared at me silently. "Naturally your aunt's upset she'll miss seeing her brother," she told me outside after I'd explained, "but is something else wrong?"

I told her about the fall and how I'd been snapping at her lately. "But it wasn't my fault. I can't be with her all the time."

"Cece, I've been planning to say that you should bottle and sell your fine bedside manner," she said. Her usual soft gray eyes turned cold. "But if you're saying unkind things to your own kin, you'll not make a good doctor for anybody."

"Yes, ma'am," I said. Those words were so unlike Mrs. Smithfield that I felt lower than a snail's tail — for a minute. Grabbing my sun hat and my lunch, I hurried around to Mrs. Bivens' house. I'd sweated up my white blouse before I'd even climbed into her wagon.

That sun broiled down on us like we were chickens in the pot. The roads outside Raleigh were so dry we stayed in a dust storm, and so full of ruts I thought ole Lissa would turn the wagon over trying to jerk through them. Each time we stopped to let her rest under a tree, we worried whether that poor ole thing would move again.

Since Mrs. Bivens was concentrating on driving and not talking, I thought back to what Mrs. Smithfield had said about my treatment of Aunt Society. Mrs. Smithfield didn't understand. I'd hardly jumped salty with my aunt at all, compared to all the years she'd jumped salty with me. Nursing her was worse than nursing Gertie. And who'd take care of Aunt Society when my school opened next month? I hoped to be going into eighth grade if the school didn't hold me back for leaving so early the spring before. Poppa and I had never talked about furthering my education, other than he knew about my dream of being a doctor. He and Momma hadn't got past eighth grade, which was normal for their generation. In light of our situation, with Aunt Society having nobody else to take care of her, maybe Poppa would think I'd had enough learning for now and make me postpone eighth grade till she got better. What a terrible thought!

"We're nearly there." Mrs. Bivens broke into my worries. "These corn fields, apple and peach orchards, pecan trees, the cow pastures, all belong to the sanitarium. Your daddy's in a nice place. Good thing he gets that veteran's pension, with him not working anymore, you know."

I agreed. But Poppa's pension wasn't as much as she thought it was. That was why he *did* work. Maybe he'd need me to work now to help make ends meet. We'd never talked much about finances. Why would we? After living with Aunti Val and seeing how we'd done without, and then splurged, I suddenly was very concerned about money and bills. I did know that we owned our house, praise God. Grammaw Lassiter had given it to Momma and Poppa when she passed on. Maybe I shouldn't play the radio so much, to save on electricity. Maybe Aunt Society had a good reason for running it only on Sunday evenings.

After toodling up a long, winding road, we stopped at a three-story white house with a wide wraparound porch. Colored people stood and sat around talking, playing cards or checkers. A couple sat in wheelchairs or leaned on canes and crutches. Heart pounding, I brushed at my hair and swiped at my blouse, which was splattered with so much mud it looked polka-dotted.

"There he is! Poppa!" I waved. He'd gained weight. In fact, his face was fat. I jumped out of the wagon before Lissa had stopped, as he stomped down the steps.

 My little girlio!" Poppa shouted, scooping me up, which he hadn't been able to do for years. I fell on his neck. He smelled like lemons and oranges. "Whew! You got big! Let me put you down. Lookin' more like your momma, Miss Hazel Eyes. Mrs. Bivens, I can't thank you enough for bringing my girl to me."

"Glad to do it, and glad to see you, Taylor," Mrs. Bivens replied, smiling. Puffing on her pipe, she turned the wagon around to situate Lissa under a tree while Poppa and I, arm in arm, stepped up onto the porch.

We sat down and Poppa began introducing me. A stout light-skinned, freckle-faced woman Poppa said was Thessalonia settled herself in a chair beside him, until he firmly told her we wanted privacy. "All right, dear," she said, and sat down farther away, but with us still in sight. Mrs. Bivens reached the porch just then. She and Poppa hugged, then she flopped down in that chair and closed her eyes.

"How's Aunt Society? She behaving?" Poppa asked, coughing a little but not nearly as bad as before. I told him about Aunt Society, leaving out the parts where she and I tangled. Poppa kept saying "Good, good" to everything I said. He said he left for the sanitarium a few days after I reached New York. "Society had Mr. Toodlums calling me most every day, agitated about the mail, or ducks and guinea hens scratching in our flower beds, or *something*, till I entertained the thought of returning home."

"She never sent me any clothes. She didn't even write, though I wrote to her."

"She can't — I thought she and Mrs. Smithfield — Laphet, come meet my daughter," Poppa said. He introduced me to a short, thick-necked man, one of his roommates. Miss Thessalonia, watching us, smiled at me. I smiled back, and asked Poppa about her. "She thinks she'll be the new Mrs. Massey, but she won't," he said quietly. "She's worse than a boll weevil on a cotton ball. I can't handle you and Society, let alone another woman." He said louder, "Can't no woman take your momma's place."

I was glad he said that. I wouldn't want anybody as my stepmother. "Poppa, how'm I gonna go to school if I have to nurse Aunt Society?" I blurted out before I'd planned to.

Poppa shuffled around in his seat. "We're banking on her getting well enough for someone else to sit with her." He leaned toward me and took my hand. His eyes were so warm, gazing into mine, that I leaned forward to be even closer to him.

"Society's had a hard life, Cece. She raised me, so I got to do as much as I can for her. Our father — your Grandpa Massey — believed that females were only good for gutting fish, scrubbing floors, cooking food, serving men. I never held to that, but see, she got her thinking about girls from him. Pappy'd be gone menhaden fishing for weeks off the coast of Louisiana. When he first got home, everything'd be copacetic, but the longer he stayed the worse he got."

I heard a soft snore from Mrs. Bivens, gone to sleep in the chair with her pipe in her mouth. "I hope she keeps her mouth closed so the flies don't go in," said Mr. Laphet. "Don't drop that pipe and set the porch on fire."

Some of the other folks laughed softly. Poppa didn't. "Listen. When Pappy drank that white lightning, he got meaner than a shark, see, and he didn't care who he bit," Poppa told me. "He beat Momma so bad one time he made her go blind in her right eye. He took Society out of school in second grade to help Momma raise us boys. Society's dream was to be a teacher, but she never got back in school."

When Miss Thessalonia bent toward our way, we walked over to a rose-draped gazebo where Mrs. Bivens could see us when she woke up, but out of Thessalonia's earshot. "Aunti Valentina told me that Aunt Society was cooking when she set fire to your house, and burned up Grammaw and Grandpa Massey. Is that what really happened?" I asked when we'd gotten comfortable.

Poppa shook his head. "Aunt Society banked the fire and emptied the ashes from the cookstove, as always. A few live coals fell through the floor cracks to damp ground, where they always died. She was very careful about fire. We went to bed, but Pappy stayed up, drinking and smoking his pipe. He set himself and the house on fire." He cleared his throat. His eyes looked very sad. "We kids got out, but Momma tried to save Pappy, so we lost them both. Society blames herself for not watching Pappy."

"So Aunti Val told a falsity?"

"No, she tells what most everybody else believed at the time." He sat quiet for a few minutes, and so did I, thinking over what he'd revealed. He began again. "Anyway, I believe Society worried and missed us so when you went to New York and me into the sanitarium that her nerves brought on those strokes."

Just then I saw Mrs. Bivens leave the porch. Poppa and I waved at her. "C'mon," he said. "I wanted to show you all around my new home." We started with the room he shared with Mr. Laphet and two other men. The room had bay windows with pretty blue and white cotton curtains that swung gently over his bed. His Bible and some mementoes lay on a small table by the bed. He told us that he attended church every Sunday, which was good, too. Sometimes he played left field on the baseball team.

"This is really nice, Poppa," I said. "You can sure get some peaceful rest here."

Miss Thessalonia headed our way. "Mrs. Bivens, help me out here," Poppa whispered. When the woman reached us, Mrs. Bivens asked her to show her where the women stayed and to bring us some sweet tea. Miss Thessalonia hesitated, then smiled and they went off.

Back at the gazebo I told Poppa about scrubbing floors, which I hadn't said anything about in my letters. "Aunti Val was fun most of the time. Miss D — I'll tell you about her, too — said Aunti'd been married, but I never knew that."

"Not much to tell. They got married, she kissed him, then he died." He laughed. "No, that's not funny. But it became kind of a legend about how great her kisses were. They both were good singers, two of Raleigh's best. They were going to storm New York and be big stars. They visited up there a few times. After he died, she moved to New York to try it alone."

"She promised to come the end of this month. Maybe you'll be able to move home by then, she'll stay, and maybe we can all be together like a family again."

"You got it all figured out, huh, baby?" He patted my cheek.

"I don't know if I'll be home by then, but we'll keep praying on it. I'm ten times better than I was. It'll be good to see Valentina, if she makes it."

"Miss D said Valentina was a butterfly and Momma was a rock."

"True on both counts. Count your blessings, Cece. Don't count your maybes." He stood up. I saw Mrs. Bivens and Miss Thessalonia coming toward us across the yard. "You're *my* rock and butterfly both, girlio!"

When ole white Lissa brought us safely back home at dusk, Aunt Society and Mrs. Smithfield were dozing on the front porch. Aunt Society seemed happy to see me, and I told them almost everything.

A few days later I went to the mailbox. Hallelujah! A letter from Aunti Val, with a postcard from Big Willie inside! The coal camp they'd stayed at in West Virginia was so awful his daddy and other miners had a big fight with the sheriff at Blair Mountain. People got killed. "My goodness!" I sat down in the swing.

Big Willie wrote at the end of the postcard, "I'm in the mines picking up coal that's fell off the coal cars. I ain't forgot about that fair. We be back maybe by then. Write me here." He gave an Eagle Rock address. My heart beat fast. I wanted to see that ole skinny bald-headed boy!

Now for more good news. I skipped over the pleasantries in Aunti Val's letter, and then read, "I can't come in August, but will by the end of September. Promise."

"Doggone you!" I shouted and stamped my foot. "You promised! I need you!" School'd be going on almost two weeks by then. Now what was I going to do?

A few days later while chasing sugar ants out of the kitchen pantry, I knocked a small sack down onto my head. Papers falling out of it scattered across the floor. As I picked them up, I smelled that familiar Tunisian Dreams perfume. Momma? I recognized Aunti Val's fancy cursive handwriting on envelopes addressed to Momma. Letters from one sister to another? After checking around for Aunt Society, I hastily tucked the sack into my waist and hurried into my bedroom, where I nervously stashed it under my pillow to read that night, when I was sure she'd be asleep.

Seemed like it took me forever to get her washed up and tucked into bed. Finally in my own bed, I opened the mysterious sack and again Momma's fragrance from the papers swept over me like her hand had moved around my head.

"Oh my goodness' sake," I whispered as I unfolded a torn sheet of paper. "Mr. Nathaniel Chavis's funeral program." What I could make out said that his funeral was held at St. Paul AME Church and that Momma and Poppa sang. It said Aunti Val and Mr. Chavis had been childhood sweethearts and had been married little more than one year. Poor Aunti. One year a bride, the next a widow. I remembered how she cried when I asked who the man was in that photograph. I guess she hadn't told me much about him in order to avoid sad memories. After he died, she moved to New York and became "Lassiter" again, until I suggested that she use Chavis for *Shuffle Along*. I hoped her taking back his name was a sign she was finally healing.

In the first letter I read, undated, Aunti Val hoped to get a position with a famous German concert singer "here in New York" — Madame Mercifal, of course. In another, Aunti wrote,

"Nathaniel's death is too fresh in my heart for me to be with you and Taylor and Celeste now that your little Emmanuel has left this world. Our family is draped with so much tragedy! I suffer so because I know I'm disappointing you, but I pray that Taylor's sister will come after all and that you'll regain your health sooner rather than later because of it." That would have been four years or so ago, since my baby brother had just been born and passed on.

Taylor's sister was Aunt Society, who at the time was still in Morehead City. Was this what Miss D meant when she accused Aunti Val of not helping the family "before when they needed you"? I found myself defending Aunti Val. She was still grieving. How difficult it would have been for her to return to so much sadness. I paused before opening the next letter. I almost felt like I was intruding into my aunt's and Momma's privacy. Who had saved these letters? And why? Poppa? Momma? Had they been left for me to read? I didn't know, but they were a far greater treasure than anything I had brought back from New York.

Aunti Val must have sent one of Momma's letters back with her own, because at the top of a letter from Momma was "Sister, I agree" in Aunti Val's hand. In that letter Momma had fussed, "She scorns the use of toiletries to perk up her skinny-legged, horse-faced self and doesn't want me to, either." *Aunt Society again, no doubt*, I thought, giggling low. "She bosses Taylor like he's still a little boy. Had I known she'd be such a pest, I'd have never agreed to ask her to move here. Though careful with my words, I set her straight three times today about her mean tones speaking to my sweet little Celeste." Praise God for Momma sticking up for me! Then at some point after that, Poppa was sent to war.

Aunti Val wrote in her return letter, "I wish I could have stayed until you get back on your feet, but at least I got there for Christmas." So she got here for the holidays. "Society lacks our Raleigh manners. I wasn't surprised to learn that she can't read and write, either."

I stopped and reread that line. Aunt Society illiterate? Poppa did say she only got to second grade. Maybe that's what he started to say about her and Mrs. Smithfield sending my clothes, but stopped. Oh, bless her heart. She couldn't write back to me. I felt a flash of guilt for being upset that she hadn't written to me in New York. But goodness gracious, she should have said something! I'd have taught her how long ago. Maybe she was ashamed. A lot of people couldn't read or write anything except their names, I knew. I was finding out that my family was closemouthed about a lot of things.

A penny postcard in the sack showed a pretty young woman and a handsome young man hugging atop a player piano with "Spooning at Coney Island" handwritten on the back. Aunti Val and Mr. Chavis! That wasn't the one he fell off of, apparently. Another showed Aunti Val standing by a seated fat White woman swathed in so many furs that she looked like a bear. On the back was a note: "Bon voyage! Valentina and Madame Mercifal."

Aunt Society must have felt quite gangly around someone as pretty as Momma with her perfumes, thick black hair, and hazel eyes. Society must have felt downright clumsy whenever fancy Aunti Val flitted down from Harlem. From their letters and from Aunti Val's own words, I knew Aunti Val and Momma probably said some really cutting things about Society, and probably loud enough for her to hear now and then. I decided to return the sack of letters back to the top shelf and not snap at Aunt Society anymore, no matter what she said or did. She'd had enough unkind things said about her.

By late August I was worrying less about Aunt Society, and more about my education. School opened September 13. Usually a parent came to school to register their children at the beginning of the term, but neither Poppa nor Aunt Society could do that. Nothing had come in the mail, unless it had gone to Poppa at the sanitarium, but I was sure he would have said something about it when I visited. Had my school and Mrs. Bracy, who was also the assistant principal, forgot about me?

And what about my school clothes? Almost none from last year fit. The ones I'd brought from New York were too dressy for everyday school wear. The nearly twenty dollars I had left would have to buy what I needed.

I walked over to the Smithfields' to borrow an old *News and Observer*, our daily White newspaper, that they kept stacked on their back porch, then settled myself on our steps. Aunt Society wheeled herself out to catch a breeze with me. I thumbed through the newspaper, eyeing advertisements. "Almost fifty cents for girls' silk hose, and two dollars for plain leather shoes! Everything's so expensive. I hate to think what a middy blouse, a decent dress, a skirt, and undergarments'll cost." I sighed. "Not to mention a new coat." I was tired of always wearing secondhand clothes, but better used clothes than none at all. I knew of a couple secondhand shops on Hargett Street, if I could ever get away.

"Like to see the newspaper?" I asked my aunt. She could at least look at the photographs.

"No. My eyes are too weak."

"Aunt Society, I don't mean to be pry, but Poppa said you wanted to be a teacher," I said carefully.

I saw her look away across the street like she was trying to remember. "Yes," she said slowly, "long ago."

"And that you had to quit school to take care of him and his brothers," I continued softly.

"Water under the bridge, Cece."

"But you know so many poems and stories, and can recite them so well."

She tapped her forehead, smiling a little. "I had a good memory, till my strokes. Why?"

"I was just wondering," I said softly, "why you didn't write me back." I didn't want to upset her.

"Oh." She shifted a little in her wheelchair. "You never knew that I can't read or write a thing but my name, did you? But all I needed was hear a poem or story just once. I could repeat it word for word," she said proudly. "Folks who don't read got to be able to remember. Book learning's all right, but you got to have the memory." She stopped and sighed. "I don't have the memory no more."

This was the longest she'd talked since her strokes. I was impressed and touched by what she said. I started to ask how she'd parsed my papers if she couldn't read, until I remembered that I'd recited my work to her. Then she'd light into me about how this or that was wrong. I'd change everything to satisfy her. But my teachers would mark *wrong* everything I changed. I finally learned to change everything back before I turned my papers in, and then I got good grades again.

I scanned the front page for stories about West Virginia coal miners. I'd watched for such news after I got Big Willie's postcard. "Let's see. Oh, no!" Anger, revulsion, and fear rose in my throat and almost strangled my words. "Aunt Society, they lynched another Colored man, Jerome Whitfield, over in Kinston, and on a Sunday morning, after they said he assaulted a White woman. Says she told them, 'Please don't kill him here in the yard.' They hung him in the woods, then shot him over a thousand —"

"No more." Aunt Society held up her good hand. "So sad. Just awful. Ku Klux Klan did that. Kluxers're servants of the devil."

"I wish Mr. James Weldon Johnson and his Colored people's group would stop them." I tightened my lips. I'd read about Mr. Johnson's organization in the *Brownies' Book* magazine, and how it was formed by Colored and White people to help Colored people get treated better. Or maybe Mr. Garvey and his army could do something.

"Can't nobody stop Kluxers." She looked at me fiercely. "They White men doing whatever nasty thing they want. Kluxers be in Raleigh, hear? They kill Colored *girls*, too."

Something *else* for me to worry about. I folded up the newspaper. I didn't feel like reading. I didn't even want to look at advertisements. When our White mailman walked up to the porch smiling and waving a fat letter at me, I stared at him. Was he a Kluxer, too? But he was nice!

I carefully took the letter. From Aunt Valentina! Inside were the Statue of Liberty photographs, and a letter from the *Brownies' Book* office, which I read first. Miss Fausett wrote that she was sorry, but none of us Butterflies won. My shoulders slumped. Then, at the bottom of a sheet listing the honorable mentions, there was my name, and "Forsythia"! I let out a Miss D–style whoop, which caused Aunt Society to jerk.

When I explained, she smiled. "I planted that forsythia bush when you were born," she said. "And I started to feel better when you played your bush piece."

"Oh," I said, not knowing what else to say. I moved on to the photographs. There I was with Miss D and the cardboard Miss Liberty, then me, Miss D, the officer, and Aunti Val. "Simply fabulous!" I said aloud. I showed them to my aunt with my thumb over Aunti Val's face.

Then I began reading Aunti Val's letter. Miss D had moved to South Carolina to be with Gertie and her folks, who'd got back together. Good; at least Miss D was closer. I wished I had her new address. And then I read, "A few of us have put together a small traveling production of *Shuffle Along*, with the producers' permission. We'll perform it at your Negro State Fair. I thought I would be in September when I last wrote you, but now I've learned that the fair will come in October. It'll be so grand. I'll arrive by train into Raleigh the day before the fair begins, be in the parade the next morning, and present it that afternoon. We'll stay at the Stackhouse. You can't imagine how happy I'll be to see you and Taylor and everybody."

"Fabulous!" I said at first, grinning. But wait a minute. Since the fair wasn't until late October, that meant she wouldn't be here for another month. I let out a big sigh.

Aunt Society opened her eyes. "What?"

"Aunt Valentina's coming for the Great Negro State Fair," I said. "But she —"

"Her? Here?" Her face turned into one fierce wrinkle. "No.

No!" She slammed her good hand on the arm of her wheelchair, then jerked the chair around and rolled back into the house.

Well, telling her *that* had surely been a mistake. I listened to her rattle through the house. But she had to know that Aunti Val was coming sometime. She would return in style, a star. Performing at our fair was a smart thing. I was positive she would land some kind of big job, like at Raleigh's Shaw University or Saint Augustine's School, or Durham's National Religious Training School and Chautauqua. She could teach drama or dance or singing, maybe. After that, she'd have no reason to return to New York, except to pack up and say good-bye to her friends.

With Aunti Val back I could have a whole family again. I could go to school, too, since she could find somebody to take care of Aunt Society, I was sure. Aunti Val was coming back to help *me*, anyway. Helping me would help Aunt Society. She could move in with us until she found her own place. Aunt Society would just have to get used to it, unless she wanted to move back to her own little dark house. Still — October!

Now, how could I get word to Poppa? I found Aunt Society sitting at the kitchen table, staring out at the back porch. "Would you like to go for a walk? It's such a pretty day," I said as sweetly as I could. "We can go over to the Stackhouse and call Poppa. You can talk to him."

She stared at Aunti Val's letter still in my hand until I stuffed it into my skirt pocket. "Well, I reckon," she said finally. I was so relieved that I hugged her. "Girlio, you just don't know that woman," she said, using Poppa's nickname for me.

Oh yes, I do, I thought, but I didn't tell her that. "Here, let me smooth your hair." I gently patted her thin white hair over the bald spot, and put her sun hat on her head. Her hair was soft and now smelled sweet from my last shampooing. When I'd offered to wash her hair, she hadn't resisted at all. I think she even enjoyed my taking care of her hair now. At least she didn't smell like pig grease anymore. I hurried to my room, got my cherries and lemonade perfume, and dabbed a bit behind my ears. When I returned with the bottle, she said, "No, none on me," but I touched some behind her ears, anyway, sure she would like it. When we were ready, I helped her down the front porch steps, then bumped her chair down them. She eased herself into the wheelchair, and we headed out.

As we walked and rolled along, I found myself staring at the White people passing us in their cars. Were they Kluxers, too? I hadn't thought much about the Ku Klux Klan until I'd read that story. When in the good Lord's world would things change for us Colored?

Seeing a yellow rosebush at the entrance of City Cemetery, I told Aunt Society that she smelled like a flower. I hoped that would take her mind off thinking about Aunti Val and the Ku Klux Klan.

"Oh?" She touched her fingers behind her ear and sniffed them. "I do, don't I?"

"Do you mind if I go by Momma's and Emmanuel's graves?" I asked. "I've been meaning to do that ever since I got back."

"Well," she said and sighed. "So many dead in there."

"They're all dead in there, Aunt Society," I reminded her.

Right then she erupted into a loud, full-bellied cackling laugh that I hadn't heard from her since she'd got tickled over a Punch and Judy puppet show at a park program a couple of years ago. She laughed so hard she had to take off her glasses and wipe her eyes with her good hand. "Go, go," she said, still laughing.

I laughed, too, glad to hear her laugh, and pushed her through the cemetery entrance. I liked the tombstones' granite angels, Bibles, intertwined doves, and other carved figures and tender wordings. Momma and I walked through here often when she was well. She'd point out the graves of people she knew, or the flowers and shrubs folks had planted in their loved ones' memory, or one thing or another. Sprucing up grave sites was something folks did every year during the last weekend of May. We called that Saturday Decoration Day, or Memorial Day, to honor not only the war dead, but all the dead. Some placed colored glass bottles or shells around the headstones. Often relatives from other places came down for their annual family reunions that weekend. Aunti Val wouldn't, though.

But today, for Momma and Emmanuel, only Aunt Society and I were there. Nobody had cleaned off their plots. I dropped to my knees and pulled weeds from around their graves. When I finished, I gently touched the headstones with my fingers. "There, that's better," I said softly. I silently promised them I'd be back.

Aunt Society pointed to a forgotten clump of weeds near the foot of Momma's plot. I pulled it up. "Looks better," she said, and I agreed.

From the cemetery we headed for the Stackhouse. Some elderly Colored people driving by waved at us, and we waved back. Aunt Society said she knew them.

"Let's go back. I'm hot." She placed her good hand against her forehead under her sun hat. So instead of our talking to Poppa, we turned around and went home, which was disappointing to me. After helping her to lie down, I chipped some ice from the block in the icebox, wrapped it in a towel, and placed it on her head. I wished I could slip out and call Poppa anyway, but remembering what had happened the last time, I stayed home.

I straightened the framed needlework of Colored menhaden fishermen on the wall opposite her bed. Aunt Society and Poppa had said the scene reminded them of Morehead City. Whenever I looked at the matching needlework on my wall, I thought of Poppa's balloon story. I wonder if Gertie still remembered it.

That night in bed, while rereading Aunti Val's letter, I found some more writing on the back, which I'd missed: "I think about you every day, Cece. Would you like to come back with me and attend school up here, if we can work things out about Aunt Society? Our schools are so much better, and you can start scouting out where you'd like to get your doctor training down the road. We'll talk about it when I get there. By the way, I'm moving into Miss D's place, so I'll have lots more room."

I rubbed my eyes, staring at her words. Go to school in New York? Was this an abundance of blessings from the Lord, or a temptation from the devil? It'd be fabulous to go to school there, but naturally I'd have to leave Poppa and Raleigh. And Aunt Society.

But what Aunti Val was truly saying was that the only move she planned to make was into Miss D's digs, not ours. Ole Truth popped me on the head right then and snapped, *Celeste, you big dummy, stop praying for your dream to come true. It's plain that just ain't gonna happen, and you were stupid to think that it would.* My cheeks started to burn. But since March I'd banked on Aunt Valentina coming to Raleigh to live with us because I wanted my family to be together. I guess I'd probably hoped she could fill in where Momma had been.

Face it, kiddo. That was your dream, not hers.

"Yeah. Well, that's that," I said aloud, heaving a long, sad sigh. I dropped the letter down onto my bed.

Then I picked it back up. But *now* here I was with this new, huge invitation! Should I stay in Raleigh to care for Aunt Society, be close to Poppa, and go to school here, or should I just take my little brown fanny back up to the Big Apple with Aunti Val and jump back into her exciting, crazy circle, where I could begin my journey for true toward being a doctor? I held my head in my hands. What would Poppa say? What would Momma say? What did I really want to do? What *should* I do?

September arrived with me more agonized over Aunti's tantalizing offer and school than ever before. I needed to get into school *somewhere*. School here was only two weeks away and I still hadn't found anybody to stay with Aunt Society. If I couldn't find anybody to do it during the day now, how in the world would we find anybody to stay with her if I moved clear to New York? The poor farm, run by the state, was out of the question. But would Poppa consent to putting her in Miss Lucille's old folks' home? Miss Lucille's was clean and decent enough. Momma and I used to go there sometimes with Christmas baskets for ladies and gentlemen she knew. But it was depressing to me. Old folks covered by blankets sagged in wheelchairs everywhere, or lay in their beds, picking at their quilts. Some cried when they saw us, because they hadn't had any other company in weeks. Weeks!

Miss Lucille's and the poor farm were where old folks got sent when they were sickly and had no home and no family to take them in. Aunt Society had family.

On Labor Day I straightened the house, myself, and Aunt Society in preparation for our annual picnic with the Smithfields. Usually Mrs. Smithfield brought food, Aunt Society and Poppa pitched in with our stuff, and Mr. Smithfield would bring Colored newspapers from cities on his train route. We'd set tables in the backyard clear of poop, and eat and talk. Then we'd have a checkers tournament, with even Aunt Society and me joining in.

This time, though, Mr. Smithfield was on the road, and of course Poppa was away, and Aunt Society was sick.

Mrs. Smithfield came with all the food, some newspapers, and a lady from St. Paul church named Mrs. Edmund. We ate fried chicken, hot rolls, macaroni and cheese, sweet potatoes, and banana pudding in the parlor. Mrs. Edmund was nice, smiling and nodding a lot, interested in everything Aunt Society said. Aunt Society behaved herself, and talked a little. I was relieved about that. Mrs. Edmund was the first real company she'd had since her strokes, other than Miss D.

After they left, Aunt Society went to her room to rest, smiling a little. *Well, that went well,* I told myself. I munched on a chicken thigh and looked through the newspapers, searching for news about New York schools and medicine.

What would I have been doing in Harlem? I imagined myself taking part in festivities in Central Park like I did on the Fourth of July, or watching another Marcus Garvey parade. Maybe Aunti Val would have taken me to Café Noir Le Grande for a big party. I laughed a little. Life in Harlem moved a lot faster than down here, that was for sure. I could have kicked myself when I wondered what Poppa was doing. While Mrs. Smithfield and Mrs. Edmund were here, I should have skipped off to the Stackhouse and called him!

Later on, Evalina and Angel Mae showed up. "I'm *so* glad to get away from Granddaddy's awful tobacco worms," Evalina said, dropping down on the steps. "We stayed out in that field all day! I drank so much water I 'bout dried up the well."

I brought them some sweet tea and the *Brownies' Book* contest letter and the new magazine. They were disappointed, but happy for me, sort of, over the results. They promised to tell Swan. "And guess what? Aunti Val's bringing a performance of *Shuffle Along* to the Negro State Fair!" I announced.

"Oh my!" they cried together.

Evalina hopped up, singing "I'm Just Wild About Harry" and cutting Charleston steps until Angel Mae shushed her. "*You* know that song?" I asked in surprise.

"You don't have to live in New York to know it," Evalina replied. "Take us when you go, please. Maybe photographers'll take our pictures with her, and — and maybe one'll get printed in the *Carolina Times*, or the *Independent*, or the *Chicago Defender*, or even the *New York Amsterdam News!*"

"I'll see what I can do," I said, trying to keep calm myself. For once Evalina didn't constantly talk over me. I guess maybe she'd learned something.

Then they started talking about school. They didn't know about Aunti's New York offer, of course, and I didn't tell them. They meant school here in Raleigh. "I don't even know if I've passed seventh grade," I said.

They looked surprised. "Well, of course you did, you goose," said Angel Mae. "Mrs. Bracy said your name with the rest of us on the last day of school. Didn't you get your grades?"

I shook my head. Angel Mae reminded me about going to the fair with the group on opening day next month. "But you'll be in school with us by then, so you'll know all about that," she said. When I mumbled off something, she looked at me funny, but let it go.

After they left, I searched around the house for letters from school. Finally I went into Poppa's room — well, Aunt Society's room for now — and asked her if she'd seen such a letter. I knew that since she couldn't read, she probably wouldn't have recognized it, though. She waved her hand around the room. I picked through a stack of papers on the dresser, and found a large envelope. Fingers trembling, holding my breath, I opened the envelope and found my report card.

"Mrs. Bracy passed me!" I screamed. Praise God for Mrs. Bracy giving me the benefit of her doubt! My certificate was there, too. I waved them around, then showed them to my aunt. "I'm in the eighth grade now!"

"Good," she said. "Now ain't that enough?"

"No!" I said sharply. I went to my room, holding my certificate. I wasn't like her, content with a second-grade education. I — I stopped. That hadn't been her fault. With a hot face, I returned to her room and took her weak hand. "I'm sorry. I didn't mean to snap. School's just so important to me," I said. She didn't look at me, but patted my hand holding hers. "You need anything?" She shook her head.

I paced in my room. *Think, girl, think!* The thought of scrubbing floors frowned me up. I never wanted to scrub anybody's floors again. But if I could scrub floors to help Aunti Val follow her dream, I certainly ought to do it for myself. Like Aunti had said, it was honest work, and it was better than being up to my elbows in fish guts. I could pay somebody to stay with Aunt Society while I went to school. Then, until eight or nine at night, I'd scrub floors and iron for people, come home, put her to bed, do my homework, and sleep, too.

In my best handwriting I began composing a letter to Mrs. Bracy. "I hope this letter finds you in the best of health and teaching well as you always do. Thank you so much for promoting me into the eighth grade. I am eternally grateful to you for this.

"Can you think of a nice, patient lady who can spare me a few hours each day from Aunt Society so that I can attend school? I'm willing to scrub floors and iron for anyone who'll hire me, so that I can pay for her services. Also, I still have the schoolbooks you so kindly lent me, and plan to return them to you. Remaining your faithful student, Celeste Lassiter Massey."

The part that I did not tell her was that perhaps this same person could take care of Aunt Society if I moved to New York. If I had to scrub floors in New York in order to keep on paying her, then I'd do that, too.

After sticking Mrs. Bracy's letter in our mailbox, I found two pieces of clean cardboard and carefully wrote "Will Scrub and Iron. Reasonable Rates" on each one. I tied them to sticks and stuck them in the front yard, where I prayed everybody but Aunt Society would see them.

Mrs. Smithfield did. She pounded on the screen door. "Girl, are you out of your mind? You've got to be preparing yourself for school, not breaking your back on your hands and knees."

"How? When I've got to stay here and take care of *her?*" I had to jump a little salty myself.

"Do your father and aunt know about this?"

"They will if you tell them. Besides, Aunti Val's coming to the fair next month and I'm sure she'll help me find someone. See, if I can get ironing jobs, I can pay for someone to sit with Aunt Society. Aunti Val knows lots of folks down here, still, and she might be able to —"

"Miss New York's finally getting down here, is she? Humph!" She huffed her short self back down the steps. She didn't tell me to take down the signs, though, so I left them up.

Waiting for someone to respond to my signs, I wrote to Big Willie at the Eagle Rock address about the fair date, and hoped he could come back, and get in school. He and I had things to share about where we'd been and what we'd seen and done — or had done to us — that kids I knew here wouldn't understand.

After checking on Aunt Society, who was resting in her room, I returned to the porch and looked for jobs in the newspaper. I found two ads from folks needing day work, but the addresses were so far away that I'd spend all night trying to reach their homes. On the front page I scanned the headlines. My eyes fell on "Negro Lynched by Mob at Pittsboro Early on Sunday." Another one, right down the road! A boy named Ernest Daniels was hanged from a tree and shot to death after a White woman said she caught him in her bedroom. Bloodhounds tracked him down and lawmen put him in jail, but other White men overpowered the jailer and killed that boy.

I threw down the newspaper. When would this stop? Couldn't they have just sent him to prison? He didn't steal anything, didn't hurt anybody, yet they killed him! Why couldn't anybody do something? I already knew; we Colored would bring the horror to our own doorsteps if we intervened. But if I were grown and a doctor, maybe at least I could get to somebody who'd been lynched and try to help him, if he wasn't already dead. Or would I dare?

I decided I didn't have to wait to be grown and a doctor to do one thing, though. I wrote a letter to Mr. James Weldon Johnson in care of the *Brownies' Book* magazine right then, and asked him to help us Colored in North Carolina about lynching.

When the mailman came around the next day, he took my letters and tipped his hat. I prayed that he mailed them both.

But while I was shelling butter beans on the front porch a little later, I began to wonder. What if the mailman read my letter and told the Kluxers? Would they come after me now? I broke out in a flush and began eyeballing every car that passed our house. When one slowed, my hand flew to my mouth, but then I realized that they were reading my signs.

Mrs. Bracy stopped by. She hugged me, sat down, and then asked about the signs, too. "Well, I haven't got any takers," I said. "I might as well pull them up. But I got to do something if I'm gonna get into school. I just wrote you a letter, too."

"I'll watch for it. This is going to be a rough — Oh, hello, Society! How are you, dear?" she said when Aunt Society made her way to the porch. "You seem to be pretty chipper."

"Taking it slow, day by day," Aunt Society said. She straightened her apron dress around her knees.

Mrs. Bracy glanced at me. "I hope you can go with us to the fair on opening day, to see the exhibits the girls have entered. There's room on the bus for you."

"I can stay by myself," Aunt Society said, "for a few hours, I reckon."

I perked up at that! I smiled so much I thought my mouth would break. She was getting better! Mrs. Bracy talked with Aunt Society a little more, but I could tell that she wanted to talk with me privately. After a few more minutes, she said good-bye, with another long look at me.

Aunt Society fanned herself with her hand. "She was nice," she said. "Who was that?"

I stared at her. "That was Mrs. Bracy. You didn't recognize her?"

"No. What does she do?"

Something clicked in my head when she said that. She couldn't be left alone, no matter what she'd told Mrs. Bracy. I went out to the front yard. As I pulled up the signs, I saw Mrs. Bracy come out of the Smithfields' house. She walked back over to me. I thanked her for passing me into eighth grade. I told her that was part of what my letter said.

"I didn't want to say much with your aunt there because I didn't want to upset her," she said quietly. "Our schools hold to the same policies as the White schools, you know, so you've got to get into school or the authorities could send a truant officer over here if they wanted to. I'm glad, though, that your aunt can stay by herself a bit now. She must be improving. "

"I thought so, too, but she didn't even know who you were," I said flatly. "I wanted to try to work, so I could pay somebody to sit with her. But it seems like she's starting to lose her memory. Aunti Val's coming for the fair and I was hoping she'd help me find somebody, but now I don't know."

I tucked the signs under my arm, remembering Big Willie and the coal mines. "Mrs. Bracy, I know kids who are out of school but truant officers don't bother them. Why can't I be like them?"

She stared at me so long I hoped she wouldn't ask for names. I didn't want to get him in trouble. "Well, glory be! Of course!" she said. She pointed her finger at me. "You can be a hardship case, like farm children still working in the fields. And medical emergencies. At least for a while. I'll talk with the principal tonight, and see if we can't get some of your classmates to bring your homework to you for the next month, say until after the fair. You know how to use your brain, Cece." She patted me on the shoulder and went back over to the Smithfields'.

I threw the signs into the air and danced the Charleston. I was actually glad to be a hardship case!

The days marched into October, closer to the forty-third Negro State Fair, and Aunti Val. Our fair was held a week later on the same grounds as the big North Carolina State Fair, the one mostly for White people, sponsored by the North Carolina State Agricultural Society. Our fair was organized along the same lines as the White one, but was sponsored by our Colored North Carolina Industrial Association. Mr. Berry O'Kelly, the mayor of Method, was president. I'd never been to Method, but I'd learned in school that it was founded by Colored people right after Emancipation and so was very historic.

Angel Mae and Swan took turns bringing and picking up my homework, so that was a blessing. I missed being in the classroom with them, but I was grateful to have such good friends. Homework in eighth grade was much harder, and Angel Mae and Swan didn't always explain the lessons clearly. I hadn't even met my new teachers.

Still, it was better than no school, because I didn't dare leave Aunt Society alone at all now. These last few days I'd fix her lunch or dinner, but she'd not eat, or say she already had. Other times she didn't eat until after I told her to ten or fifteen times. I also had to make sure she swallowed all her pills. Not that she refused to take them. She just didn't swallow them until I told her to. She kept forgetting to do so many things. When I told Mrs. Smithfield, she allowed that Aunt Society was probably succumbing to old age due to her strokes.

Angel Mae told me that she and Evalina wanted me to take them to meet Aunti Val when she reached the Stackhouse from the train station. I shook my head and nodded toward my aunt's room. "Can't leave her. She's not doing so good."

"I thought she was getting better," Angel Mae said.

"She was, until I told her Aunti Val was coming." They laughed, but I didn't. "It's the truth. That's when she started going down-hill again."

Chapter Twenty

The evening before Aunti Val was to arrive, Mrs. Smithfield came over. "Good news, Cece. Mr. Smithfield said he'd stay with Society while you go meet Valentina at the Stackhouse," she said.

"Oh, hallelujah!" I grabbed her around the neck and hugged her until she squirmed.

"Listen, I had to promise Alton that I'd bake a Lady Baltimore cake just for him," she said low as she straightened her hair and dress. "He's doing this for *you* because he feels bad for giving Society that bell. He thought it'd be funny to have her ring it. "

While she was in with Aunt Society, I ran over to Evalina's house and told her. Her mother, Miss Josie, sat and listened and shook her head. She and Aunt Society hadn't spoken to each other for years because of Miss Josie's ducks' and guinea hens' poop.

The next afternoon finally arrived. My heart thumped so fast I could barely breathe. The star was on her way! I wore my organdy frock and my pumps, with my hair twisted into a neat bun, and cologne behind my ears. I wished they were pierced so I could wear Momma's pretty baubles.

I went into the kitchen, where my aunt sat at the table, to make sure she was situated before Mr. Smithfield came. "Angel

Mae, Evalina, Swan, and I are going to the Stackhouse for a few minutes, but Mr. Smithfield'll sit with you," I reminded her for the fifth time that day.

She drank some sweet tea. "Why?" she asked.

"Well, the fair starts tomorrow and we want to — uh — see the people coming in," I stammered. She hadn't asked that before.

"Which people?"

I hesitated. She'd know soon enough. "To see Aunti Val," I said.

Silence. She drank some more sweet tea and stared out the back porch door.

Mr. Smithfield arrived at the front porch with a newspaper and his cigars. "I want an autograph," he whispered.

"All right. Thank you so much!" I whispered back, and took him to my aunt. "Aunt Society, I won't be gone long. Aunt Society?" I stood by her until she lifted her good hand briefly, then dropped it into her lap.

"Just go," she said in the coldest voice I'd ever heard. "Just go. Just go!"

"She's mad at me," I told my friends at Evalina's, blinking back tears. "She hates Aunti Val."

"Does she like anybody?" Evalina asked. After complimenting each other on how fine we looked, we hit Hargett Street. "Have you found someone to watch her so you can go with us to the fair tomorrow?" she asked.

"No. This might be the closest I get to the fair," I replied. "Tarnation!"

I was finally out and free at last, for a little while. Hargett was full of cars and Colored people moving about. Chanting "tarnation," we switched our hips up the street, and got looks from menfolks! There were plenty of places to stay in Durham — called the "Old Black Wall Street" because it had so many Colored businesses — so many folks stayed over there, too. Mr. Toodlums was so tied up with guests I had a hard time getting his attention. "She hasn't checked in yet," he finally said.

"But she said she'd be here by this afternoon," I told him, trying to keep the disappointment from my voice. "She —"

"Oh, she's in town. Mr. Shepperson picked her and the other show folks up at the train station. He took them out to the fair so they could rehearse. You girls wait on the divan in the corner so you don't be in the way."

After waiting for over an hour, I had to leave. I was so let down tears burned in my eyes. Now when could I see her? Would she come to the house? Angel Mae, Evalina, and Swan left with me. I knew they were sore at me that they had worn their good silk hose in the dust for nothing. But for once everybody stayed quiet, even Evalina. We said good-bye at our usual corner.

Mr. Smithfield was in the porch swing, smoking and fanning himself with his newspaper, when I returned. "Your Raleigh aunt's fine," he said. "I swear, I'm sorry I gave her that bell! She about near played a song on that thing, ringing it so many times this afternoon. Where's your beautiful New York aunt?"

"At the fair practicing. Did Aunt Society recognize you? She did? Well, that's good." I hesitated. Mr. Smithfield was a man of the world. Maybe he'd have an opinion that Mrs. Smithfield and Mrs. Bracy couldn't give. "Mr. Smithfield, Aunti Val wants me to go back to New York with her," I said softly.

Mr. Smithfield drew in a long puff of his cigar, studying me. "Oh, no," he said, blowing out a stream of smoke. "You don't want to do that. Society nearly talked my ear off about how she prayed you wouldn't go off from her again." He stood up. "I got to head on. Maybe I'll see Valentina tomorrow. Cece, don't leave this ole lady," he said once more. "I swear she'd have another stroke if you did. She called you her baby."

"Her baby?" I thanked him, and then I peeked in the kitchen, where she still sat, iron-faced. Her baby? "I'm back," I said, though she could see that. "Can I get you anything?"

"No. She here?"

"Yes, ma'am, at the fair."

Aunt Society lowered her head and fingered the frill on her apron dress. I helped her to go sit on the back porch so she could watch the sun go down. She liked that. Just in case Aunti Val stopped by that night, I fixed some more sweet tea and set our prettiest glasses out on the sideboard in the parlor. We had half a pecan pie from Mrs. Smithfield, and I'd fried chicken yesterday. It wasn't much but it was the best I could offer.

Just then somebody knocked on the front door. *She here?* I rushed to the porch. It was Miss Josie, Evalina's mother. "Evalina told me you didn't think you could go to the fair with the girls tomorrow," she began. "If your aunt doesn't mind, I'll sit with her tomorrow. You just tell me what I need to do. Neighbors got to look out for one another, when they can."

"Would you? Oh, I love you! Aunt Society, Miss Josie's here."
I led her through the house to the back porch, wondering if my
aunt would remember her. Miss Josie'd been one of Momma's
good friends. She hadn't stepped foot into our house, though,
since Aunt Society had moved in, when they'd started battling
over the bird poop.

Aunt Society looked up at Miss Josie curiously. "It's Evalina's
momma," I told her. "She wants to sit with you tomorrow so I
can go with Mrs. Bracy and them. Ain't that something? I can
give you your medicines before I go, and have everything fixed
for you."

Aunt Society raised her good hand up to her mouth. "Mercy
me, really? I haven't seen you in years."

Miss Josie sat down and they exchanged pleasantries. I brought
her out some sweet tea, but she declined the chicken and pie.
We talked over plans for tomorrow. She'd be over by nine thirty.
Mrs. Bracy's bus would be at her house by ten. After she left,
Aunt Society smiled bigger than she had in days. "I'll be glad —
glad to see her. Don't nobody come to see me no more."

"Well, I'm really happy that you remember her," I said,
relieved.

"Yes," she said. She kept staring at me. Then she asked, "Now,
who was she, again?"

Tears sprang into my eyes as I tried to make her remember who
Evalina's momma was. How could somebody remember things
one minute and forget them the next? I even mentioned the duck
poop. "Oh, yes," she said. "I see them ducks. They're pretty."

I burst out laughing through my tears. "You like them?"

She nodded. "Course, I don't go out in the backyard no more."

She stood up and I walked her back to her room. She'd been unsteady on her feet lately. I glanced at the framed needlework picture of the fishermen on the wall. On impulse I took it down and wiped off a thick layer of dust. Attached to the frame's felt back was a yellowed piece of paper with Poppa's handwriting: "Presented to my baby Celeste Lassiter Massey on her first birthday."

My mouth fell open. Below it was Aunt Society's quivery signature. "You did this?" I held it out to her, and pointed out her signature.

"I made both of 'em, for you," she said. "Matched set. They won first place premium at our fair. See, that's my name. I wrote it."

"This is beautiful work. And you remember doing them for me. But what," I asked carefully, "does 'my baby' mean?" Was I about to get another BIG surprise? Oh, heavenly Father, please, no!

"Elizabeth wrote those words," she said slowly. "I teased your Momma, calling you *my* baby. Fat brown toes. Big hazel eyes. I planted that bush for you. You played that bush song for me when I was so sick, and it made me feel better."

I listened, amazed at her sudden clear memory. And then I recalled that she had told me before how my violin playing had made her feel better. I gently rubbed my aunt's weaker hand.

We sat there studying her embroidery. Suddenly she looked up at me, and stared. She lifted her good hand to her mouth. "I'm sorry, I forgot your name."

I looked into her eyes, filling with tears. So did mine. "I'm Celeste, Cece, your — your baby." Tears rolled down my face. "And you're Aunt Society, remember?"

"Are you going to leave me?" she whispered. "I just don't know what I'd do if you left me all by myself."

"No, ma'am, I'm not gonna leave you," I told her. "I'm gonna stay right here with you, right here in Raleigh."

She touched my chin with her good hand. "You promise?"

"I promise." I kissed her wrinkly cheek. "Well, I mean I got to go to the grocery store and things like that," I said carefully. "And out with my friends."

"Well, of course," she murmured, and closed her eyes.

With trembling hands I replaced the needlework on her wall, then I went to my room. I lay down on my bed, and had a long, sad cry. That was that for going back to Harlem with Aunti Val. But I think I already knew that when I read her invitation. In a bit I got up, and swept floors, dusted, cooked, and straightened for Miss Josie tomorrow. I fell into bed around midnight. Aunti Val didn't show up.

The next morning I showed Miss Josie where everything was. I'd already written instructions for Aunt Society's medicines and food. Miss Josie was as loudmouthed as Evalina was, but Aunt Society didn't seem to remember that part about her as Miss Josie talked with me.

"Aunt Society, do you know who this is?" I asked. "Sometimes she gets a bit forgetful," I told Miss Josie.

"Course I do. That's Josie with the ducks," she replied. We laughed. I told Aunt Society that I would be right back, and not to worry about anything. She said all right.

When I climbed onto Mrs. Bracy's rickety bus at Evalina's, the other kids cheered. "Why're they doing that?" I whispered to Angel Mae.

"'Cause you're finally on the bus and we can go," said Evalina, who'd heard me.

"Quiet, children, quiet." Mrs. Bracy stood at the front of the bus. "You all know that Celeste hasn't been able to attend school due to sickness in her family. Cece, your letter touched me so that I read it to Mrs. Edmund and Miss Addie and some other members of our women's group at church. They all cried. They're going to come take care of your aunt every day so that you can go to school. I think they're also going to talk with your aunt's church and woo them into helping again. The power of your words, Cece, and the power of the good Lord all work together for good."

Everybody applauded. "Oh, my, God is good! Is that why Mrs. Smithfield brought over that lady to our house on Labor Day?" was all that I could think to say.

Mrs. Bracy bent over and whispered, "She was sizing up your aunt. She'd heard the horror stories."

"Can we go now?" Leon shouted from the back of the bus. Mrs. Bracy nodded to her husband, who was driving, and we pulled off for downtown and the parade. While Evalina, Angel Mae, and Swan jabbered around me, I was trying to get my brain reorganized. St. Paul had just freed me up to go to school — and to New York! But I'd promised Aunt Society I'd stay home with her. I had to keep that promise, didn't I? Or did I? Would she remember my promise?

We swarmed off the bus and jostled for the good spots along the parade route. Shaw University's band started out first, followed by Mr. O'Kelly, our fair's association president, and the other dignitaries in fancy cars. I recognized Mr. Lightner, the businessman, and Miss S. L. Delany, our fair's Superintendent of Art and Literary Work. She'd read some of my poems last year, and liked them. One of her brothers was a doctor, and a sister was in dental school in New York. Her father was Bishop Delany at Saint Augustine's. I'd forgot about her. Maybe her family could help me when the time came. The uniformed parade and fair marshals on horseback reminded me of Mr. Garvey's African Legion and his auxiliaries, except that I knew these folks. I stood straighter and waved proudly.

"Look, look, in the red cloche hat and green feather boa!" I shouted, pointing. "See, sitting in that Pierce-Arrow. It's my Aunti Val! Aunti Val!" I kept screaming until she finally turned my way and, standing up in the car, blew me a kiss!

"She's so pretty!" Evalina yelled. We jumped around and hollered until Mrs. Bracy hushed us. After my aunt rolled by, I wasn't much interested in the rest of the parade. Afterward, we returned to the bus and rattled away to the fairgrounds.

"No wonder you loved living in New York," said Swan. "She looks so glamorous! I bet being with her was like living with a queen."

"It was that, all right," I said, smiling so she wouldn't question my answer. "You think your entry will win, Angel Mae?"

"Probably not," she replied. "I had to replace the lids on my jars three times before Momma said they were on right."

"Our fair shows off what we Colored have accomplished each year from all over the state in farm, field, home, and health," said Mrs. Bracy, who'd been listening. "It has to have the highest standards. They can't give first, second, and third place premiums for just anything."

"Yeah, but those rules are still calamitous," Angel Mae whispered.

We drove under a gigantic WELCOME TO THE GREAT NEGRO STATE FAIR banner into the fairgrounds, already packed with people. We piled out of the bus into steamy, smelly air. "Pig poop!" Angel Mae pinched her nose so she wouldn't have to smell the stink.

The boys and Evalina wanted to see the pigs, cows, chickens, and lambs, and watch the motorcycle and horse races first. We other girls wanted to see the home economic demonstrations in the women's building. We all planned to hit the midway, scream on the rides, and eat cotton candy. Mrs. Bracy, however, said we had to listen to Governor Cameron Morrison first. Then we were to see how our kids did with their entries and view exhibits from Saint Augustine's School, A&T College, and the State Negro Deaf and Dumb School. After that we'd be free to do as we pleased. We stood out in the steamy, funky, hot autumn air while Governor Morrison flapped his lips about how fortunate we Colored were to pick tobacco and cotton in his fine agricultural state of North Carolina. Our Colored leaders Frederick Douglass and Booker T. Washington had come to our fair and spoken in past years. I'd rather have heard somebody like them — but they were dead — or Mr. James Weldon Johnson. Had he gotten my letter yet?

As we walked around, I kept looking for Big Willie. I had told him in my last letter about opening day and that I planned to be there. With so many people, though, it'd be almost impossible for us to see each other. Still, I kept up my hopes.

A few older girls and boys won premiums from Raleigh, but

none of my friends did. Best peck of oats! Best collection of vegetable seeds saved from a home garden! Best bale of hay! Best home-cured country ham! Best beef cattle, best dairy cattle, best hog! Best pig, for boys' and girls' Pig Club, which was what Evalina had wanted to enter. Best cake, pie, cookie, butter, cheese, jelly, and jam! Best fancy needlework and millinery, where Aunt Society had won first place so long ago! I wondered if she was behaving for Miss Josie. Bless her heart, I hoped she wasn't worrying over whether I'd come back to her. If she even remembered. I'd be back, the Lord willing. That thought didn't dismay me, either. I just wanted to see what Aunti Val was going to say.

At last Mrs. Bracy let us split up. Angel Mae, Swan, Evalina, and I and some other girls shot off to find Aunti Val's show. We looked and looked through the fair program and finally found a listing for *Stride Along Show with Val Chavis.* "Wonder why they changed the name?" I said. I'd have to ask her. We found the performance area, actually a large room, and settled in. The stage was tiny compared to the Sixty-third Street Theater.

When Aunti Val strutted out in a silky short red and black dress, green feather boa, and slinky see-through pumps, men whistled and ladies gasped. So did we! She looked like a hoochie-coochie woman! This was much different from the Oriental and other outfits she wore for *Shuffle Along* in New York. Instead of a full orchestra she had a drummer, a pianist, a trumpeter, and a bass player. After introducing herself and the musicians, she pranced back and forth, belting out her songs. She was truly the star!

Too soon, the show was over. Everybody applauded, whistled, and stamped their feet like they did in New York, and rushed to the stage, but nobody threw flowers. After several minutes of waiting, the other kids from our bus left. Angel Mae, Swan, Evalina, and I hung in there. Finally Evalina said we should leave, too, but I shook my head. When we took our eyes off Aunti Val to peer around, the stage lights dimmed, darkening the room. When I looked back, she had disappeared!

"How'd she get away from us so fast?" Swan wailed. "Nobody's here, Cece. We got to go!"

"I'm staying right here till I talk to my aunt."

"But if you don't get on the bus, you'll be stuck here," Angel Mae said. "Somebody might grab you in the dark."

I folded my arms. "I got robbed in the train station in Washington, D.C. I kicked the man who did it. I ain't scared." I told them what happened.

"Girl! Ohh!" Swan breathed while Angel Mae just smiled broadly at me, nodding.

"Shoot, I'm scared of you now," said Evalina. "But even so, you oughta c'mon with us." I shook my head again and watched my friends leave me in the dark room. Of course I was scared. Just telling them about that thief brought back the fear I'd felt. What if a Kluxer showed up?

"Valentina Chavis," I called. Nothing. I climbed some steps leading onto the dark stage. What if she had returned to the Stackhouse, or had gone to our house? I didn't want her and Aunt Society to meet without me there. She might say something to upset Aunt Society. I saw from Aunti Val's letters that

Aunt Society could never talk smart like Momma and Aunti Val did, bless her heart. Now she could barely get out her words. Just then I thought I heard someone say my name, but I couldn't see anybody as I felt my way around backstage.

Faint voices reached me from somewhere. Following the sounds through shadowy hallways, I reached a sunny bay window in a corner. Aunti Val laughed. Her shapely brown leg, with the silky red dress lying above the knee, slowly swung up and down. The motion caused her pump to bounce on her great toenail. The rest of her was stretched out on a broken-down divan, she had that green feather boa around her shoulders, and she was holding a cigarette! At least it wasn't lit. A man with a camera and another one with a notebook sat smiling by her on rickety-looking chairs.

When she saw me, she sat up, smiling, and threw open her arms. "Come, come! Gentlemen, my darling niece, Celeste! Oh, it's so good to see you!" Smelling like cherries and lemons, she swooped down on me and hugged me while the photographer popped pictures. She wore so much powder and lipstick I could see it caked on her skin.

"Aunti, you were marvelous!" I whispered. "I'm so proud of you!"

She introduced the men as being from a Colored newspaper in Charlotte. Remembering my manners, I walked back out into the hallway so they could finish the interview. A tall, skinny, bald-headed boy with long dimples and thick eyelashes stood there smiling at me. My mouth flew open.

"Hey, girl, you move like a cat in the dark," said Big Willie. "Didn't you hear me holler for you back there? I came to your aunt's show 'cause I didn't know where else I might find you." He looked me up and down, grinning. "Girl, you look — different. I like it, too."

"Big Willie!" I threw my hands to my mouth. "I — I — it's you." All I could do was smile and smile. Big ole skinny boy, lump of coal still on his handsome dark face.

"Celeste, are you still there?" Aunti Val called.

"Come on, m-meet my aunt," I stammered. My mind was awhirl. Lord sure knew how to answer prayers. I shyly took his hand. It was warm and hard.

"Oh, my, who do we have here?" Aunti Val said, and I introduced him to her and to the newsmen. "So you're the young man Celeste has talked about so much. Pleased to meet you."

He jerked his head at them. "I'm pleased to meet you, too," he said, and his voice cracked. With a big smile, the photographer told Aunti Val that he would see her later at the Stackhouse, and the newspapermen left.

"I gotta go find Momma and the kids," Big Willie told me. I turned from Aunti Val to him, not wanting him to leave so soon. "We'll be right out," Aunti Val said. "We'll meet you in front of this building in just a few minutes."

Big Willie looked at me. "Told you I'd be here," he said. That long dimple in his right cheek appeared, like a wink.

Aunti patted the divan for me to sit beside her. She was just bubbling. She said Miss D and Gertie and Gertie's parents were living together in Charleston and might even pop up here for the fair. "Miss D credits you with improving Gertie's health by having her drink that goat milk and leave Ex-Lax alone," she said. "And how's your father and your aunt?"

"Poppa's better, still at the sanitarium. He's not sure when he can leave. Aunt Society's — well, her memory's getting worse. Are you rich yet from Mr. Garvey's shares?"

"Good gracious, no! The value of those shares sank like rocks thrown in the river. But no matter." She tapped me on the knee with her fingernail. "Monsieur Le Grande's teaching me about this New York Stock Exchange, where you can buy all kinds of shares. I've bought quite a few, since I'm making good money from *Shuffle Along* and the café. If I do it right, I can be a millionaire by 1930. Isn't that fabulous?"

I nodded, but shouldn't losing her money from Mr. Garvey's shares have taught her to be more careful with her money? "I thought more folks from the show would come."

She played with her feather boa. "I couldn't take anybody from the show because it's still on Broadway. I called it *Stride Along* because I couldn't use the real name. I can't keep performing it under that name for long, though." She leaned closer. "Enough about me. So are you ready to move back with me and go to school in Harlem? You'll love it, Cece."

She looked so much like how I remembered Momma.

But Momma always told the truth. "Aunti Val, how were you able to come down here if everybody else is still on Broadway? They let you go, didn't they?"

Her face froze for a second. "What makes you say that?"

"Because they wouldn't have let you leave if you were still working for them, would they?"

"But see —" She sighed. "All right. I had a falling-out with one of the leading ladies. The producers were willing to let me do *Stride Along* and return, but that ole jealous heifer raised a stink and made them cut me loose. But it's all right. I'll get something else bigger and better. You'll see. Tell me you'll come, darling!"

I stared at her. Now I understood. I was so glad I hadn't told anybody that I was going to go back to Harlem with her. "Because you need me to scrub floors with you again to help pay the rent. I couldn't go to school all day and scrub floors all night."

"No, no, it's not like that. I — I just like having you around, honey. But yes, it would be nice to have your help. We wouldn't have to scrub floors." She trailed off. "We could work out something with your schooling."

"Aunt Society needs my help, too. You could stay with us, get a job here," I said.

"Celeste, I promised you in my letters I'd come back, and though it took a couple of changes, here I am. I didn't promise that I'd *move* back. If you misunderstood my promise, I'm sorry. But Society would drive me into hysterics with her criticisms and her country ways. My wings would fall off." She swung her leg harder.

"She's been a lot nicer since her sickness," I said quietly. "But now she's having memory problems. If I leave, she's apt to have another set of strokes."

"Well, that makes sense. Society was crazy about you. She'd never been around baby girls until you came along. She adored you. I never could understand why she got so hard on you. I guess after Elizabeth died and you became her charge, Society got scared. Sometimes folks think being overly strict shows their love."

And sometimes folks think working you half to death teaches you responsibility, I said to myself. *And now you're set to do it again.* "I thank you for the offer, Aunti, but I'd better stay here. Aunt Society and Poppa really need me. I guess I'm just an ole rock, like Miss D said."

Aunti Val laughed and flicked her boa at me. "That woman believes that everybody's either a butterfly or a rock. After she got to know me, she said I was a butterfly and Elizabeth was a rock. True, I had a million projects going and I don't think I completed any. When I moved to New York the first time, I'd planned to make a career there. Then I came back to Raleigh, was miserable, had tragedy, and then I went to Harlem and hooked up with Madame Mercifal. Then I got you and *Shuffle Along*, and now here I am again. So what? That's life. I love what I'm doing." She shook her shoulders. "Being a butterfly's not a bad thing like how Miss D describes them. Butterflies are beautiful, adventurous. We touch the sky!"

She leaned toward me. "Did you know that when you-all started up your club, Elizabeth named it the Butterflies Club after me, for those very reasons?"

"Is that right?" Having a club named after you was a big deal. We loved our club name. Well, that put a different light on her ways. Sort of back to where I had thought of her before I went to New York. I stood up. I didn't want to miss Big Willie. He might be waiting for me. And I needed to get back to Aunt Society. "Well, Aunti, can you promise me one thing?"

"It depends," she said slowly.

"That when I'm old enough to be a doctor, you'll help me get into a doctor's school in New York, or somewhere?"

"Oh, sure," she said. "I might have my own mansion and a big fine car. After all, I'll be a millionaire from the stock market. I might even be able to pay for your schooling."

Aunti still had her head in the clouds. That was all right, too. Me, I thought I was going to be better off as a rock. Was Big Willie a rock or a butterfly? Coal was closer to rocks than bugs!

I helped Aunti gather up her things, and we walked outside. The warm October autumn sun was setting, but the Negro State Fair was going full swing. I didn't see Big Willie, but he was around somewhere. I'd find him. "I better get back to check on Aunt Society soon," I said.

"I plan to stay for a few more days. We'll go see Taylor. I'll see Society, too, and some friends around town. There may be something going on here that I don't know about. You never can tell where butterflies might land. Look, I have something for you." She dug into her big purse and gave me a small box. I opened it up and laughed. It was Tunisian Dreams, Momma's cologne.

Author's Note

My challenge in writing *Celeste's Harlem Renaissance* was that I had not lived in either New York City or Raleigh, North Carolina. I had to study the history of Harlem and North Carolina before I could even begin to write this novel. I had lived in Durham and love that town, but I chose Raleigh because I wanted my character to have the experience of living in the state capital. I practically lived at the North Carolina State Archives, the North Carolina Museum of History, the State Library of North Carolina, and the Wake County Library System's Olivia Rainey and Richard B. Harrison branches.

In September 2004 my husband Zack E. Hamlett III and I vacationed in Biloxi, Mississippi. I drove to Hattiesburg, Mississippi, to use the University of Southern Mississippi de Grummond Collection, where my repository is. There I read *The Best of the Brownies' Book* (edited by my friend Dr. Dianne Johnson-Feelings), which profiled the NAACP's *The Brownies' Book*, the distinguished African American children's magazine (1920–21), edited by Jessie Fausett, which Celeste loved. In May 2005 my husband and I spent two hours in Harlem—my first time there. In December 2005 we visited the Indianapolis, Indiana, neighborhood where Madam C. J. Walker operated her hair salon. Two esteemed elder friends, Mrs. Winston Collymore and Mrs. Mary Carter Smith, told me about their unique New York and coal-miner childhoods that I couldn't have researched otherwise.

To gain authenticity in clothing, buildings, food, and other artifacts of 1921, I turned to fashion books and period photography. The late South Carolina photographer Richard Roberts' excellent photographs provided assistance, as did old photos of folks at Duke University's Rare Book and Manuscript Collection of photographs, and those displayed on Web sites like Lee Cook's. When I e-mailed Dr. John Kenrick (Musicals101.com) for information about the musical *Shuffle Along*, he informed me that the show opened twice—on May 21 for a private audience and on May 23 for the public. Dorothy Phelps Jones' *The End of an Era*, and *Culture Town: Life in Raleigh's African American Communities*, by Linda Simmons-Henry and Linda Harris Edmisten, were an important part of my North Carolina research. Poppa's story about the girl and the balloons is based on a dramatic event that allegedly occurred November 15, 1883, in Morehead City, North Carolina, according to a weekly newspaper called *Kind Words*, published by the Home Mission Board of the Southern Baptist Convention of Atlanta, Georgia. I read about it in *A Pictorial Review of Morehead City, 1714–1981*, published in 1982 by the Morehead City Woman's Club, which recounted the *Kind Words* article and the backstory. Was it true? *Kind Words* seemed to think so.

How can one write historical fiction without including real personalities? Since Celeste is fictional, real people could not have talked to her, of course, but I'll mention some figures from the book who are important to North Carolina history and that everyone everywhere should know more about: concert singer Caterina Jarboro (born

Catherine Yarborough) of Wilmington, North Carolina, who truly was in *Shuffle Along* early in her career; Caleb Bradham of New Bern, North Carolina, who invented Pepsi Cola; Thomas Day, furniture maker; educators Dr. Charlotte Hawkins Brown and Berry O'Kelly; Sadie Delany and her father Bishop Delany; North Carolina governor Cameron Morrison, and Raleigh businessman Calvin Lightner. Jerome Whitfield and Ernest Daniels were two African American men lynched in North Carolina in 1921, horrendous murders described in the book. Durham's North Carolina Mutual Life Insurance Company, and the school known as National Religious Training School and Chautauqua are also real. The school is now the distinguished North Carolina Central University, Durham. Saint Augustine's School is now Saint Augustine's College, Raleigh. Its Agnes Hospital ceased operations long ago. Shaw University continues. Big Willie's account of the clash between coal miners and the sheriff's men, one of several in American coal mining history, was the Battle of Blair Mountain in August 1921. The North Carolina Negro State Fair closed after 1930.

Eleanora E. Tate, Author
November 26, 2006

The author invites you to read more about her research at the Web site she maintains, www.eleanoraetate.com.